AMERICAN WEATHER

Charles McLeod's fiction has appeared in publications including *Conjunctions*, *DOSSIER*, *Five Chapters*, the Pushcart prize series, and *Salon*. A Hoyns Fellow while at the University of Virginia, he has also received fellowships from the Fine Arts Work Center in Provincetown and San José State University, where he was a Steinbeck Fellow. *American Weather* is his first novel.

CHARLES McLEOD

American Weather

VINTAGE BOOKS
London

Published by Vintage 2012

2 4 6 8 10 9 7 5 3 1

First published in Great Britain in 2011 by
Harvill Secker

Vintage
Random House, 20 Vauxhall Bridge Road,
London SW1V 2SA

www.vintage-books.co.uk

Addresses for companies within The Random House Group Limited
can be found at: www.randomhouse.co.uk/offices.htm

The Random House Group Limited Reg. No. 954009

A CIP catalogue record for this book
is available from the British Library

ISBN 9780099542223

The Random House Group Limited supports The Forest Stewardship
Council (FSC®), the leading international forest certification
organisation. Our books carrying the FSC label are printed on FSC®
certified paper. FSC is the only forest certification scheme endorsed
by the leading environmental organisations, including Greenpeace.
Our paper procurement policy can be found at:
www.randomhouse.co.uk/environment

Printed and bound in Great Britain by Clays Ltd, St Ives plc

For my family, my friends and the State of California

AUGUST

1

The blonde tennis star is in a robe on my sofa. She won't stop asking me questions about my wife's external defibrillator. It's late afternoon, the first Sunday of August. Link prints are back in and here on my shirt, with its French cuffs and broad collar, are thin chains of gold in a plaid sort of pattern. They look like the cords for men's pocket watches. They say: I own Time. They say: I am powerful. The shirt is bright white. I am deep bronze. I'll throw the shirt out in a month or two, tops. The tan stays year-round. In winter I turn slightly orange. I'm forty years old. I'm wearing board shorts. I'm worth about thirty-five million. My house, in the suburb of Piedmont, California, makes up one-fifth of this total. On my west-facing oak deck are a half-dozen chaises; they look at the Bay, at the bridge, San Francisco. Today, heavy smog: fine, brown, acrylic. Smog promotes fear. Smog makes me money.

'You really don't mind if I borrow this?' the tennis star asks me. She's left the red clay of Rolland-Garros early again, losing the second round to an unseeded Belgian. Some of her friends down in Indian Wells are throwing a taser party for her. Michael Jordan will be there, as will Ringo Starr. The gala will take place on a twenty-acre compound at the base of a very steep canyon.

The house and the lot are both owned by the Feds; the celebs will arrive in camouflage Hummers.

'It's fine to take it; someone there can read joules?'

'We rent out some doctors from down in the Burbank.'

'Up,' I say. 'Burbank is up from there.'

The tennis star's mouse face scrunches tight. She's thinking. Her small mouth's thin lips press in on each other. Today I read *The New York Times* to her while she showered. Her sexiest attribute? Her injured left shoulder. You do not get rich via standard perspective. Yes, her toned arms. Yes, her pert ass. Yes, her long legs, like twin camel towers. But the scar on her shoulder, and the bone chips below it – this is what makes my heart thump in my chest. To know that on days marked by shifting barometric pressure, the star, once she's older, will writhe from discomfort. To know that while showing some kids at some camp the proper way to hit a backhand volley, something will pop and she'll curse tersely in Russian. The shoulder is fault line; the shoulder is wrath. The shoulder's war is a war of attrition. It is items like these that provide my net worth. It is items like these that build five-car garages. Some say this country is coming apart. My Rome is not burning. My Rome has not fallen.

'How is your son? He is at his new school?'

I nod. I am looking out, at the water. 'Muhammad Ali's doing fine, I think, thank you.'

'Make Nike give me more TV commercials and I'll fly back there and see him. Surprise him. We get a hotel. We'll do things together. We'll buy things on eBay. We'll outbid all others.'

'I'd love that, Yi-Yi' (my nickname for her), 'I really would. I'll keep it in mind and we'll rain check on it.'

'But the season, you know. I get so busy.'

4

'Yes, the season,' I say. We both laugh and it's a fun laugh, a laugh of shared joke. My white Gucci loafers are calfskin, eight hundred dollars.

'I'm sure you'll try hard.'

'I will try one ounce of hard for each dollar they give me.'

From the baby monitor I've set up in the living room comes a low, metal grunt, made by my wife. These are phantom sounds, physicians assure me: ethereal, arbitrary issuances. I walk over to the device and turn down the volume.

'I'll talk to Nike later this week. What was your favorite article today, in the shower?' Yi-Yi's big secret is that she can't read. Perhaps two dozen people know this about her. And really, who cares? Does her sport involve thesis? Does her drop shot require thorough knowledge of Dickens? It doesn't. It requires that her sports bra make her chest shapely. It requires good teeth and a surplus of smiling. It requires that she squeals when she hits the ball, emits a shrill sound not unlike major orgasm, so that you, the white male sitting at home, will keep watching. The problem with the player who started the grunt was that she was ugly. Prototypes are rarely spectacular. So some people I know paid to have her put out of commission. Our currency? What we gave the guy with the knife? A pallet of assorted sugar cereals. He wanted ten boxes of Fruit Loops, ten of Apple Jacks, ten of Corn Pops and so on. It cost maybe two hundred dollars, plus shipping, to get Horse Face shivved in broad daylight on international television. The subconscious lesson? *La morale inconsciente?* Loud ugly people get knives in their backs. Not true, though, for loud gorgeous people.

'I liked the story about the people cloning panda bears,' Yi-Yi tells me. 'I think it would be a terrible thing if panda bears ceased to exist in the world.'

'And you consider the panda bear as remaining in existence

5

even if all the panda bears that are left are clones of the actual panda bear species?'

'I don't think that anyone would know the difference. They look the same, right?'

'They do,' I say. 'Exactly. At your party: will you be tasered, or will you be doing the tasering? To my understanding it's either/or, top or bottom.'

'I am mainly watching, but you're right,' says Yi-Yi. 'Almost always either/or. Some are switching, though. Spike Lee is a switch. Billy Jean King, she is switching.'

'I'll get pictures to my email in a week or so, then.'

'And the machine will come back in a courier truck.'

'Yes. DHL. You know what to do?'

'Three gold-star stickers on the bottom right side with the word "armadillo" in tangerine Sharpie.'

My cell phone is vibrating. The limo is here.

'It's time to go,' I say.

'OMG,' says Yi-Yi. She bounds from the couch and the robe drops to the floor, a puddle of black silk on the hardwood.

Yi-Yi gets dressed and we kiss at the door and my house, while not empty, is silent again. I loathe silence: it affords contemplation. It allows for the fog of the mind to clear out. The machine that I make is loud. It burns hot. It needs you to remain under perpetual cover. It needs you to lube it with fear, lust and haste. It needs tears in your eyes and sweat on your face.

It needs to always keep running.

I eat a big meal of dog on my deck. The Vietnamese identity-theft ring I employ brings me steaks of it. They're cut very thin – how you often see veal – and I bread them in flour with a pinch of cayenne and then fry them in oil on my eight-burner range, with two egg whites and hash made from corn beef.

Whenever I can, I eat breakfast foods: bacon or pork chops or omelets or sausage. It's a trick that I learned before I dropped out of college. That Food Pyramid that the Feds conjured up? Total bullshit. Done to save farmers. Eat that many grains and see how you feel. Force that much fruit down your gullet. My body needs protein; I am a wolf. I hunt and I howl and I wander forlornly. I am a ghost of the tundra. Migrate where you can, where you want, on a whim. I follow your tracks. I stay one hill behind you. I feast on your sick and your lame – and your well. I propel you until I destroy you.

Below my wood deck are four weeping cherries, arranged in a square around an oversized porcelain vase on a pedestal. My house, on the crest of a very steep hill, was built in the shape of a wishbone. The kitchen and deck comprise the bone's base, with two wings curving eastward, symmetrical. Between these two wings are a lawn, a small pond. There are roses, chrysanthemums, forsythias. A column of poplars – the Italian variety – stand at the back of the property. Postwar, this plot housed a colony for artists; ten tiny bungalows stood across its half-acre. The rich came here to paint, to write verse, to snap pictures; a darkroom once stood where I've put in a sauna. The compound's destruction was the key selling point. I loathe art, and crave its obliteration. Were there no art, I would not be an orphan. Instead, in my dreams, Klees pock and melt. Instead, bulls trample Picassos. And Cezannes are graffitied and Rauschenbergs bulldozed, and Pound, in his room, is given no pen, and Da Vinci is hung, and Hendrix is aborted. Art is false pretense. Art connotes peace: if war eats your block, or disease, or a mall, no art can be created. Art takes and takes, wanting so much. I give and give, and ask little.

I put down my plate and stretch out on my chaise and here is the sun and here is the sun shining through me, my skin slowly changing, my body consuming and producing, the crows hunched on sun-brightened wires, the dragonflies and yellow jackets landing then buzzing then landing again, the lemon trees still in their planters. The Bay's marine layer is just past the bridge; in minutes, its gray will crown San Francisco. Downhill from my home stands the home of the Burgstroms: a cream-colored Tudor worth maybe four million. The electrified fence that I've had wrapped with fake ivy has killed two of their cats and, before that, a puppy. The Burgstroms no longer own any pets. This saddens me; pets are big business. Pets need to be bathed. Pets need to be fed. Pets need to be housed over summer vacations. Pets get in fights. Pets get hit by cars. Pets need their limbs amputated. And leashes for walking. And small rubber toys. And round granite headstones to remember them by, when direction of sojourn means meeting of maker.

Mrs Burgstrom floats now in her blue-tiled pool, in a white rubber cap and strapless black one-piece. On their roof is a telescope, for looking at stars. One son's at Dean-Witter, the other at Merrill. Both have tall wives with thin hips and slim feet. Both of these women would look gorgeous in rags. Instead, Valentino, leased German sedans. Rings inlaid with diamonds, each gem the size of the pit of a cherry. And in exchange for these gifts, a womb which will ripen: nine months of weight gain then pain then C-section, followed by breast pumps and throw-up and diapers, and with the weight lost and the crib still and silent, the two Burgstrom sons and their slim-footed wives will grow damp and moan under high-thread-count sheets, and repeat the process exactly once more, and begin, very slowly, to hate one another, as the husbands work late, though they aren't really working, and the wives have lunch dates where nothing is eaten, and the children, both boys, grow, quickly, up, and get into Stanford, and get into Princeton, and have too their own wives, and their own pairs of children, and buy houses with pools, which their wives will float in.

Wind off the ocean, pushed through the fog. Mrs Burgstrom ascends her swimming pool's ladder. The sun sinks to dim orb past the white marine layer, and bathed now in soft light is Berkeley, is Oakland. Goodnight to Napa, its acres of grapes, its Zagat-applauded French bistros. Goodnight to the Golden Gate Bridge and its jumpers. Goodnight to the hobos of South and North Berkeley, pissing in yards filled with drought-tolerant flora, who through the small hours will slur incoherent – goodnight to their beards and their fleas and their fears, goodnight to their laughter and problems. Goodnight to artists' lofts dotting west Oakland, where vegan subversives silk-screen scoop necks to the tinkle of crack vials breaking. Goodnight to Lake Merritt, its gray murky slough. Goodnight to Hayward, the county courthouse, its surplus of piquant redactions. Goodnight to the South Bay, its orchards of pixels. Goodnight to the city named after St Francis; goodnight to the tight and steep hills that comprise it; goodnight to North Beach, goodnight Noe Valley, goodnight to the Mission and Western Addition and long-idle shipyards of Bayview/Hunter's Point; goodnight to Nob Hill and the Castro; goodnight to the Haight, goodnight Pacific Heights, goodnight to Parkside and SOMA and NOMA, goodnight to the Sunsets, both Inner and Outer. Soon, switches flicked to keep out the dark. Soon, the consuming of Sunday-night dinner, the small fork then the big one, the spoon and the knife, sweaters and slacks, napkins of linen, the cooking of beasts slaughtered six states away, brought here by Eisenhower's Interstate System – five million mouths chewing five million meals as stomachs expand and dusk, bruised to death, is wondered at mutely then promptly forgotten.

I put food in a tube that runs down my wife's throat. The bedroom's near-dark, the lights kept on a dimmer. I scrub my wife's feet with the same sort of stone one uses to remove lime from porcelain. My wife is past gaunt. Her ribs show through the sheets. Each day new hairs loose onto her pillow. My wife dyed her hair blonde but is really brunette. Her straight matted locks look like a half-painted wall, like a project unfinished. And here the done nose, the bridge sculpted to perfect. And here the blue eyes that don't ever open. And here are my hands on the clasp of her necklace, her back slightly lifted, her breathing tube pressed against the wall of her esophagus. The noise deepens some, the machine working harder. One year of this. Four separate seasons. One year of baths with a bowl, a damp sponge. One year of massaging thin calves and thin fingers. The doctors say grim. The doctors say stasis. The doctors give chances that involve single digits. And I say you're wrong. I say you don't know her like I know her.

A key in the lock: Esquido is here. Esquido's our nurse. Esquido's Salvadorian. Esquido was once part of the MS-13s, one of the most evil gangs on the planet. Their ways are perhaps best described as parasitic: they figure out who is selling what where, then kill lots of these people and enslave the remainder. They grew up in jungle towns, orphans of orphans. They worked for cartels as sadistic guerrillas. They hack men with machetes in area malls; they control the Richmond dope trade, every kilo. My friend Frank Gaines, not a nice man, works for the Feds out of their LA office. He was part of a raid on a house down in Watts; Esquido was caught climbing out of a window. This was bad form, per the MS-13s' governing tenets. You kill all you can and if capture is imminent, you kill yourself – there aren't any prisoners. Esquido did neither, and was thus marked for death. Hid underground by the Feds for eight years, they removed his tattoos and altered his cheekbones. Esquido takes pills that lighten his skin. Esquido has learned how to speak without accent. Esquido was trained as an R.N. while lamming. Esquido's real name isn't really Esquido.

'How is she?' he says, shutting the door. Early last year, the first week of February, men broke into my home while I slept. They planned to tie me up and then take things. Both were parolees with no gang affiliation. Esquido was in my home's den, not sleeping. The men's paths diverged, a tactical mistake. They lived bound in my basement for over a week. My son never knew the intruders were here. Afterward, Esquido presented me with two mason jars: one filled with teeth, the other with fingers.

'Her eyes twitched,' I say. 'They're doing that more. I know it's nothing.'

'It's not nothing,' says Esquido. My friend Frank Gaines has promised me this man until my wife dies, or until she gets better.

'I fed her already and I changed her necklace. The tube bumped her throat. If you'd double-check that everything's fine there.'

'Of course,' says Esquido.

'I'm out for the night, then,' I say, and Esquido nods once and I leave the bedroom. In my office I change into slacks and black oxfords and slide one of my laptops into its neoprene sleeve. It's full dark outside. The air's gotten colder.

I leave my home's hill in my small silver Prius. My suburb is still, its main street elm-lined and empty. Piedmont is home to three banks and two churches. There's a small barbershop, one high-end market. The Veteran's Center is set between the police and the fire departments. There's a community pool; my son swam for their team. Across the street, his old high school, the source of his exile, the setting for him beating a classmate unconscious. My town has six stoplights, about ten thousand people. My town has no motto. My town's motto is: Money. At the base of its hills, where it borders with Oakland, are tall iron gates with chains wrapped around them. As legend has it, these gates were installed for keeping out have-nots in times of peril. They haven't been closed since I was alive; few things, however, are purely aesthetic, and on some occasions, in pre-dawn's small hours, I've seen city workers, their truck's lights turned off, checking the locks and oiling the hinges.

Telegraph Avenue runs north to Cal-Berkeley and south to Jack London Square, and Oakland's marina. The waterfront's air smells of salt and pollution. My top-floor king suite looks out at its docks and its jetties. Boats with their sails wrapped bob on the water. The whole room is pastels: hues of nausea, of weakness. The drapes are light salmon, the bedspread mint green. Wallpaper that would best be described as eggs, fainting. All these shades chosen from the same base ideology that gets fusion jazz into so many elevators: finding things that all will like is quite hard; finding things that all will hate is much more achievable. Placation is the Siamese twin of distemper. Here's your cheap room: do you see these wan colors? Can you feel, deep inside you, how much you dislike them? And do you remember that were you much richer, you would not bed, shit and shave in such places? That these sorts of interiors simply aren't seen by those who drive Beamers and clutch Prada clutches? That that demographic gets mints on its sheets? And flat-screen TVs? And sleek fancy headboards twice lined with firm pillows? Not you, though, small friend. Here, hairs by the drain. Here, every wood surface fiberboard laminate. And the lamp needs a bulb and the ceiling fan's broken and the windows won't open more than two inches, the management's unspoken belief being, in regard to the last of these items, that if this is the sort of place you must stay in, a window fully opened will be used as a portal to an afterlife that must be at least a bit better than an existence you've managed, somehow, to cobble and eke, a life of malaise and microwave dinners, a long string of months lived paycheck-to-paycheck, a life of clipped coupons and loans upon which you've defaulted, and for this, low ceilings, exterior stairs, a TV that whines while you watch it, and for this, brown carpet (the room's dark exception), a cake of thick shag iced with the fluids of decades of guests, while the fatcats drink gin in big lobby bars, and don't wake in the night to the noise of airplanes overhead – instead this place, that feels like you're living in a trash can the day after Easter. Get mad. That's what I'm after. That's why this room looks like it does. You've paid for it already; I don't want you in it. I want you to hate it so much and so purely that you go out and spend cash so that you'll feel more worthy. Bring back dumb gifts for your undersmart kids, *des petits cadeaux* for that spouse you know not what to do with. This room is not here to make you feel at home. This room is not here because you're on vacation. What this room is is just better than jail. Shop. See the sights. Get some fries at the Arby's, located next door. It closes at ten, due to near-constant robbings. I hope, sincerely, you had a nice stay. Now return to your rock, its slick, dark underbelly.

In the small single drawer of the king bed's nightstand, I remove the phone book from beneath the Bible. Escorts is found just before Escrow, and just after Escalators. I call the first place I find with a 510 number. A woman's voice answers. Her tone says, I am bored. Her tone says, I spend long hours of my day accommodating perverts. She is, perhaps, a mile away, in a small ground-floor office without any windows. The building is filled with these sorts of suites, blank sterile chambers with low overhead leased by dreamers and scammers, the stupid and brave. There are rows of phone banks; there are rows of computers.

'I want an escort. A woman,' I say. A boat's galley lights up, out on the water.

'What type of girl do you want?' the woman asks me. I am trying to imagine her happiest moment, that scene in time where the sun shone upon her. What was she wearing? What sat in her hands? What was the name of the pet that had loved her? Doing so is my job, and I'm always working.

'She needs to have arms. Both arms,' I say. 'Legs are of lesser importance.' I unzip my Mac from its neoprene sleeve. The woman says nothing for two, three, four seconds.

'Are you there?' I ask. 'Did we get disconnected?'

The bored woman sighs. We all have a sound that we're best at.

'I need your first name.'

'My first name's Esquido.'

'Okay, Esquido, and where are you this evening?'

'I'm staying in a king suite down at Jack London. Do I get the privilege of learning your name?'

The bored woman's typing now. 'My name is Rachel, Esquido,' she says, leaning on the middle syllable of my alias, to show she's not stupid, and that her name's not Rachel. So many masks and codes and passwords. So much emotional binary.

'And Rachel, what are we wearing tonight?'

'We're wearing clothes, Esquido.'

'Are they sexy clothes?'

'Not really,' says Rachel.

'Well, what kind of clothes are they?' A man climbs the stairs of the boat with the illuminated galley. He points to the stars and then pulls down his pants, and pees in the water.

'Do you want me to hang up, or do you want a girl at your hotel room?'

'I don't want you to hang up, Rachel. I'm deeply sorry. What I was wondering, and what I did a poor job of wording, was whether you are, in your line of work, forced to dress up. Is it office wear? Is it business casual? Or do you work in sweats and camis and such?' And I do want to know, because Rachel's employed, which means that she has disposable income. Maybe not much, but at the very least some, and clothes let me know how she wants to spend it.

'I've got on blue jeans and a sweater, Esquido. Where are you staying and what's your room number?'

'I'm at the Breezeway, room 325. But Rachel, please, who makes your jeans? Are they from a thrift store? Are they designer jeans? Is your sweater a crew neck? A long thing that ties?'

More typing now; I can hear the sharp clacks. A phone rings on Rachel's end of the line. Dumb, lonely men, nervous and hungry.

'My clothes are not used. I need a card number.'

'But Rachel, the jeans. Just tell me that. Are they Levis? Express? Did you buy them at Walmart? Were they a gift? Who knows your size? And what *is* your size, Rachel, if you don't mind me asking?'

The phone line keeps ringing; Rachel's maybe alone. 'I need to go, Esquido. Like right now.' Rachel is stressed; this exhibits work ethic. I give her my card number, my security code.

'Rachel, okay, but answer me this: how much would you say you spend per week on gasoline for your vehicle? And when you fill up, what else do you buy at the gas station? Mints, maybe, sometimes? A soda or two? And Rachel, what else would you buy if you could? What is it you want that's not being offered?'

'Jacinda is a hot brunette with all the right moves. She's tall, and she used to be an exotic dancer. Jacinda will take you to the heights of passion, and leave you wanting more. Goodbye, Esquido.'

Rachel hangs up. Goodnight, sweet Rachel. May the agency give you a raise for your poise in the face of such wanton indelicacy. Please know this land has plans for you. Keep working. Keep praying. Keep spending.

The peeing man descends the stairs to his galley. From my hotel's small lot comes the sound of a car frame shaking from bass. I open my room's door and step out to the shared asphalt landing. Here is a Caddie on Daytons with Sprewells. The car is grass green, the windows tinted to onyx. The rims' name, Sprewell, is derived from the former Golden State Warriors basketball player. This man choked his coach in the middle of practice, then returned later and promised to kill him. And for this, hubcaps named in his honor: shiny chrome things that when a car moves at a high speed cycle, slowly, backwards. Their image is one of confusion and whimsy and danger and status, and in this way pays homage to their namesake quite well. Sprewell's gone from the league but lives on here, in Oakland.

The Caddie takes off as fast as it arrived. Through the windshield's thick glass I catch a glimpse of the driver, a man wearing a baseball hat and sunglasses. So many masks and codes and passwords. So much emotional binary.

I watch Fox for ten minutes, then CNN. The big breaking news? In our new global world? Where everyone and everything is connected? Where one can know all with a few clicks of a button? Where we can all organize? Where we can all matter? The big breaking news is that early this evening a girl hung herself in Frankfort, Kentucky. Kylie Mae Heath was sixteen years old. Kylie Mae Heath was a virgin. Kylie Mae's friends were part of a 'club' where they had to bed at least one male peer by the semester's conclusion. Kylie Mae Heath alone failed to do so. Swift retribution: her car's tires slashed, her MySpace and Facebook pages gone friendless. In her school's long halls she was turned to pariah, and one day at lunch someone dumped pasta on her, and one day, during gym class, her backpack and cell phone and sandals were stolen. And then, the next week, some boys, all juniors, went to the middle school that Kylie's brother attended, and there stole his skateboard, and knocked him unconscious. These acts were enough for Kylie to fashion a noose, and then tie this noose to one of the rafters in her parents' home's basement. Fox has on a pastor; CNN a psychologist. Why, tell us why, plead the newscasters.

The pastor and shrink give their status-quo answers: if we worshipped more, if we knew ourselves better. But that's not why this item is big breaking news. This item is news because it's Sunday, past nine. This item is news due to marketing trends and understanding the television-watching demographic. This item is news because on other channels are cartoon sitcoms and plot-heavy cop dramas. This item is news because those who watch news, at this time, on this day, have been understood by execs as low-level unstable, and biased, and zealots, and won't watch the filth that's on other channels, that coarse, smutty fiction without virtue or god. Those who want news at this time, on this day, want two things at once: to feel worse and feel better. This demographic – stern widows, the sick – must own its self-loathing to best revel in it. This demographic is low, constant moan: a cave-thing, albino and sightless. It needs its own voice beamed back at its feelers – it subsists on recognition of echo. It's the grandmother rotting away in her mansion; it's the blood-diseased uncle in hospital gown, who blames the woes of his body on the Dems, immigration. And thus young Kylie, wood-hard on a slab in a morgue in Kentucky, her corpse now a springboard for Nielsen share. Are you faith-based? Fox has rented a priest. Do you crave ethos? The shrink teaches at Harvard. The wrapping is different, but it's the same present: a gift that keeps giving because you want and let it. And now the newscasters thank their paid guests. And now the newscasters vow that in minutes you'll get to see young Kylie's mom, standing on the lawn of her home in Frankfort, her eyes like a raccoon's, her life wrecked forever. Wait; please just wait. We promise you sustenance. We promise you reverberation. We promise you hate that you'll translate as love.

In the meantime, please watch these commercials.

Three raps on the door – my project's arrival. I get up from the bed and turn on my Mac and cross the brown rug and crouch at the peephole. I see no pimp hiding. I see no one else. I swing the door open. 'Jacinda,' I say. She typifies cliché. She is the Socratic ideal of hussy. Her makeup's foundation is like skin on warm milk. Her cherry red lipstick looks as though applied with a roller. Her hair, dyed to black and done up in a bob, appears closer to wig than genuine fibers. Her faux-leopard half-jacket is too small, polyester. Tiny black hot shorts. Diamond fishnets. Red open-toe heels, the ankles unbelted. Is there some rack in the agency's chamber? Some poor row of costumes from which all must pick? Jacinda's chest, fake, spills from her corset. Her calves look on loan from a pro football player. I thank Rachel profusely. Jacinda is perfect.

'Hey, baby,' says Jacinda, and pushes in past me. Her scent is amalgam of armpits and perfume, a compost of wilting rose blossoms. She sits on the bed as though this were home, as though this place possessed for her distinct comfort. Her eyes are deep brown and too close together. She digs in her purse. She takes out a cell phone; she takes out two condoms.

'Like sands through the hourglass.'

'What'd you say, baby?'

'Forget it,' I tell her. 'I want you all night. Until sunrise. Roughly eight hours.'

'I can't do it, baby. I've got people waiting. I've got other clients I've got to go see.'

From my slacks' pocket I take out a sheaf of clean bills. They're bank-bound: fifty one-hundreds.

'This is five grand. Will you stay until dawn.' I pose this as statement. Jacinda stops burrowing through the pouch of her purse. She meets my gaze. We have a winner.

'I don't do anal. You can't piss on me. You can't beat me up. And there's no way I'll kiss you.'

'Absolutely,' I say. I throw the bills on the bed. 'Jacinda,' I ask, 'are you familiar with Microsoft Word? Do you know how to craft a text document?'

'You mean, like, type? On a computer?'

'That is what I mean.'

'Well, yeah,' says Jacinda.

'That's perfect,' I say. 'That's really good.' I shut the room's door. I turn the lock's deadbolt.

'Jacinda, what I need you to do, when you're ready, is sit down at that chair, there, in front of that laptop.'

Jacinda obliges. Her hips swing like a bull's. I'm guessing size 12. I'm guessing 180. Jacinda sits down. The room's floor shakes a little. Right now, in China, a factory worker is sewing the stitching into a new pair of hot pants just like the ones that Jacinda is wearing.

'Are you comfy?' I ask. 'You have what you need?'

'Oh wait, my purse,' says Jacinda.

'I'll get it,' I say. 'You just stay there.' The black mini is vinyl with buckles of chrome. I put the phone and two condoms back in its belly and set the accessory down on the bureau.

'What are we going to do?' asks Jacinda. She is anxious. She made it, I'm guessing, through ninth, tenth grade. High school like a dress on a changing-room bench: ill-fitting, forgotten.

'What you're going to do, Jacinda, is this: you're going to write down everything that you want, or have ever wanted. You're going to include these items' details: what color they are, their type, size and shape. This list can derive from free association. The list does not need to be chronological. Feel free to jump backward and forward through time. Let one thing draw another thing from you. But the list must be complete as you can possibly make it, and you must include, when you can, why you want or wanted these items. You have until dawn to complete this assignment.'

Jacinda stares blankly. Her dumb eyes won't blink. When I was fourteen, and cleaning out my parents' house in preparation for auction, I found a possum down in the basement. It was crouched at the sill of a ground-level window. In my hand was an orange extension cord I'd just finished coiling. My dad had once told me that opossums were so dumb, you could hypnotize them into falling off things. I uncoiled a half-foot of the thick orange cord. I swung this length back and forth in front of the tensely clutched rodent. Ten seconds passed, then fifteen, then twenty. The animal's eyes watched the cord swing; they were bright black and tiny, and soulless. I kept at it: even and slow, patient swings. The animal's body relaxed as I neared a minute. Its haunches sat down and its tail spread out. I gave the cord slack, the arc growing wider. The possum's front paws moved past the sill's lip. Its eyes went back and forth, its mind lost to the motion. When I brought the plug down on the crown of its skull, the possum fell stunned to the basement's stone floor. I crushed its head with the heel of my boot, then went back to packing.

'Did you know, Jacinda, that possums are the only marsupials that live on the North American continent?'

Jacinda's sloped nose almost reaches her teeth. 'What's a marsupial?' she asks me.

'A marsupial, Jacinda, is so many things. But it's also just one individual thing. Do you understand what I want you to do?'

'You want me to write down all the shit that I want.'

'That's right,' I say. 'Every last item.'

Saga: a Pikachu Pokémon doll; a thrift-store Nintendo her stepmom wouldn't buy her. Games for this console: Duck Hunt and Punch-Out, Tetris and Metroid and Mario Brothers. Brown Mary Janes with red satin bows. A bright yellow backpack with CatWoman on it. A passport. A degree from a college (read: collage). O-ring poly halters, backless, from Macy's. Free coke from her dealer. Courvoisier. A stretch Hummer limo with sunroof and hot tub. A red Schwinn three-speed with white plastic basket. *This ring that I saw in da city w/ Leesa – it had hella emuhrulds on it.* A hot pink tracksuit, velour, made by Juicy. Picture frames, tampons, Chicken McNuggets. A 58-inch flat-screen TV. An iPhone. An iMac. Bras by La Perla. Prada sunglasses. White satin sheets. Free auto insurance. A Pick-A-Path book called *The Dungeon of Monsters*. A pit bull named Biggy. A sleek private jet. A masseur and a personal trainer. Two full-length fur coats, one of hare, one of sable. A skybox for every Raiders home game. *For those fuckers to parole my dad outta Folsom.* A house in Lake Tahoe. A house in LA. A bed that sleeps ten. A yacht that sleeps fifty. Couches in leather. Couches in suede. *I saw this gun once that was pink – a revolver. I want that gun, like four of those guns. I want one of those guns for each of my houses.* An Xbox. A website. Her own perfume line. *To cut off the balls of each man that's fucked me.* Her own pool. Her own beach. *My own fucking ocean.*

Jacinda smokes Newports. Jacinda types slowly. At ten after one, around three hours in, Jacinda runs out of things to write down. I turn on the TV and then mute the volume. Jacinda stares at the box, its blue screen of bright colors. I sit inches away, in the room's other chair. Jacinda bends over to remove her heels. I set down my journal, its copious notes, and push my capped pen into her fleshy shoulder.

'I can't take off my shoes?'

'I'd prefer if you didn't.'

'But they're hurting my feet.'

'And yet you chose to wear them.'

'I hell of did not choose to wear these. The agency says that I gotta wear heels.'

'And who was it,' I ask, 'that forced you to work there?'

Jacinda says shit man, which isn't the answer. The answer lies in the things comprising her list. The answer lies in the Sprewells, spinning, slowly, backwards. The answer lies in Esquido, right now at my home, curled up with Proust beneath a plaid blanket. The answer lies in bank fees and house liens and crime rates, in numbers that don't stop compounding, accruing.

And the bulimic preteen. And the weekend jet skier. And the wan soccer mom lost to Lustral from Walgreen's. And the all-summer tourist inside his RV. And the Vanity Queen with her Botox appointments. And the elderly widow alone on her couch; on her TV set are tanzanite bangles. The man who is hosting this QVC hour has the same chin as her husband once had. The bangles are bright. The bangles look charming. The bangles are shown from a variety of angles. She is undone by their glow, by their wonder. My Lambs, my Lambs, here is Your church. Here is Your altar, Your nave, Your stained glass. Here are Your pews and Your steeple. Remain pious always. You are safe here. Listen not to the spendthrifts, the bear-market false prophets. Their words are untrue; they've been licked wet by evil. Fight those dark thoughts of downturn, of recession; our republic is sun-kissed, without pox or canker. Dear flock, devotion: Your faith is each day. Rest little. Stay scared. Buy often.

Around three a.m. Jacinda breaks down. Tears turn her mascara to narrow grey streams. Her upper lip shakes like a newly born kitten. Her list, single-spaced, is roughly four pages.

'I can't do this no more,' Jacinda says through her sniffles. 'This hella sucks. I ain't ever gonna get this stuff and this was fun for like a second thinking about getting all this stuff but now it sucks and I'm tired and just want to go home.'

I stand up and grab the bills from the bed. I take out one single hundred. Here is Ben Franklin, his smiling face framed. At dawn, post-Jacinda, a three-hour nap, then the Bay Bridge, a full day at the office. Above the room's bureau, on the wall, is a mirror. I stare at Jacinda's dark, beady eyes. Her face's reflection, from nose to chin, is cut off by the laptop's monitor. Behind her, my starched shirt tucked into my slacks, my black leather belt, my hand holding the hundred. I own Time. I am Powerful. I flip down the laptop. Jacinda stares at its logo. I bend all the way down to the cuff of her neck. I press the bill to her cheek, drying her tears. I press hard, and then wipe off the other.

2

My name is Jim Haskin, and it's my job to make you You. Not the small you, the lowercase, the intractable you, not the first you, the true you, not the you of unbiased judgment; not the you who will help your elderly neighbor rake leaves in autumn and shovel come winter and water come summer, and pick up their paper, and take to them supper, not you the dissenter, not the you of love unconditional; not you the good parent, not you the free tutor, not you who will talk for as long as you want with the store clerk, the teller, the waitress; not the you who still knows how to cook, how to bake, not the you who can change their own tire; not the you who can name your sky's constellations; not the you who has given up soda; not the you who picks trash up from off of the street and repairs it to some place more proper; not you the hand-holder, not you the weigher of options; not the you who turns shirts that are stained, ripped or wrecked into rags for the floor of the bathroom; not the you who can sew on a button; not the you who can sit very still on a couch or a bench or a seat of a bus, turning a library book's pages; not the you who keeps taped to the door of the fridge the number for their state representative; not you the scribe, not you the philomath, not you the sesquipedalian; not the you who still looks at the

24

afternoon light of a Sunday with the bare grace of wonder; not you who is staid, not you the succor, not the you of no mistress or ex-mistress or mistress-to-be; not the you who writes letters, those small noisome things; not the you who can do their own taxes; not the you who is happy to walk down the street because you know your city and you know your neighbors, and know too the names of the trees that you pass, and know also the names of the birds on their branches, and what types of clouds are right now overhead, and what days of what months mark the passing of seasons, and tells drivers at nighttimes to turn on their lights, and stops well before crossing pedestrians, and sleeps soundly and dreams and knows when to indulge and does possess inner resources, and does not think, as the poet once said, that *life, friends, is boring*; not the you of the mind like a trap made for bears; not the you of no party alignment; not the you who has placed, per federal law, a five-year moratorium on firm offers of credit, and has also stopped getting thick mailers of coupons, and removed your name from catalog lists, and does not own a cell phone or mp3 player, and does not have in their closet a near-lake of shoes, and more ties than they know what to do with; not you the aplomb, not you the fomenter; not the you who dispels the contumely, the flouters, and does curse but rarely and spends within range; not you the roisterer of viral malaise, who is not too ashamed to let loose in ways healthy; not the you who thinks twice; not the you who checks labels; not the you who cleans up; not the you who stays after; not the you who calms down before violent action and thereby avoids both regret and shame (I need you to have those: hit harder, hit often); not the you who can find on a map the Black Sea, not the you who can find on a map Costa Rica, and also the Balkans and Burma, Peru, and can locate yourself amongst all this terrain – remain who you are and what you want to be in the face of subversion, in the face of debasement; not the you who tries daily to do what they can; not the you who staves off, not the you of the well-balanced diet; not the you who attends monthly community meetings, who knows when they are, at what hour they meet, and where they are held, and just how to get there, and which topics, on that night, might be discussed, and demands to know why, and always wants better, and raises their hand and puts thought into words, and lets not their thoughts be usurped by the language of others; not the you who is critical; not the you who is patient; not the you who is even and open and public; not the you who dislikes but supports nonetheless, not the you of the complex position; not the you who is happy with what you possess, not the you who is happy not possessing; not the you who lets the other person go first; not you the observer, not you the fact-checker, not the you who keeps at it in the face of complaint; not you the supplicant; not you the line striker; not the you who packs out all the things they brought in; not the you of greased elbows and dutiful ethic; not the you who pulls over on the side of the highway to wait for the tow truck with some total stranger, only to watch them beg off and say *help's on the way but thank you, thank you for stopping*; not you of the scales, not you of the fulcrum; not you the big tipper, of present unearned, not the you of guerrilla altruism, not the you who is charming by being yourself; not the you who is loyal, not the you who stands guard, not the you who could but won't do it; not the you of no diamonds, no makeup for face, no shots for smooth skin, no breast augmentation, no pills for erection, no treatment for baldness, no pump for your penis, no contact lenses that alter the iris, no dye for your hair, no ink on your skin, no piercings thrust through some soft bit of flesh, no three-inch wedges that blow out your ankles, no silk pocket square to make your suit pop, not the you of good thoughts; not the you of no watch; not the you who embraces the holidays of foreign religions; not the you unconcerned with what others may think; not you the uncertain; not you the imperfect; not the you of deep breaths nor the you of cloth diapers; not the you who is humble, not the you undeserving; not the you who keeps track; not the you who leads through example; not the you who is kind, not the you who is lucid; not the you that deep down you have truly always been.

Fuck that you; it gets me nothing.

The You I make is brand-name. The You I make is prime-time. The You that I make is a status update. The You that I make is a wireless router. The You that I make is Your favorite shape. The You that I make is Your favorite color. The You that I make cannot have enough. The You that I make covets and covets. The You that I make is a five-star review. The You that I make hates all of Your music. The You that I make wants to eat healthy but won't. The You that I make fears their spouse, loathes their marriage. The You that I make sees a shrink twice a week: this world is so awful, what could have made it? The You that I make has more house than You need. The You that I make buys books You don't finish. The You that I make prefers magazines, their short blocks of text next to pretty, pretty pictures. The You that I make distrusts the valet, and parks in an alley, and is mugged after dinner, and in turn succumbs to racist ideology that I did not make but brought out from in You – think of Michelangelo, the sculpture there always, in Your slab of marble. The You that I make likes shopping online: the malls are too full of the wrong type of people. The You that I make has not been on a bus since the last day of grade school. The You that I make is a driver. The You that I make hates the bus, that long beast, so sure of its tonnage that it blocks Your lane while helping out others that I have helped make, but these others not You, these castoffs are scourge, and their Mongol ways are both base and invasive. The You that I make is proud of Yourself when You drive by the bus and flip off its driver. The You that I make is somewhat overweight. The You that I make puts strain on your organs. The You that I make, without morning caffeine, would implode while both weeping and screaming. The You that I make, when you pass by a bum on the street, is sure they're a drug addict, because You're a drug addict, but don't view yourself as an addict of drugs, and therefore despise the addicted. The You that I make likes to pout like a child when the You that I make doesn't get what You want. The You that I make is sure You're being watched, and the You that I make's right to think so. My You is a truckler. My You hoards time. My You is fop and subaltern. The You that I make comes in five different flavors. The You that I make loved the season finale. The You that I make owns the boxed set that like You has been digitally remastered. The You that I make weeps out-of-control when the commercial comes on for pets sick, lame and orphaned, but when they show the number that allows you to help, You dry Your eyes and then change the channel. The You that I make hasn't voted for years. The You that I make owns five dozen sweaters. The You that I make is not worth full words, and will BRB, and is LYAO. The You that I make, no matter what You make, is not making enough, keeps getting passed over. The You that I make has kids that need shots; the You that I make has kids that need braces, and cleats for athletics, and tutors for Spanish, and the right kind of friends and a primary role in this year's Winter Holiday Pageant, and needs also decals for the back of the car, each family member represented as sticker, stick-figured, one single column of crudely done drawings, all holding hands: please see how happy, please see how united. Please believe what you see and leave us alone and let us drive back to our four-bedroom home of quiet dysfunction. To the You that I make. To the self that I crush. To belief that's put out like a pan that's caught fire. To loud pipes of lead. To poor water pressure. To sex toys and end tables and espresso makers. To a thing made of things that must be replaced with other things that are faster, and sleeker, resplendent, as the You that I make is the new You, the now You, the You who is scared, the You who is perfect, the You who will chew what You've been told to eat, the You of true greed, the You of acts violent, the You who feels small, the You who feels slighted, the You of divorce, the You of depression, the You of a narcissism so expansive and base that it functions as both sea and anchor; the You who hates men; the You who hates women; the You who will turn on the TV without thinking; the You of cards made for credit and debit; the You of the mortgage and 401K and portfolio that You're slowly growing; the You of the website; the You of the pantsuit; but above all the You Who Buys Items, because when You Buy Items You are strong, and You are well, and when You Buy Items You're like everyone else but You are also very much better, and when You Buy Items You buy Yourself time, and when You Buy Items You show that You're trying, and when You Buy Items it's just not Your fault, and when You Buy Items You're lord and not vassal, Your house now a castle, Your lawns not just land now but kingdom, and when You Buy Items Your flag flies on its pole, and when You Buy Items You own drawbridge and moat, and when You Buy Items You have both sword and armor, as out there are dragons and bugbear and demons, mythical threats with claws on their feet, and great and wide wings, and mouths that breathe fire, and You'll perish quickly if You're not prepared, and away goes Your jester and away goes Your mutton, but when You Buy Items Your walls are much thicker, Your escutcheon known, Your allegiance unquestioned.

And when You Buy Items you are a warm and blue day in our Nation of nations.

It's Monday, and the Bleach Boys need something new. My office on Battery Street faces east; its dual panes of foxed glass look back toward my home and the mainland. In between, the Bay Bridge: its long columns of cars, the spiritual grace that true gridlock affords me. On top of my desk of white pine and black leather I keep a pair of high-end binoculars, made by Steiner. I use my Safari Pros nearly each day. I can check on my Flock without being seen, without interfering. It's eight-thirty a.m. The lines scoot and then stop, then do it again, then again. My Lambs' morning commute is like having a seizure. I spin the Pros' scope with one of my fingers. Turn signals blink; a woman is singing. A man loses the cream in his filled maple bar and throws the thing down and hits his car's ceiling. The sun has burned off the Bay's nightly fog, and the cars' painted roofs gleam like coins tossed as tithes into the basket of collection. The ad firm I run, American Weather, takes up one-half of this side of the building. My assistant, Andrew, is openly gay. He's single but hopes to be married soon via Prop 8, California's bill on gay marriage. A Yes vote on Prop 8 means No on Gay Marriage. A No vote means Yes. Andrew has reminded all at the office of this repeatedly. Andrew grew up in Georgia and his voice is an amalgam of fey whine and slow drawl. His voice, right now, is talking to me through my phone's intercom system.

'Hey, Jim, hey, y'all's appointment is here.'

'Okay, send them in,' I tell Andrew. 'Thank you, Andrew.'

American Weather employs twenty-five. We do more with less. I do next to nothing. My Senior VP, Simerpreet Sweeney, takes care of the ins and the outs of the daily operations. I pay her well. She both loves me and hates me. The former because she gets to play boss, the latter because she actually isn't, and feels that she should be. Simerpreet went to Yale not once but twice. Simer's dad's white, her mom Bangladeshi. I'd asked Simer once what surname she'd used on her school applications. Her mom's maiden name is Akhtar. We were up at a bar at the top of Nob Hill.

'The one that worked better,' Simer had told me.

Past this, the office is faux-socialist: people do certain tasks and have certain titles, but mainly are nine-to-five wards of my state, happily babysitted. The new collar is No Collar, especially out west, and especially here, in San Francisco. This toned-down aesthetic makes good and fine sense for an ad firm like American Weather. This is because we are Green. Green as a field. Green as the Charles on March 17th which, being Green, we did not approve of. American Weather will design you an ad only if your product and line and soul, body and mind are eco-friendly. We do organic and solar and cruelty-free. We do hybrid, upcylced and hydro. We sell exercise bikes that can power light bulbs. We sell shoes made of hemp and car tires. If it doesn't use gas, or the parts of dead beasts, or damage our streams or our air or our soil, we design ads and we sell it. My firm's won awards from the State, the EPA. My firm has been featured in *Newsweek* and *WIRED*.

All that's the front room. The back room is me. The back room is why the Bleach Boys are here. The back room is exactly the opposite of Green. I call the back room the Red Room.

The door opens up and the Bleach Boys push in. The duo resembles the product they make: artificial, toxic, icterine. Both men are Caucasian, and tall, and quite thin. Wan, jaundiced faces with terse down-turned lips. Cheap pinstriped suits that fit rather poorly. Bleach sales, it seems, have gone through the floor. Their product's main plant, near Oakland's port (and the hotel where I spent the night with Jacinda), has been in the news as of late, and not for good reason. A *Tribune* reporter, a year or so back, caught wind of run-off: each night around three, the plant emits gallons of hazardous agents into the Bay's ecosystem. This isn't new. The plant's been here forever. The bleach plant predates Kaiser's shipbuilding yards. It predates Prohibition. The bleach plant was here when Oakland had *farms*. And bleach was and is quite important.

However.

Oakland's estuary is a small strip of murk used more by hookers than by sea creatures. Its weeds, dirt and straits are largely ungoverned. The doomed come here with syringes, with condoms. It functions, too, as an ad hoc graveyard for the near-constant gang wars of West and East Oakland. But at six in the morning, three days a week, the city's crew team arrives to set up its sculls on the water. The Oakland Strokes is comprised of high-school juniors and seniors, many of whom come from families in Piedmont. The rest are from way up in Oakland's rich hills. Poor people don't row. If they did, the Bleach Boys would be in less trouble.

One day, last April, their races complete, the Oakland Strokes team, at five in the morning, came to the estuary for one final practice. Two hours before, the plant had had a problem: some switch was not flipped and instead of ten gallons of hazardous waste being hurtled through pipes and into the Bay, out went thousands of gallons. This was the bad stuff: lye, heavy metals. Things that once in bloodstreams deform unborn babies. And the team members, feeling cocky, and against better judgment, but also upholding a decades-long tradition, finished their pulling and then left their boats, and jumped headlong into floating biohazard.

Two of the teens are now permanently blind. Four more contracted hepatitis. There were lesions on skin, hair falling out. Infections of staph. Vascular problems. In short, a disaster, and again, less so, if these teens had been from a more modest tax bracket. Instead, though, rich white kids, their lives largely wrecked. Instead, the Associated Press picking up coverage. Lawsuits and bomb threats. A grim fiscal quarter. And so now they sit, the Bleach Boys, concerned, in chairs on the other side of my desk. The men's names are Doug Combs and William Luttrell. They've paid big money and they want big answers. This is how cash is made hand over fist. This is how my ad firm affords vegan foie gras on birthdays.

'Mr Combs,' I say, 'Mr Luttrell, the product that you represent is one of humankind's necessary evils. For so long, without bleach, there's no brightness, no sterilization. Without bleach, the microbe rubs us from the face of the planet. Your company's founders were smart and good men with true and pure vision. And yet we've reached a point, as a society, a species, where your product has become a microbe itself. Our planet is dying and you help this along. There are autoclaves now, other modes of sterilization. You saw the picketers. You heard the bomb threats. You feared, I am sure, for your safety. None of this your fault – you went to college and fought the good fight and found yourself gainful employment and reproduced, and these attacks on the item you happen to sell have transformed into attacks on your person. You are Doom Merchants. You are Where the Finger Points. You look in your rearview when driving your car now. You call your wife on the hour, every hour. You have been vilified beyond measure. All because you happen to run the PR arm of the nation's most successful bleach company.'

Mr Combs is my age: forty-two, forty-three. Mr Luttrell can't be out of his twenties. State schools but good grades. Middle-class parents. No going-without but still gazing up. They have all they need but something's still missing, and they can't figure out what it is. Americans.

'But you represent evil to the masses, gentlemen, for different reasons than you may think. Your enemy here is not the tree huggers, nor those maimed teens. Your enemy is your own public image. The product you sell is part of Times Gone. Bleach hasn't kept up with the changing face of this country. Bleach is the railroad. Bleach is stonemason. Bleach is the bleak and black soot of industrialization. Bleach, Mr Combs and Mr Luttrell, is Dickensian. Our nation is service now, and research and idea. The smokestacks are empty. The die casters are dying. Bleach is long winter with only a wood-burning stove. Bleach needs to be fun. Bleach needs to be sexy. Bleach needs to realize its place in postindustrial America.'

From a switch on my desk I dim the room's lights, then press a button adjacent. On the wall behind the Bleach Boys a screen descends from the ceiling. The men look at me and then turn their chairs.

'Men of Bleach,' I say, 'I give you the Hypo Beach Party.'

Cue fade-in of shoreline. Cue blue water, blue sky. Cue overdub of saccharine pop music, that big summer hit that by autumn has vanished. Zoom in on a banner that reads HYPO BEACH PARTY, the waves breaking behind it. Cut to the partygoers themselves: girls in their late teens, playing volleyball in low-rise tankinis. Cut to boys of the same age barbecuing hot dogs, their twin rows of abs both firm and bronzed. The boys drink from red cups. Their blond hair is frosted. The volleyball leaves the court and sprays sand onto the calves of the boys' oiled bodies. Happy consternation, followed by revenge: a girl picks the ball up and one of the boys dumps the contents of his cup onto her face and head. Shoulder-shrugging and smiles, and also young love: the dumper and dumpee have made a connection. They grin sheepishly at one another. The song reaches chorus.

Cut to the water: azure, pristine. At once erotic and virginal. The camera's submerged and, crashing now into frame, a pair of young snorkelers. Shots of a reef, small mottled fish. Schools of these fish fanning left and then right, moving as a singular entity, glittering. Cut to a moray, perched in its cave in the reef. Cut to an octopus skimming the sea floor. The snorkelers are the young lovers from moments before. They have found an activity that they enjoy doing together. Ten seconds of quick cuts of these two in fins. They walk out of the water in nearly no clothes, holding hands and their snorkeling equipment. The song is still playing, the happy pop song, the maxi-singled ditty that moves many units. The couple, exhausted, flop down on the beach.

'As we can't show them actually *fucking*,' I tell the Bleach Boys, 'we imply it here. They have done something together that is nearly as intimate. They are barely clothed and, by the end of the act, exhausted.' The Bleach Boys only keep watching.

The boy nudges the girl in the ribcage with his elbow. She leans into him against his shoulder. The camera pulls back and pans to the right: down the beach are their cohorts, still playing, still eating.

End scene. Lose overdub. Cut to nighttime: a concert, a raised stage, tiki torches. An alt-rock quartet, tattooed and goateed, plays live for the attendees of the Hypo Beach Party. Cue this band's music, melodramatic, a catalyst for beer-drunk youth to believe themselves creatures of very deep feelings. Quick cuts of each member of the alt-rock quartet, then a cut to the crowd, the tan boys and girls. They've put on tight tank tops and longer board shorts and sarongs with tropical prints on them. All hold the same plastic cups as before. Some are holding striped vinyl beach balls. Cut to one of these boys throwing his cup into a blue plastic bin that reads *Recycle*. Cut back to the stage, the camera behind the crowd now. Heads bobbing. Raised fists. Lighted lighters. The Beach Party banner is feet over the band. The guitarist breaks into a solo and our young lovers, wanting time to themselves, walk down the beach toward an unmanned bonfire. Cut to the two sitting down on a towel, in front of this fire. Drop the song's volume. Zoom in on the couple.

'Do you think that we'll ever go to a party this cool again?' the boy asks the girl.

They gaze at each other, faces inches apart. The boy's tone is one of drowsy fulfillment.

'We'll make sure we do,' says the girl. They smile and gaze longer, then lean in for The Kiss. Cue fade-out. End scene. End promo.

I leave the screen down and turn the lights up. The Bleach Boys, eyes blinking, turn their chairs back towards me.

'The Beach Party, Mr Combs and Mr Luttrell, covers every one of your bases. You have fun. You have food. You have nature, untouched. You have people preserving this untouched nature by recycling their red plastic drinking cups. You have young and tan bodies. Everyone happy. You have people swimming in the water. You are taking back the environment that your product wrecked. The name of your product, bleach, has been supplanted by the much friendlier word, beach. A single letter's difference, but all the difference in the world, and yet these two words are so strikingly similar that in some ways the mind cannot divorce one from the other. You are saying: Bleach has a place by the sea. You are saying: Bleach makes the beach better. What you sell now is not lethal if consumed, but instead sandy, and jaunty, and pleasant.'

Mr Combs is uncertain. The hair on his temples is gray. But Mr Luttrell, the younger one, is smiling. He gets it. He understands the subversion. He understands the fallacious distraction, the ball-and-shell agitprop of what he just saw. His grin is the grin of the snorkeling boy from the commercial.

'My model calls for a half-dozen of these parties over Labor Day Weekend: three on the West Coast, where the crew team's small tragedy has had the most coverage. The remaining three parties will be spread over the rest of the country. I'm thinking South Padre and Miami Beach and Michigan's Upper Peninsula. If funds allow, we can move the last of these to the shore of Chicago. But certainly Santa Cruz and certainly Ocean Beach, here in the city. Perhaps Stinson. It will depend on permits. If worse comes to worse we can fake most of these and/or pay off county officials.'

'This all sounds expensive,' says Mr Combs. 'I was quoted a number by our CEO and I don't see how we can maintain that number.'

'You're assuming,' I say, 'that admission is free?'

'It isn't?' Mr Combs asks me.

'It's expensive,' I tell him. 'It isn't. It will cost forty dollars per person. I've got a rum company on board. We're going to raffle off hybrid cars. There will be bottomless soft drinks. Gentlemen, you forget that you are part of a group, a consortium. Alumni of sorts. Corporations that rose through the ranks on their own and now at the top stand united. Yes, you're going to have to shell out up front. But, Mr Combs and Mr Luttrell, this is damage control that comes also with profit. My team has shown a gain of as much as 10K per event. Chump change in the big scheme, but then you can't put a price on changing your image for the better. And people will help you. And your lawyers have informed you already, I imagine, that most of these lawsuits have no feet to stand on. The estuary was wrecked long before this unfortunate incident and, even if you are the prime culprit in said polluting, there's burden of proof, statutes of limitation. They'll bring in chemists the jury won't like: bright men and women who will sound way too smart to the box's dumb dozen. You'll take some hits, but it won't be season-ending.'

Mr Luttrell, still smiling, gazes down at the carpet. I've awed him, an easy trick to pull on the young. I've also failed to mention a lot of specifics: that those who attend will not look like the young men and women in the mock-up, which was compiled by a friend of mine, Henry Stine, down on a lot at Universal. Instead, fat hicks and their near-feral children: The NASCAR crowd, shit-faced on tall boys. Bands that haven't broken Billboard's 100 since Ollie North put his hand on a Bible – washed-up one-timers truly thrilled to be playing a venue that isn't a state fair or birthday party. Store-bought hot dogs. Mosquitoes and heat. But then, I sell ads, not reality.

'How fast do we have to move on this?' Mr Combs asks me.

'Fast but not so fast,' I tell him. 'Take a day or two. See if someone else has a better solution. I can only imagine what your PR unit currently looks like. Do you sleep at hotels now? Do your children cry because you and mommy are fighting? Because of the stress of all this? The weight of all this?'

'Doug, why are we waiting?' Luttrell asks his cohort. 'Let's get the ball rolling.'

Combs looks at Luttrell and then back at me. 'Twenty-four hours?' he asks.

'Twenty-four hours,' I say, and stand up from my desk, and hold out my hand for both these men to shake. Nothing will change in twenty-four hours.

The Bleach Boys shuffle out and I sit back down.

Simer comes in about two minutes later.

'Who the fuck?' Simer asks. My Senior VP possesses the mouth of a sailor. She's six feet in heels and around 125 pounds and does yoga each weekday and most weekends. She, too, owns a small silver Prius. Today, Simer is wearing a sheer Furstenberg blouse of pure silk, an abstract design in black, purple and white. High-waisted plaid pants in beige, cream and teal. Her size is 2L, and this outfit, on most, would look clownish, utterly stupid. Not so, however, for Miss Simerpreet Sweeney. Her black hair and big eyes and tan, perfect skin have been the catalyst for divorce for five area surgeons. Simer likes doctors, men who can fix, because Simer is quite apt at breaking. Simer doesn't have friends; instead, she has projects. Her life, like mine, is about deconstruction. For those whose job it is to analyze humanity, it's really quite hard to behave in ways standard to humans.

'Reps for a bee farm up by Lodi,' I tell her. 'Scientists, thus the poor clothing. They claim they're months off from making honey into gas.'

'Bullshit,' Simer says.

'That's what I said,' I say.

'Aqua,' Simer says.

'Aqua,' I tell her, agreeing.

In fifteen years of steering my ad firm's small ship, I have been fooled exactly once. This was right before the tech bubble vanished. A company calling itself Aqua planned to use injured whales as workhorses off the coast of Hawaii. While being nursed back to health, the blues and the orcas would swim tethered in circles, and generate power. Hawaii's senator had supposedly gotten on board, and papers were provided showing PETA's approval. But what Aqua needed was word-of-mouth to generate capital: for AmWe employees to talk to their friends, who would in turn talk to their friends and so on. We got calls from Virgin: is this for real? We got calls from GE and Lucent. We got calls from attorneys representing billionaires who did not wish to be indentified at this juncture. All hoax and idea: Aqua, in truth, was two MIT dropouts living in a basement apartment in Cambridge. One month of hype and then fallout, the joke up. And because I, like my friends, am not a nice person, and believe that poor acts deserve repercussions, arrangements were made to have Aqua extinguished: their cars disappeared, then their bank accounts' money, and then, by fire, their headquarters in Cambridge. The last of these items received one inch of text in a weekday edition of the *Globe*'s Metro section. And that was the last that the world heard from Aqua.

'I'm getting raw bar – do you want raw bar?' Simer asks, but I wave her off and she turns to leave and her shoes are Kate Spade and backless and black, each heel as thin as a pencil. I click my mouse's left button and on comes my computer. The *Times* site has the Dow down over two hundred: subprime, stagflation, car bombs in Iraq. East Texas refineries, per a tropical storm, not refining. My ad firm's off big so far this quarter. The bright, spritely shops full of virtuous things are taking a killing, as are the green companies that make the safe soaps, the sweatshop-free totes, the rainwater collectors. If what's on the horizon does come to shore, I'll be dipping into my own net worth in order to keep my business.

I turn off my Mac's screen and look back out the window. Here is the semi with Ha Jin container; here is the semi with blue Walmart signage. The lines scoot and stop; a horn bleats, then another. The herd wants to always keep moving. Here is exhaust and overfull bladders and mp3 players and people on Bluetooth and kids watching kid shows on tiny TVs placed in the headrests of front seats of minivans.

And I say Amen, and I say God Bless My Children.

3

Dear Dad,

The school psychologist wears only plaid ties. I wonder what this says about him.

Hello from the Hilltop! It's really damn damp. I imagined humidity different, somehow, but it's a difference that I can't describe, which I find upsetting.

Only the varsity athletes are back: there's another three weeks until classes. I've got my mile time down from six minutes to five. Please learn this name: Cameron Nash. He's my competition for keeper. A senior. A smoker. Suspended last spring for cruising. Cruising, Dad, is being out after hours, and with the perceived intention of entering a dormitory housing the opposite sex and having relations with one of its residents. Cruising is viewed as trespass, as crime. Cruising is very soon what I hope to be doing.

The buildings are red brick. There are quads of green grass. We are perhaps two hundred yards from the shore of the Atlantic. The main drive up to campus is lined on both sides with big sugar maples. The brochures provided really are correct: it's that picturesque, that seaside-beatific. Most of the world could be blown to smithereens and you wouldn't know it here, in Newport, Rhode Island. Parents' Weekend is October 16–18, so let's make a deal, Dad: I start in goal for that weekend's game against Milton and you be here to stand on the sideline and watch me. Agreed? Consensus?

Thank you for securing for me my own room. I like my room. There's a plain wooden desk. There's a bed on wood stilts, and space for a sofa below it. I have a view of the ocean. I know part of this place was about, in some way, me becoming a 'joiner,' a person who appreciates the company of my peers. We both know, of course, that this won't happen, and your adherence to pragmatism in this regard is appreciated. I like having my very own space to come back to. I like things being just as I left them. Please say hi to Mom, even though it's sort of pointless.

Did I tell you what Esquido told me before I left? So the MS-13s' sign is the devil horns – you know that sign, right? The pinky and index fingers up and the rest curled down? They do it at metal concerts and then also sorority girls do it because it's symbology that's been assimilated into mainstream culture? Esquido told me before I left that in the '80s, when the MS-13s first got up here from Columbia and Guatemala and Honduras, they picked up that sign FROM heavy metal concerts. I think most people assume that if one is in a gang, they necessarily listen to hip-hop. Not so, however, for the MS-13s, and so I want to see if my English teacher will let me write a paper about this? Like how listening to a different genre of music, specifically metal, allows the MS-13s to think 'outside the box' when it comes to strategy and tactics and tenets of governing ideology? I'm sure they won't let me. I'm sure I'll be writing about the Lake Poets' use of nature imagery. Guess what: they liked Nature, especially lakes. Guess what: they disliked technology. Show me the poet with thinking converse to this. Show me the poet that lives for the Panzer.

My dorm, named Bismarck, as in Otto Von, is on the east end of campus. My room's single window looks eastward. Beyond it, in this direction, are two playing fields, a low wall made of stones, then the path to the beach and Atlantic. This beach is called Second Beach. A two-lane blacktop cuts off the path and winds north, up to Third Beach. (New Englanders, it seems, were not so inventive when it came to nomenclature.) Up at Third Beach is a base for Marines: barbed wire and gates, a bunch of low cream-colored buildings. They're meant to blend in with the sand that's around them, though this doesn't work – I can see them quite clearly. Now and then, a truck leaving, a Jeep with no top. I see no one drilling. I hear no gunfire. What could go on there? I'm curious.

Newport is stuffed with the trundling obese: tourists with families and cell phones and cameras. The cobblestone streets (town's a mile west, and everyone just calls it 'town,' and not Newport) are too narrow for cars to go in both directions at once. I like seeing them try. I stand on the sidewalk and watch the drivers get mad – what good is history if I can't drive my Range Rover through it? Tradition vs. Progress, replete with collisions. The drivers get out and yell at each other in the shadow of statues, of monuments.

Coach Blitzer is Swiss, and short, and quite tan. We wake up at six. We stretch and go running. The girls' field-hockey team often runs past us in the opposite direction. There's a girl toward the back, the last third of the line. I don't know her name yet, but will soon. We do suicides: sprints from one end of the field to each line on the field and back again. But the best part of practice is Bull in the Ring. You may know at least a version of this, Dad, from when you played football. In football, if I have it right, one person has the ball and the rest of the team forms a circle around them and the ballholder must try to break through the ring. In soccer, it's different. In soccer, everyone has a ball except for me, the goalie. I'm in the middle of the circle, on my knees. The coach calls a name and the owner of that name then kicks the ball at me. I have to locate this person and then block the ball, which is coming at my face, at my chest, at my crotch. The rest of the team is five feet away from me.

There's no way to block out everything, Dad, but I do the best that I can with it. At night, before bed, I don't think of home. I don't think of you or of Mom or Esquido. Instead, Coach's voice, my gloved hands at chest level. The foot poised to kick. The ball coming toward me.

The school shrink, Dr Dimler, He of Plaid Ties, has mandated that I keep a journal, one entry every two weeks.

My first entry was only one sentence, which was this: *I am sixteen and three thousand miles from home.*

But then it's really too hot out for deeper self-analysis. See you in October.

Love,
Connor

P.S. – our mascot: it doesn't make sense. St George slayed the dragon but we're called the Dragons, but the name of our school is St George's. We're the St George's Dragons: we are what we kill? How draconian.

4

The Bleach Boys say yes the following day. I make dozens of calls. I send dozens of emails. I fax permit forms to Texas, to Marin, to Michigan. My will is beamed up to orbiting satellite; my will is transported through fiber-optic cable. South Padre's on board, as is the Upper Peninsula. Miami Beach says no so I call my guy at Disney, in Orlando. They're happy to do it: fax everything through. Who's going to play here? We need all ages. We need white and Christian.

I phone Henry Stine, Media Kingpin. Wind pouring through his end of the line. I can hear the purr of an engine. Sometimes I wonder why those in LA even choose to buy houses.

'Henry,' I say, 'how are you?'

'You had a birthday, you little shit, and you didn't tell us.'

'I am under no such obligation,' I say. My office, the Red Room, has maroon-colored wallpaper with gold fleur-de-lis running vertically down it. My office has a fern and a ficus.

'How many years? Which one was this?'

'I turned forty, Henry,' I say.

'Forty!' screams Henry, and he really does scream, and I hear the screeching of car tires, a horn, Henry calling someone a wet hairy cunt and screaming it, really screaming it. 'I remember forty. My dick worked. I hate you.'

'This doesn't seem like such a great time.'

'These are the best of times,' Henry tells me. 'You know where I'm going? Right now? As I speak? I am driving to Nogales, Arizona. Why that border town, Jimmy, you ask? Why that filthy and lawless hamlet? Because, Birthday Boy, Nogales is going to be the onsite headquarters for the next big reality program. Picture this: Mary Kate Olsen in rags, crossing the desert. Her mascara is running. She's been bitten by a snake. Not a very poisonous snake, Jim, but a snake nonetheless, and her ankle is swollen, and she's chain-smoking, but it isn't helping. With her also: Randall Cunningham, former Philadelphia Eagles quarterback. Debbie Gibson and Richard Marx and that fat guy with the moustache from *NYPD Blue*. You remember that show? Dennis Franz. That's that fucker. Remember how you got to see his bare ass every week? Dennis Franz's fat, pimpled ass? Remember, Jimmy?'

'I don't remember his ass as being pimpled.'

'I'm talking pre-filming, Jimmy, pre-filming. You should have seen what had to be done. Imagine whitewashing a pair of Virginia baked hams.'

'You're getting ahead of yourself,' I tell Henry.

'I am,' says Henry, 'you're right there. The program: *Coyotes*. Celebrity wash-ups go incognito from Mexico into America. They're led on this trek, on this FUCKING VISION QUEST, Jimmy, by hired guides, known on the immigration circuit as coyotes.' Henry pronounces coyotes in a faux-Spanish manner: the kai to a kee, the tees to a tez.

'Are you there?' Henry asks. 'Are you listening, Jimmy?'

I tell him I am.

'So these fuckers, Richard Marx and the Olsen girl and Franz, they start off in some decaying slum village maybe two hundred miles from America. And the coyote is leading them. But THEN,

Jimmy, THEN, it's like a pick-a-path book. You see, Jimmy, they have all these choices. They reach a river: do they cross it at night? They encounter a dust storm. They run out of water and Randall Cunningham has to carry Debbie Gibson on his shoulder. On his shoulder, Jimmy! Holy shit! And the coyote: can he be trusted? The group has a finite amount of American dollars, and the coyote DOES get them across the river at night, but then wants more money! And each step of the way, the team has the choice of dismissing the coyote and hiring a new one, but this costs, Jimmy, and they have to SAVE AT LEAST SOME OF THEIR MONEY TO PAY THE VAN DRIVER!!!'

'The van driver,' I say. Henry is bald and in his mid-fifties. Henry, I think, has been self-medicating.

'The fucking van driver, Jimmy! The guy who's going to take them from Nogales to their new meatpacking jobs in Montana! That isn't cheap, and the coyotes, Jimmy, they always want more, and can our small gang of celebrity immigrants TRUST them? And there's border patrol and Minutemen, Jimmy, and scorpions. And the host is that asshole from that show where they eat things for money! You know that guy, Jimmy? That fucking walking ad for hair plugs and penile enlargement? Okay, I stop. I calm down. I cease. What do you need? I'm guessing that this call is business.'

'I need September's spreadsheets a tiny bit early. I've got festivals lined up for the Beach Party, and I need to see which bands are available.'

'Done and done. My promo went well, then,' says Henry.

'It went very well and I thank you for it,' I tell him.

'When I pull over at this gas station forty miles up and after I pee I'll send you the spreadsheet. Lunch next month. And Jimmy?'

'Yes?' I ask.

'Dennis fucking FRANZ,' and then Henry hangs up on me.

From AmWe's main office comes the sound of a gong being banged. This means something quite good has happened. One of our ad reps, Tugba Hussein, brought back this gong from a trip to Kyoto. Tugba is Turkish-American. Her first name is pronounced just like the name of the brass and cumbersome instrument. Tugba does not shave her armpits or legs. Tugba owns a four-thousand-dollar mountain bike. Tugba goes on weekend retreats in the Santa Cruz Mountains where she lights incense and chants and communes with the redwoods. Tugba buys T-shirts of organic cotton that cost sixty-five dollars. Her alloy water bottle costs twice that. Tugba pens sub-par ghazals and haikus and tacks them to our office's Free Spirit Space, a wallboard constructed from recycled cork and scrap metal. Tugba's bracelets are bamboo; her dress flats are vegan. She once spent nearly two weeks of her life in a tent hung from the side of Cal-Berkeley's Campanile. The UC Board of Regents wanted badly to chop down a large grove of old-growth redwood trees in order to build a new playing field. Tugba was against this construction, so she and two of her hairy coeds slept one hundred feet off the ground, over the side of the building. The Regents cried safety first, and brought to them food laced with low levels of ketamine. Tugba and Friends refused this cuisine for the first seven days and then ate it, their bodies so starved that the pairing of horse tranquilizer and protein wreaked havoc on their gastrointestinal systems. In short, the trio of would-be activists came down from their perch due to painful constipation. The trees were buzz-sawed the very next weekend.

For me the gong functions as cue, as alarm, as one minute to curtain. I stand up from my desk and take a deep breath and walk down the short hall outside of my office. I peek through my blinds of recycled bamboo. Andrew is sitting on his ergonomic stool. He's tied the tails of his dress shirt across the front of his stomach. The top of his green microfiber thong has risen above the waist of his gray pinstriped dress pants. Across the thong's hem, in bubblegum pink, read the words NO ON PROP 8. Andrew's barefoot and bidding on something on eBay. I open the door. Andrew closes the window.

'Hey, Jim, hey,' says Andrew. 'We got the Evermore account.'

'Oh my gosh that is SO great,' I tell Andrew, as I am no longer my true you but the Me that is seen by those I employ: the bumbling altruist, the ad man with heart, the aw-shucks progressive. This mask is both simple and comfortable. All I must do to pass off this disguise is be spineless and nearly retarded with glee and hold no opinion that might be considered offensive to any disenfranchised person or entity. In short, I just have to be Californian. 'We should totally have a party,' I tell Andrew.

'Say, Jim, you know St Isidore Memorial, right? That church where all the prostitutes get their AIDS medications? I was, like, thinking, Jim, it would be cool to do a fundraiser there. Do some advertising for Evermore and get some break dancers and stuff and have a poetry slam.'

I have worn this mask for so long that its strap no longer tugs at the back of my head. I just listen and nod. I just play along. Break dancers and crack whores and throngs of slam poets. Yes, yes and yes.

'Andrew, that's a great idea; I thank you. And Andrew? Your thong is sticking out of the back of your pants and I just wanted to let you know this not to interfere with your personal aesthetic but to communicate TO you that this specific aesthetic detail might be unwanted BY you? Wow, I just feel so blessed right now. Do you feel blessed, Andrew?'

'Oh my God I so do,' says Andrew. He claps his hands together, fingers upturned, tight and quick claps, like an epileptic, praying.

'Would you maybe want to get that thong's rise down a bit?'

'Sure, Jim,' says Andrew. He stands up and aligns his pants and T-back. Michiko Gonzales runs over. She bends down and gives Andrew a hug and a kiss on the cheek.

'I'm so happy,' she says. 'And I'm totally voting Yes on Prop 8!'

'Do you mean that you're voting No on Prop 8?' Andrew asks.

'Yes,' says Michiko. 'Wait, what?' she asks Andrew.

Around the office, my employees are involved in a variety of celebration rituals. Brianna and Brenda, both in-house ad reps, both twenty-four, have taken out noisemakers from the drawers of their desks. Tugba has put on finger cymbals. Kelton Chen, Layout, in a mute gesture of joy, has projected onto the ceiling the single word CONFETTI. Simer stares at me from the room's other end. Arms crossed, she leans against the door frame of her office. I pretend not to notice. I gaze out at the mirth. At American Weather there are no dividers, no cubicles. These things have been found to inhibit lively fun. Instead, our workplace is designed to mimic, roughly, the floor plan of a second-grade classroom. The firm's walls are painted in primary colors: stripes of dark blue and deep red and bright yellow. Desks sit in groups, facing each other. There are chalkboards on wheels, a wall-mounted pencil sharpener. All of this aids in sustained infantilism, an effect that I work very hard to maintain. It allows my firm's team – nearly all early twenties – to retain psychological insulation, a trait that for them functions largely as milk does for puppies. They want things their way and cannot be bothered. They're products of divorce who got everything they wanted. They grew up under Clinton, the empyrean reached, the Eastern Bloc beasts of the Cold War all vanquished. They hated their parents, who paid for their cars and their four years at Skidmore, at Vassar, at Pomona, where their professors, ex-potheads, minds lost to white guilt, regurgitated portions of decades-old theses about Emily Dickinson as closeted dyke and Dickens as Marxist. They listened, then didn't; they fucked and took drugs. They found causes that got them through winters. And with their degrees they left those institutions with a simultaneous belief in and contempt for the common man, something that they had glimpsed, on occasion, from car windows. They couldn't sell out but they needed good money. This is the demographic I choose to employ: dilettante, liberal capitalists. Ab-crunching pagans. When training new hires, or on Green Field Trips (work days where our collective packs into vehicles and burns gallons of gas to venture out and make our community more eco-friendly) I remind my small team that compartmentalizing one's life is unhealthy and outdated. No longer do we exist in an era where we daily depart from the home world to the work world and then back again. Such boundaries are ersatz and rigid. No, I tell my bees, here, at this firm, we are modern and fluid and better than that. Tear down these divides and Nirvana will follow. And they all eat it up like burgeoning cultists. These aren't the minds that will govern the future, but they think they are, and I'm happy to let them.

I cough once, for attention, and then wave my hands. Today I have on plaid madras shorts, handmade by a collective of Peruvian weavers and sold by white people at PC Boutique on Valencia Street in the Mission. My silk-screened dress shirt (the inks are soy-based) is brown and white stripes, the design orange diamonds. My flip-flops are made from used bicycle tires and discarded rope from docks wrecked by Katrina. It's tough, at times, to dress within character, to put on then accept that certain clothing pairing that passes me off as Unmatched Mission Statement, as a billboard for my public and false ideologies. My bees have stopped buzzing. They're looking at me. I smile until my eyes start to narrow.

'My friends,' I say, 'my team, my Army for Peace, today we have won another Un-Battle. Today, the corporate overlords, and their modified food, and their shoes cobbled in Thailand for cents on the dollar, and their oil-swilling, grotesque non-hybrid cars, today these despots recede just a bit further on the scalp of humanity. With our expertise, and passion for good, and our mind's fortification through blended fruit drinks, we will create an advertisement campaign that does the architectural wonder that is the Evermore Towers true and good justice. I want all of you to take the rest of the day off. I want you to leave here and wander the city – consider our parks, our streets, our museums. Consider the sun and all it provides. Consider buying something at one of your favorite stores, something that will commemorate this wonderful day: a new yoga mat or a video game or a long and bright scarf knit by Nepalese monks.'

'There's a sale at Greenhound, I'm going, who's going?' screams Brogan McCovey. Brogan works in Media Planning. She went to a boarding school in the same athletic league as the school that my son is attending. Brogan has four dogs, all purebred spaniels. Brogan enjoys scrapbooking. Brogan brought her scrapbook to her job interview as proof that she liked scrapbooking. Brogan has gifted me ten songs on iTunes. Brogan is often seen bouncing. Her internal landscape, I am very near sure, resembles the children's board game CandyLand: gingerbread houses and candy-corn streets, a sickeningly sweet, brightly hued, boring adventure.

'That's great, that is just such a great idea,' I tell Brogan and everyone. 'Who else owns pets? Who else might go with Brogan and buy something eco-friendly for those creatures that add so much to your lives?'

Michiko Gonzales puts up her hand, as does DeKwan O'Riley.

'That's wonderful. Michiko, Brogan and DeKwan are going to go buy vegan pet treats and hemp leashes and consider, just maybe, how pets might fit into our Evermore campaign, how we can import the animal kingdom as viable design component. Does anyone have any questions for me?'

There are, of course, no questions. What I have just done is this group's wet dream: a day of pleasure had under the guise of professional input. Simer enters her office, shutting the door. There is the sound of keys jingling on key chains. Brogan walks toward me. Her straight brown hair is pulled back in a ponytail tied with the shiny tin handle of a Chinese takeout box. I know this because last week she spent nearly eight minutes relating the story to me.

'Jim, HI, and thanks for this day and I'm just so excited to go be out in the city and thinking about how to make the city, like, different and better and stuff. Um: I don't really know how to say this but I'm having an Emossue? With Dina?'

Emossue is short for Emotional Issue. Emotional Issues are taken quite seriously here at American Weather, as are the combining of words.

'Okay, Brogan, this sounds like a big deal. Take your time here. Do you think that you're ready to talk about this? It's okay to start crying. Never hide your emotions. Crying IS strength, not NOT crying.'

Brogan starts crying. As a child of fourteen, I once sat in a car for four hours with my collarbone shot through the top of my shoulder. My eyes stayed as dry as a desert.

'Okay, so like Dina? She's stealing from me? Not like my things here at work but from this website? Etsy? They sell handmade stuff and like vegan candles and you can set up an account and then store things that are your favorites and there was this shoulder bag made from old billboards that I totally wanted and Dina knew I wanted it because I showed it to her on the Etsy site and then she created an account on the Etsy site and she bought it and brought it to work today and like totally didn't say anything but walked by my desk with the bag on her shoulder and it was so emotionally devastating?'

I have a very standard-looking face. I have brown eyes and brown hair and a nondescript nose and lips of a very average size and proportion. I could rob a person at knifepoint and they couldn't give a better description than the one just supplied. I am totally forgettable. This, most often, suits me quite well, until I am forced to convey emotion. As Brogan pouts, and then starts to cry, I try to widen my eyes. I try to show that I'm invested. But even with years upon years of practice, I know I am still not producing the right gestures. I know, for instance, that the corners of my lips should turn up, thereby forming a small smile of compassion. I know that I should cock my head a few degrees, that such an angle aids in implying sympathy. But I simply can't do it. Instead, my lips curl downward, mutinous. Instead, my eyes lock and go filmy.

'Brogan, this is just awful,' I say. 'I am sorry that this situation has overridden the joy that all creatures should feel in every second of every waking hour. Let's resolve this. Is Dina here now?'

Brogan nods. 'She IS,' she sobs. 'She's in the Dream Pod watching *The Simpsons*.'

'Well, I'm going to go talk to her in a manner where everyone can leave here happy. Okay? Does that sound all right? Can you just hang out at your desk and maybe find something else on Etsy that you'll enjoy buying?'

'I guess,' sniffles Brogan.

'That's great, you're being really brave,' I say, and pat her once on the shoulder, my arm at full distance, so that no one can sue me or otherwise construe that through this shoulder touch there are hidden lustful motives. And, truly, there aren't – I fuck my employees in ways that have nothing to do with intercourse.

The Dream Pod is next door to Simer's office. It was, at its architectural inception, a conference room; it was meant to have chairs, a large table, a phone. At American Weather, it has beanbags, a plasma TV. There are black lights and sleeping bags and docks for iPods. There are headphone jacks lining the room's wall at waist height, so people can watch DVDs of *South Park* while others sleep soundly. In the Dream Pod, it's always time for a time-out. In the Dream Pod, there's a cooler filled with bottles of organic fruit tea.

I knock once on the Dream Pod's thick plastic door and when no one responds, I open it. Curled in a fetal ball lies Dina Phelps, Graphic Designer. Dina is almost thirty years old and is dressed like a tween post-spree at Hot Topic. Her black army boots reach up to her knees. Her checkerboard skirt is a mini, six inches, with striped tights, pink and green, underneath it. Today Dina wears a sort of smock/cloak, formless and black with a long pointed hood that runs down the length of her back to her tailbone. Her strands of dyed hair have been dreadlocked to knots. Her lip rings number six, their hues comprising a rainbow.

'Dina?' I ask, and nudge my employee's curved back with the sole of my flip-flop. On the plasma TV, Homer Simpson eats radioactive waste and is taken to an area hospital. Dina wears headphones over her ears, the device's long wire wrapped around her lean body. Dina has effectively returned to the womb, strangling herself with bright, happy colors. The contact from my flip-flop causes Dina to unfurl. The headphones unplug from their jack in the wall and the room fills with sound, an ear-splitting melange of dialogue and orchestrated music. I jump from the pitch at the same moment Dina jumps upon realizing that I'm standing over her.

'I don't want to talk about it,' Dina says, and then plugs the headphones back into the wall. She reaches up under her very short skirt and from inside her tights pulls out a pack of Paul Newman's Mint Patties. American Weather has no HR department; these tasks are handled, normally, by Simer. Simer, however, is not really good at being kind, so I am left now to play surrogate parent, because Dina's own parents, aged Baby Boomers, had a hands-off approach when it came to parenting, and instead let their child always get her way as long as she brought home strong report cards. I bend down and my knee pops and it takes near-pious reserve not to swear profusely and punch Dina in her dreadlocks. Instead, I take the TV's remote control from its spot on the rug and press the mute button.

'Hey, Dina, this is really hard for me and I don't want to come off as the enforcer here, but Brogan is having an Emossue, and we need to resolve this so all of us, and thus the world around us, can be truly peaceful.'

Progress: Dina sits up. She rips open the Mint Patties and takes out a cup and nibbles, murine, at the chocolate.

'So Brogan told me that she had a tote bag made of billboards in her Favorites page on Etsy?'

'It's not like that means it gets to be hers,' Dina tells me.

'Well, Dina, if I can, may I ask you if that was an item that you truly wanted? That is, I am inquiring here about your motives for purchasing the ex-billboard tote bag?' I try to smile warmly. I try to imagine what a 'warm smile' would be.

'The world is filled with chaos,' Dina says. She crumples up the Mint Pattie's brown wrapper and stores it in the leg of her over-tall boot.

'This is true, this is so true, but I'm wondering, Dina, is this the message that we want to promote here?'

'No, I know it isn't,' says Dina.

'So do you think that the tote bag is something that you might be using often? That is, when you wake up in the morning, and after you've checked your email and eaten, and dyed your hair maybe and put on your makeup and chosen your outfit and you now have to accessorize that outfit, is the billboard tote bag essential to the outfit of your choosing? What I'm asking here, Dina, is whether or not you might be able to look into your future and see where that bag is going to be in it. Because, I think, Dina, I think that Brogan sees that bag as a very important part of her future. I think that Brogan may wake up in the mornings ahead and, after grooming her spaniels, really strongly consider that her life is somewhat bereft without the billboard tote bag in it. Do you know what I'm saying, Dina?'

The question, sadly, is not rhetorical; I have no idea what these turds comprehend. The problem with turning the masses into obedient dogs is that they understand little English.

'I think I know what you're saying,' Dina says, and with a few more minutes of coercion I am able to get Dina to stand, and then walk to her desk and give over the tote bag to Brogan. The two women hug and tears spring from eyes and they walk out of AmWe actually holding hands, the tote bag over Brogan's shoulder. I watch this play out from the dark of the Dream Pod. *The Simpsons* episode finishes; the animated family stand in their yard, gazing out toward the sunset and a burning pile of car tires. I turn off the TV and repair a bottle of fruit tea to the recycling bin in the corner, walking out of the Dream Pod just as Simer opens the door to her office. She has on an all-black yoga outfit, skintight, the top spandex and midriff, more bra than shirt. Were I a different person than I am, but I am not that sort of person.

'The Evermore's big, Jim,' Simer says. She winds her hair into a ponytail and bands it. 'We need it bad, too. You've seen the numbers?'

'I've seen the numbers,' I say.

'Scary shit, Jim,' Simer tells me.

'I know,' I tell her.

'You want to come over? Figure out what to do? I don't cook but I know where to order from.' Simer poses akimbo, her chest pushing out.

'I'd love to but I love someone else.'

'But that someone else can't fuck you,' says Simer.

I say nothing, my stance firm, and Simer backs down and fishes her keys from her Coach tote of pebbled lime leather.

'You know,' Simer tells me, 'Matisse once said, "I don't paint things. I just paint the difference between things."' She sets down her purse and wraps her arms around me, her chest pressing close, her lips grazing my ear lobe.

'I can't stand Matisse,' Simer whispers, and she picks up her bag and then leaves to do yoga, and so ends the waltz of the office, its four-step graceless and base. The story of these days sums only to maw, without arc or even true narrative, my bees absconding, fleeing yet again from the prosecution of duty and ethic, ideas they know not what to do with, here, in the realm

60

of safe tap water, in the realm of pornography downloads, in the realm of one hour or less and add friends and drive-thru and low APR and no payments until 3050. America is a bright coat with fur collar, bought used. America is ten million Hungry Man dinners, the brownie dessert burning the roof of one's mouth, and not quite enough, and way too delicious.

Ten minutes later I'm past the front doors of my building on Battery Street, the light through the fog in thick golden-white beams, coating the row of parked Vespas and Harleys, and here is the Sikh sitting stunned in his taxi, beyond tired, his turban off-kilter, the car engine in neutral as his Bluetooth device again starts its chirping; and here is the family of lost German tourists, in cameras and tight khaki shorts and white tube socks, and black walking sneakers, searching for brunch in a strange foreign city, both of the children obese and headphoned, trailing behind in enormous bright backpacks, jet-lagged, unhappy, as I head south from Pacific toward Jackson Street, past a huge moving truck with its lights on and ramp down, past black Starbucks lids left in dry filthy gutters, past hydrants graffitied with Sharpies, past bus stops where men sleep next to their wheelchairs in clothes donated by the dead and the wealthy, as walk signals blink and car alarms sound and a man screams a coarse and high lunatic scream and flags fly on their flagpoles. Here is the city, bursting with math, wrapping itself up with wires and iron, with signage and warnings so we can slide cards through machines and get things that we need or desire, as neon fills tubes and beacons light up: guide your ship here, this cove has a dock, this port is open.

At Hinckley Walk I head east toward Davis Street and the Bay Bridge and the slips for the ferries. New Century

Commons is thirty stories of apartments, each with a deck and a fireplace. Its lobby houses jade plants, a fountain. One of four penthouse suites on the Commons's top floor is leased by myself, under a pseudonym. This place has functioned for over five years as pied-à-terre and base of operations for patrolling my employees' online activities. Alone now, the mask off, I step out of the elevator and onto the hallway's plush golden carpet. Living here also: a lawyer to the stars, a whore of the Mayor's, a rich plastic surgeon. These people know me as Willie McGee: anonymous, corporate and loaded. If our paths cross there are nods but no conversation – fins are sewn into our gabardine suits; they lace our shoes, they are both belt and buckle. We swim mute in our sea on the thirtieth floor, sharks of the heavens.

I swipe my key card and my door's tumbler tumbles. My apartment's furnishings are expensive but few: a brown leather sofa; a red Persian rug; a desk, a chair, a computer. A bed in the bedroom. Light falls in squares from window to floor. I sit down and bring up the screen on my desktop and here is a list of IP addresses connected to servers on employee computers at American Weather, as the New Church of Purchase has blind and pure faith in these plastic contraptions that function for them as songbook and pew, stained glass and buttress. I sit now with my Lambs for confession. Tugba Hussein is cheating on Thor, her partner-per-Wiccan-hand-fasting-ritual. Brogan has joined an online découpage club. Andrew's been outbid on eBay. Julia Jones, who works with DeKwan and Kelton in Layout, has a sister who's manic-depressive. This sister, Katherine, won't take her meds and has now fled her MFA studies at UNC-Wilmington where, in between bouts of the crazies, she wrote double reverse sestinas about having sex with her best friend's dad in high school.

The Trojan I use to access my employees' emails has the simple and appropriate title of Beast, and was created for me by a man who at one point worked for one of the largest biotech firms on the planet. For a short while this firm produced a drug called Supinal, used mainly for conscious sedation: if one needed a camera put up their ass, or their wisdom teeth out, or the tubes of their penis cut and tied off, hospitals employed Supinal. The drug worked so well that the firm decided to make a prescription-only version thereof, something the sleepless could keep in their homes and use when they wanted or needed. My wife, Denise, had never slept well. Now she sleeps always.

The hacker, whose full name is Kyle Adam Kim, and whose Social Security Number is 448-78-9237, and who lives in Boston, at 883 South Channel Street, Apartment 2A, is the owner of one of the many lives I have wrecked per their affiliation with the biotech firm. Kyle owned a car and this car went away. Kyle had a girlfriend who left him. Kyle had two bank accounts, both of them drained in the very same week, and then drained again, and then Kyle was evicted from his spacious townhouse in a nice part of Lowell, Massachusetts. After this, Kyle was supplied with a choice: quit the biotech firm and come work for me or have his parents deported to Korea. Kyle chose the former. At the biotech firm, Kyle's job was computer security, preventing cryptoviral extortion attacks and DoS jobs and firewall breaches, so the firm's equations – math of high wealth, chemistry that yielded its magi mansions and Beamers – could be kept in its virtual vault quite securely. To do this, Kyle had to be better than hackers, which he himself was during his time at Brown and is again now, as he rots away in a seedy one-bedroom on the outskirts of Southie. I'll never meet Kyle and he'll never meet me and as long as he keeps doing his job he can eat turkey with his mom and dad on Thanksgiving.

Julia Jones, sibling of Nut Job, has a credit-card bill in real need of paying. Julia has fallen on hard times, it seems. Fodder for subprime, her fiancé and she now can't make payments on their split-level Edwardian flat in posh Noe Valley, land of the Cooper and panaromic views and people romping through trust funds like children in fields of clover. Her husband, a victim of cutbacks at Yahoo, has taken on contract work as Webmaster for internet sites specializing in everything from animal porn to salt-water taffy. Through these four months of creeping foreclosure, Julia has retained composure at work – were it not for Kyle Kim and his patching and malware, I'd think Julia was faring quite nicely. Instead, though, desperation: a loan from her Dad, the sale of her cream-colored Honda Accord, replete with ski rack and moonroof. And delivered, it seems, this very morning, a response from a couple needing donors of eggs, Mr and Mrs Dan and Pam Deane who can pay 20K for the life that resides in Julia Jones's ovaries, life she can sell to maintain her life, or the one version of it that she deems worth living.

Per my keystrokes, the sum from the Deanes disappears. I do the same for Andrew's outbid notice from eBay. I suspend three employees' Netflix accounts. I delete the response from Kelton Chen's broker about dumping his AIG stock pre-September. Gone too is a sonnet from Tugba's paramour. I add my Lambs' names to e-based mailing lists for lingerie stores and car dealerships, for reminders from multiple chains of hotels and new offers from car-insurance companies. Dina Phelps will not know that in her hotmail, this hour, was an update that Switchblade Petunia, her favorite band, has cancelled their show at Bottom of the Hill. She *will* learn that she can buy Viagra at cost. She will learn that a Somali man wishes to deposit, in Dina's bank account, his dead uncle's millions.

The purpose of this is its purposelessness, its coating the minds of all that I can with a veneer of bright consternation, of filling back up each to-do list, so those in my flock never venture afield and find themselves lost and alone in some figurative forest, where the novel is read, the exhibit seen, the time to deprogram located. Instead microbouts of weekly annoyance, long minutes on hold while Celine Dion croons and we wait for some prophet to solve all our problems, to complete us, because when we can't rent or download or sell off, we live lives absent of faith and devotion. Our souls are empty. And my flock is a flock of the pious near-always, but even the pious have moments of doubt where they too make poor decisions, and do go to the book-signing and hold signs in protest and utilize public transportation. This, Lambs, is fine, for we all stray from faith. Know I am here to nip at Your legs, to guide You back home through the fog and the darkness. Here, Lambs, is the farm, its outbuildings and silos, here is Your pen and Your comfy straw bed: eat and then sleep and then wake up again. Know that my methods are cruel means to good ends. Remember who's loved You through shearings and winters.

The sliding glass door that leads to my balcony faces south, and overlooks much of the rest of San Francisco. Past Montgomery Station, past acres of mixed use, past the brick plazas along Market Street, stands the Tenderloin, future home of Evermore Towers. Evermore Towers will be four-by-four city blocks. Evermore Towers will have parks thick with maples. Evermore Towers will have a tranquil fake stream, an outdoor movie projector. Evermore Towers will have, on each shower, a hologram of the planet, our planet, a laser-cast picture of Earth that appears on the shower after ten minutes of water usage, reminding its tenants that we are indeed part of a global community in which drought will soon be a near-constant problem. Cotton from blue jeans bought at Goodwills will function as the Towers' insulation, so that drafts never sweep across floors made of recycled plastic. All of this in the heart of the crime-slicked Tenderloin, blocks from St Isidore Memorial Church and its lost, filthy congregation, a flock that combined does not own one blouse of raw silk, or gold bracelet from Gump's, or sport-fishing vehicle.

I log off, my sermon and good acts complete. Above my computer, hung from the wall, is a photo from 1984, when I was fourteen years old. I'm wearing blue overalls and standing between long rows of almond trees, my brown hair in a bowl cut. This picture was taken near the town of Crows Landing, east of Berkeley and Piedmont, where the Bay Area recedes into farmland and Stanislaus County. Arranged in a group are Mr Hand and myself and the three friends that I have on this planet: Henry Stine and Frank Gaines and Ned Akeley. On the left edge of the shot one can see just a bit of the dormitory at Mr Hand's orphanage – part of one wall and one window. The almond trees seem to go on forever, receding to thin grainy lines in the photo's far distance. Mr Hand's in black pants and a black jacket vest with white collared shirt underneath it. His hair is ear-length, and silver, and brilliant, and he has on his deep black felt trilby hat. Henry and Ned stand on either side of Mr Hand, and Frank and myself, still minors, stand in front of him, one of our caregiver's hands on each of our shoulders. The sky is pure blue and trapped in the photo, midflight and forever, is a quartet of vultures riding the mid-morning thermals. The birds are perhaps a half-mile up, and form there a near-perfect circle. They scan the ground, wings out and heads down, searching the world for the dead and the dying.

5

Dear Dad,

Our cafeteria's huge. Its ceiling is high and its floor creaks from use. Along one wall is a fireplace to keep us warm while we chew. The wood walls are the color of toffee, and old, and ringed with portraits of past headmasters. The men in these portraits wear what look like judges' robes, black garments that show only the knots of their ties, their shirts' starched collars. There are stacks of white plates on a big iron cart. There are machines that dispense us our beverages. Popular dinner entrees are white fish in white sauce, Salisbury steak, meatloaf. Down a short hall between here and my dorm is the door to the school infirmary, and whom have I seen leaving the infirmary three times this week, Dad? The girl from the back of the field-hockey line, wearing each day some new blouse and skirt, and carrying each time some shiny new purse that looks very expensive.

This girl's name is Sally Ashton.

Sally Ashton's in my year. She just turned seventeen. Sally Ashton grew up in Manhattan. Her hair is light blonde,

blonde almost by default, blonde because it can't really be white because Sally is not quite albino but near it, her eyes blue but just barely, her skin pale though in the past weeks it has turned a shade roughly the color of bubblegum, as it remains really damn hot here.

Last weekend, I walked into town to buy a fan and then walked the mile back, the device assembled by me on the street corner, its box abandoned, so that I could carry the fan over my shoulder. The sand here works its way over everything, Dad: the grass, the cobblestone, the concrete. Between town and St George's is First Beach, the tourist beach. On this beach, with her parents, was Sally Ashton. Cocked at an angle was a bright, wide umbrella that Sally sat under, reading. She had on black shorts and a bright red tank top, and kept moving her feet back and forth in the sand as though she were sitting on something with pedals. I watched her for a full fifteen minutes. I've not heard her speak though I have heard her laugh as the varsity field-hockey team practices right next to us and her laugh is the best laugh, a shrill anxious thing, like she's surprised she can still laugh at all. But her room-mate, Perrin Thune, is able to get her to do it, and Sally lifts her head to the sky and the laughter drifts over from her field to mine while I stand in goal and pretend not to listen. We catch each other looking and then look away, like this is some game neither of us is quite sure how to play yet.

My team runs two miles each morning now. Coach Blitzer stays behind not out of sloth, but from fostering in us, he says, independence, in believing we can and will do it. And all of us do, save for Cameron Nash, who after the first half-mile or so breaks off from the group and sits on a park bench and chain-smokes. Our four fullbacks – Dreyton Stropp and the Furr Twins and Richard Mann – all grew up in the rich Boston suburbs. Our center half-back, from Spain, has attained the inappropriate nickname of Nacho. He's flanked by Brit Timms and Luke Maynard. Both are the progeny of Hartford area insurance magnates. Brit and Luke are short and fey and unsure, and will build themselves up later in life through working, in some way, with money. When Nash goes to his bench and pulls out his Camels, the Hartford boys look at each other. Both then start running faster. As if to say: we are scared of what we don't know but if we keep running we don't have to know and will probably wind up better for this lack of knowing. Someday they'll hawk T-bills from skyscrapers.

Our stars are our forwards. Last year, we made it to state and lost badly first-round and are expected, this year, to do better. Coach Blitzer chews toothpicks that over the course of the day begin to dissolve, at which point he eats them. Our forwards are Ford Probst and Brad Hauth and Hayes Chase. Ford's from Alabama, Brad grew up in Maine, and Hayes grew up not far from Sally, on the Upper West Side of Manhattan. No one here, not one other person, is from California.

When Cameron Nash is done with his butts, he hides them under the park's monkey bars, amongst the cedar chips there to provide padding for falls. He joins back up with the line as we run by colonials set back from the street, their huge sloping lawns trimmed to perfect. Nash makes a point of cutting in right in front of me and I never say a word about it and when I stay mute he looks back and then smiles, and his eyes are like wolf eyes, this weird yellow-green, and his smile stretches, I swear, nearly to his temples. I meet his gaze and when Nash turns back ahead, I look at his shoes, lifting and falling. Between the yards of the colonials and the narrow asphalt street are short, sloping ditches of grass; these aid in controlling rain from summer storms and snow in winter. Coach Blitzer wants us to stay right on the road's lip, and as I said, Dad, no longer runs with us.

Dr Dimler has yet to bring up my assault. Tuesday's tie was Bannockbane: beige with brown, white and orange running through it. Thursday's was Black Watch. His hair resembles that of an aging Dominican friar. He asks about you and, more often, Mom. I tell him I like you: you provide me with advice; you provide me with the best education you can. I tell him that I understand there's a trade-off in life in regard to providing: that a parent has a choice of earning as much as they can but then are gone for long swatches of time, or they can be around much more often and provide less materially. I tell him I remember sitting in our living room when I was young, watching cartoons and eating some cookies, and hearing the door of the garage start to open – a rush, Dad, a push so compelling that the TV went off and I stopped eating cookies and ran to the back door and watched as your car seemed to glide into its parking spot. Dr Dimler then asks me if I feel differently now. I tell him I obviously do – what sixteen-year-old is going to spring from the couch and run to greet Daddy? I'm not autistic. But I know what the doctor is trying to ask and it's this: have I found other heroes? That, barring desertion or abuse, every child worships their father and then, at some point, usually post-puberty, the child begins to locate other models on which to base the rest of their years, the father remaining part of this mixture, this amalgam, but necessarily diluted in prominence. I told this straight back to Dr Dimler, and he said that I'll probably do pretty well on the PSATs. I told him that I'd already taken it once: top 3%, just dandy.

Ford, Brad and Hayes all reside on the same floor, the third floor, of Bismarck as I do, along with Dreyton Stropp and the Furr twins. Two other rooms remain vacant. After dinner, Ford and Brad leave open the door to their double and play Skynyrd or Cream in the evenings, and Hayes and the Furr Twins and sometimes myself pack onto their tapestry-covered sofas and talk soccer and talk about girls. Sally Ashton's name has come up only once, when Hayes said he met her at some event for SG in Manhattan, and that she had on this floor-length black velvet coat and asked him two separate times if it looked like a small piece of thread was attached to her ear, and kept touching at the ear that she thought it was attached to. The consensus was 'loser,' and the conversation moved on, but there's something in Sally, a strange sort of loss, a compelling, beguiling incompleteness. When the ball comes her way during practice, she's dismayed. When she talks to her friends, her eyelids sort of shiver. She seems trapped in her mind, the acts of her days either task or distraction. And I want to ask her, do you know why that is? Because I'm like that too and it makes life really hard and I have no one to talk to and don't know what happened?

There is a rock outcropping here, Dad, just southeast of the boundary for campus. Twenty feet high, its uneven face gazes out over the still-warm waters of the Atlantic. It's wild land, owned by the city or state – no one can build here or they would have already. Bushes with sharp leaves and dark purple berries dot the uneven top of the cliff; they seem to grow out of the stone itself, though obviously this is impossible. A grove of pitch pines, along with other, smaller trees, must be managed through to get there from the street that runs past our campus. I can see this grove from my room's single window and one Sunday, with nothing to do after Chapel, I decided to walk there, hopping the low stone wall past the playing fields and ducking my way through the trees' branches. I emerged onto the cliff's plateau, the stone gray/pink and striated to permanent ripples, exacted, I am assuming, by centuries of wind sweeping off the Atlantic. Looking out from the top of the cliff and back in the direction I came, I could see Second Beach to the northeast, its long spat of sand, and then behind it Third Beach, and the Marine base. Third Beach faces north, up toward Cape Cod and the rest of New England. A field of reeds turned tan by the sun separates these two beaches. I sat down on the uneven stone (its color, I think, is very near to cooked salmon), and listened to the waves and watched seabirds hover, their wings out, feet from the side of the cliff, still enough to seem connected by strings, a part of some nautical diorama. I stayed here through the afternoon, skipping dinner, the sky turning purple then gray, and I realized that what I was waiting for was the sun to sink into the ocean. Which was stupid, as I'm in Rhode Island. Instead, as the last bit of lavender left and low tide hushed the ocean below me, I got up to leave and heard noise in the bushes that grew near the trees and saw, for the first time in my life, a fox. In the thin light its fur seemed to glow slightly, the orange not flame but ember, a middle form between two things, an idea emphasized by the size of the animal – while full-grown, it was small enough to seem trapped in perpetual adolescence. It stood poised, its ears up, ready to flee back into the small plot of woods but then didn't. Its wide mouth made it appear to be smiling. Have you, Dad, been honored with moments like this? With scenes of near-magical grace? And after such moments did you consider if you deserved them? The fox stood between me and my route back to campus and I thought of Mark Norris, his wrecked bleeding face, and the creature spun on its hind legs and ran away into darkness. I managed my way back to the street bordering school and hopped the stone wall and walked over the playing field, back to my room, where I ate a banana and granola bar in silence.

I'll write again after the semester has started. It will be strange to see the quads teeming with people, to sit in a classroom, any classroom, again. It's an odd thing, the brink, that thing between things: the seabird so near the lip of the cliff, the fox at the copse's rough boundary. I imagine that Mom inhabits a space in some way like this, her body in our world but her mind faraway.

Please tell her hi.

Love,

Connor

SEPTEMBER

6

My name is Jim Haskin, and I am an ad on TV. The ceiling in my den is twenty feet high. The overlong room has a nook for my desk; its windows face west, and Lake Merritt is lit, a nice string of lights strung around it. Above the fireplace mantle is a plasma flat-screen, 65x54 inches. Let us all gather for this nightly drug, this light without heat, this machine that transforms and also disallows transformation. Let us regale and absolve it, and in doing so regale and absolve ourselves, our dreams numbed, our sins forgotten. Let us believe its fictive representations. For if we believe, and are true of faith, we can do what Man's sought since He hunted mammoths: reinvent nature. And crops can be sown where there were once trees, and towns can spring up next to ports on our rivers and oceans, and ore from the earth can be reaped and shaped, and things can be made that connect these port towns and in turn allow for more towns between them, as the more things we build, the more we can believe that we matter – that were it not for us there wouldn't be rain, light or lichen, that our explicit schema of ethics and ways is what lends the ants legs, and the walrus its fins, and the bushes their berries, and all of our waste goes magically away, and the meat that we eat is red cubes under plastic. Let us remember we're better than beasts. Let us remember that God will sweep it up later, for were this not the case we wouldn't have brains that knew of His Love and His Wrath and the ways to synthesize plastics, and shape glass in a manner to be flat and thin, and make circuit boards smaller and fit more pixels per inch, and dream up docudramas for the eight p.m. Sunday slot on the American Broadcasting Channel. It is with God's grace, my Lambs, that we are given culture, that next type of nature, and we must not forget all that culture provides, and for this Mankind, in the image of God, created television.

Sexy Assassins is Nielsen gold: a trio of trollops solves crimes, wearing little. On tonight's episode, Lana, the adventurous blonde, is kidnapped by an Angolan terrorist cell and kept locked in a basement, where water drips on the chest of her teal PVC corset. Natalia, the brunette, and Meena, the redhead, must save their trapped friend by having their nerdy male sidekick, Binh, hack into a global positioning satellite. This ruffles the feathers of Colonel James Holt, their patriarchal government liaison. The agents' code name is Project Amazonia: a privately funded Special Ops Unit. When Uzbeki jihadists try to poison the wells of Middle America, it's Project Amazonia that's called in to stop them. When an ambassador goes missing in the jungles of Brazil, it's up to the ladies to parachute in wearing camouflage bodysuits. Natalia's the leader; Meena is artsy. Lana would rather be dating. Each episode's plot is roughly as complex as a maze on a kid's dinner mat at a Denny's. Conflict, crisis, resolution. D-cups. Private enterprise saving the Feds' faulty ways. Reagan is gone but his ways live on in the box in your residence.

Ten minutes into 'The Angola Virus' and after Lana is stuffed in a van while out jogging in pink velour skimpies comes the first set of commercials. My latest creation, ISCI code AMWE 8872, is in pole position. It is stupendous. It is unique. It is a polar bear, drowning. A full twenty seconds of real-time footage: the white-furred animal, starving, leaves its small bit of ice floe to dive into the sea and find krill, find something, its mind now a slave to its stomach. It can't get back up and out of the water. We watch it. The long claws clamp down, dig in, but the bear does not have the strength left within it. Three seconds of struggle. Seven seconds. Arctic water is some of the clearest in the world: here is the white corpse, sinking. One pan to the next ice floe, just off the screen: the bear's cub, calling and watching. Circling the floe. Stopping. Circling. Cue overlay of the web address for Habitat for Humanity. Cue fade-out. End of commercial.

The next ad – this one for dryer sheets – comes on, taking the minds of the majority of viewers: the bear dying will be unremembered, fever dream, lost as it is in the brightly hued nightly parade of televised images. And should the bear's image bob up at points later, when the viewer is driving to the drive-thru, the office, there will be one of two possible outcomes. The first is that our driver, torn through by guilt and only now realizing it, will indeed give to my client. The second outcome is an overwhelming feeling of worthlessness and/or self-loathing; soul trauma, after which our driver must do something to forget that the car that he/she is driving is wrecking the soil, the ocean, the planet. And so he/she goes shopping, buys something nice, something cobbled overseas, something sleek, something fast and independent. Something that gives the powerless power – the new Bluetooth device, the red diamond fishnets, the side-zip, calf-length white leather boots, the black automatic weapon. There is nature and culture: the bear or the mall. You can have one but you cannot have both. I profit regardless.

Now back to *Sexy Assassins*.

Just after ten I bring tea to Esquido, who sits in the over-stuffed shepherdess chair I bought in Paris early last summer. The wood frame is walnut, gilded and carved, the upholstery a luminous turquoise. Esquido sits cross-legged, the reading lamp on, an antique edition of Proust's *La Prisonnière* spread open on his blanketed lap.

'The commercial was on?' Esquido asks me.

'It was.'

'And you were happy with it?'

I shrug. 'It does what it needs to.'

'It shows death,' says Esquido.

My wife, before coma, redid our bedroom: there was to be a renaissance of sorts, with Connor approaching his time to be leaving for college. Denise decided on *nouveau rococo*: lots of motion and brightness and prints. The bedroom's wallpaper is cream with green vines running down it. The bed's duvet cover matches Esquido's reading chair: turquoise and gold, in stripes of pure silk. I spend most nights on a cot by my desk in the office.

'It shows real death,' I tell Esquido. 'Not American death. American death isn't real. American death isn't permanent death. It can't be.'

'But people die everywhere,' says Esquido. 'The end is the same.'

'The means, though, are very, very different,' I tell him.

'We're off to promote?' asks my nurse aide, closing his book.

'We are. And you can't prove it,' I say.

'I can't prove what?' asks Esquido.

'That it's the same in the end for everyone,' I tell him.

'Life is unbalanced. The cosmos equates and death does this math.'

'I can't believe that,' I say.

'Why not?' asks Esquido.

'Because,' I say, 'it's just not American.'

We take the Prius to Connor's old school. In my car's trunk, and covering my car's back seat, are a variety of items we'll plant on the school grounds: spent cans of Coors Light, flyers for area gun shows. Piedmont is silent; the rich are all home, clicking at keys and pushing at buttons. Behind drapes of sheer silk sit shadows of people, mute from the glory of wealth and doing all they can to stay silent, to maintain it.

Denise and I moved to Piedmont when Connor was five. I'd worked my way up to full Art Director at the SF ad firm I'd been at since leaving college. I found the job simple: keep the masses entertained. Create what can't be forgotten. Boredom is this country's most richly understated sickness. I made ads for dog food, for bug spray and blue jeans. I made ads for a Drug-Free America. My wife and I rented a two-bedroom apartment while we saved and saved, knowing the future as vague but expensive. Our home was filled with things we'd found used: cheap lamps from thrift stores, mismatched and second-hand couches. When I got stressed out, my wife told me to breathe. When I was still working past dinner, Denise told me to stop it.

Connor started hitting children when he was three, during his first month in preschool. The place was only blocks from our house; Denise walked our son there each morning. We met with the director: are there are problems at home? How's your boy's eating, his sleeping? But it wasn't these things, and Connor was smart: the school had said we could enroll him at two, but we'd waited.

'The problem seems to be he's aware that he's different,' the director told us while Denise and I sat in matching olive vinyl chairs, surrounded by the hand paintings of children. 'We think that he's internalizing this, and when he can't internalize it anymore he goes off the deep end. He just blows up.'

'He internalizes it?' I'd said. 'He's three.'

'Just tell us how to fix it,' Denise begged the director.

'But we don't know what's wrong. It's not ADD and it's not OCD. Connor loves tasks. He loves being busy. When it's time for recess, though, he won't go outside, and when we make him do it he starts crying. Another child will approach him and he pushes them away, and when they come back again he gets violent.'

Our doctor said General Anxiety Disorder. He prescribed Ritalin; Denise and I agreed. We kept Connor on meds for two years of his life, our three-year-old son, once vibrant, once bright, now a middling zombie. At the kitchen table, at home, Connor would drool on his food and stare at the pea-colored, wall-mounted phone. At school he fell asleep almost daily. Denise and I fought not from opposing viewpoints but from the fact that the cure seemed worse than the problem and, even though we hated the changes in our son, we were seemingly powerless to do anything about it, a fact I considered on my morning commutes, the BART train lurching and screaming its way under the Bay's brackish water.

In '95 my firm landed an account for a new allergy drug. We ran print ads, bright full-page things in the back of *Golf Digest* or *People*. Two years later, the FDA released revised guidelines for Direct-to-Consumer broadcast advertising. What this meant was that drug firms, once forced to include all the risks and side effects of their product, could instead offer up a toll-free number for people with questions. No longer did the ad itself need to include a laundry list of things to consider; instead, only the most major risks needed to be told, and these could be fitted in at the end of the television ad, in a single breath and by a man talking very, very fast, so fast that it made the consumer not want to pay attention.

At home, Connor's mind had all but shut off; he'd developed dizzy spells, was emotionless, lethargic. We took him back to the pediatrician once every few weeks.

'But he's calm, right?' said the doctor. 'He's getting along? Fitting in?'

We told him yes, we guessed that he was.

'Well,' said the doctor, tapping his pen on the side of his clipboard, 'then the drug's doing what it's supposed to.'

My firm's client had invested hundreds of millions since filing the patent on the allergy drug during Reagan's first term. It wanted TV spots, and it wanted these to do something that no ads had done since the time of snake-oil liniments: sell drugs not with knowledge but image. Provide feeling, not fact. Turn negatives into positives. And thus I came up with The Heaven Campaign. The Heaven Campaign deified medication. The Heaven Campaign made folly of logic. The Heaven Campaign also made my ad firm rich, and brought me enough clout to venture out on my own, and with the help of my friends start my own business.

In The Heaven Campaign there is video montage; there is narration and CGI and bright colors and music. Young urban professionals wear white linen clothes. They sit out on the grass, on picnic blankets. Everyone's teeth shine. Everyone's faces are numb from their smiling. In the Heaven Campaign people fly in hot-air balloons. In the Heaven Campaign parents hug kids and the kids hug their parents. And at the end of these ads, like the bright, shining sun, the little white pill sits in the middle of the sky and the people on the ground, in the balloon, in the park, they worship it, worship the pill for all that it does, give thanks to the pill as though it were Jesus, as gone now is allergic preoccupation, the need to stay in, to brood, think and dwell, the need to consider the human condition. Instead, in The Heaven Campaign, there is optimism and joy and relief. Instead, in The Heaven Campaign, there is transcendence.

I park the Prius on a side street near the school's football field. Esquido and I gather our things into trash bags. Included is the new Miley Cyrus CD, seventeen issues of *NASCAR*

Magazine, promotional materials for the U.S. Marines, twenty-five cartons of cigarettes. My three closest friends in the world, in one way or another, are invested in all of the items above: they own stock, they want war, they want people addicted. And the high-school demographic wants only two things: to have money and be told how to spend it. AmWe's client base is represented as well: there are energy bars and bamboo yoga pants, hemp jewelry and jars of organic face cream.

We strew items on the football field's grass and its red rubberized track, then head up to the gold-painted bleachers. Esquido sets down a copy of the Miley CD, then looks down the length of the stadium seats, to see how far one item sits from another. On a night not long after my wife went forever to sleep, Esquido had a rare confessional moment. He told me about an initiation ceremony the MS-13s had for their child soldiers. Not far from their barracks was a pond filled with alligators. These alligators weren't there naturally; someone had put them in there, and the pond had grown overpopulated. The men would wrap loops of steak around the boys' wrists and make them hold out their hands over the water. What the men didn't tell the boys was that the meat had been soaked in turpentine, and the alligators wouldn't go near it. If the boy didn't cry, he joined the gang. If he did cry, he was killed the same night, and fed to the alligators.

We walk up a steep and short hill to the campus, Esquido and I going our separate ways to cover as much territory as we can. In the night's silence I hear the flop of glossy reading material hitting pavement. I walk down a red-tiled exterior hallway, in the direction of Connor's old locker. Off the meds, my son largely reverted to the person he'd been, but part of him, too, never fully came back. A sad blankness, like a film, sat over his eyes. There were bouts of rage that seemed to arrive out of nowhere. With puberty, this cycle of grief, anger and grief increased and increased and then seemed to stop altogether. Denise and I were joyfully relieved; our son had returned, and couldn't be better. My wife went into coma later that year. Connor put his classmate, Mark Norris, in the hospital seven months later.

I rip open one of the cartons of Kools, sprinkling its contents over the ground as though I were feeding corn pellets to chickens. I hang hemp bracelets on door handles and make a small stack of all-natural deodorants next to the door of a bathroom. I send fourteen Miley Cyrus CDs down the book-return chute for the library. As I'm turning to leave, a light comes on in the main office window. From my spot in the shadows, I watch a custodian push out his trashcan-on-wheels. He goes for his key clip attached to one of his pants' belt loops.

'Hey,' I say, walking toward him. 'Wait a minute.'

The man's tall and thin with dark closely cropped hair, a very big nose and thick and dark glasses.

'Can I help you?' he says, looking around, trying to tell if he's about to get jumped, if this is a set-up.

'You can,' I say. 'But I don't know if you will.' I'm guessing jail time, a string of small crimes, possession with intent, maybe car burglary.

'Shouldn't be up here, man,' the janitor tells me, pushing his glasses back up the bridge of his nose.

'I know, but I was dropping off books for my son. He's at home right now, and applying to college. He needs his MedFile. He's applying online. Do you know what a MedFile is? That thing that the State says all minors need to have now, if they're in public schools? It proves that they don't have swine flu? My son needs to scan this thing in with his college application.'

There's of course no such thing as a MedFile at all, but the janitor's eyes quickly skimming the ground assure me that he doesn't know this.

'It'll just take a second,' I say. 'I know Principal Welks. He's an acquaintance of mine. You can stay in there with me the whole time. You can watch me.'

For all I know, this man beats off in the school's sinks. For all I know, this man worships Satan. But he also pays rent and has a shitty job, one largely reliant on being subordinate at nearly any cost.

'Come on,' I say, and take out a hundred from my brown leather wallet. 'I know you're in charge here. It's just a MedFile. It'll be back in the morning.'

The man looks around once and pockets the bill. I follow him into the Principal's office. The last time I was here was to sign my son's expulsion papers. I did this prior to picking him up from the Piedmont police station. In the car, driving home, my son next to me in the passenger seat, I'd told him he was going to school back East, away from what was happening at home. I'd told him that it would be a good thing, this change, and that he'd be getting a great education.

'So you're sick of raising me?' Connor had said.

'I'm not,' I'd answered, 'but I'm out of choices.'

'Maybe, when you ship me off, I can pretend that you're dead, like your parents are. Maybe I can pretend that you're done existing.'

I'd pulled the car over to the side of the road, in front of a house where a little white dog was taking a dump on a trimmed, perfect lawn.

'Is that what you want?' I'd asked.

'I don't know. Is it what you want?' Connor had answered.

We sat there in silence, and when this went on a minute more I put the Prius in gear and drove my son home, neither of us answering the question.

Principal Welks's file cabinets – there are three – are unlocked.

I find the form that I signed some months ago. It's the original. It will be burned. My son's teenaged past will not get to haunt him.

'All done,' I tell the custodian. 'Have a good night.' I walk past him and then spin around. 'You almost done here? On the grounds?'

'I do the office last,' says the janitor.

'Great,' I say. 'That's really great. I'm glad your day's almost over,' and shove the end of my now-empty garbage bag down into my chinos' side pocket.

I walk back down the hill, toward the field, toward my car. I turn a corner and Esquido is standing there, waiting for me. I nod my head and he falls into step and we continue in silence all the way to the street, where I depress the unlock button on my Prius's key chain.

'What were you doing up there?' Esquido asks.

'Some tidying,' I tell him. 'For Connor.'

'You shouldn't have to do that,' Esquido tells me.

'He's sixteen. And do you have a son? Are you a parent?'

'I was a parent to many children,' says Esquido. 'I told ten-year-olds to cut off people's ears. I told teenagers to rape their own cousins. They did what I said. Your son doesn't listen to you. Your son is going to cause you many problems.'

I stay silent and turn over the Prius's weird engine. Headlights turn the corner and a car, a mid-80s cream-colored Buick, stops beside ours, facing in the opposite direction. A trio of men, all Latino, stare at me and my nurse aide, the driver rolling down his window. He has on a plain white T-shirt, a gold necklace with the Roman numeral fourteen on it.

'You know how to get to the freeway?' the driver asks. Esquido leans over the car's middle console and says maybe two dozen quick words in Spanish. The Buick's driver looks at Esquido

87

and then at me. He has a thin mustache, a finely shaved head. He nods once and then keeps driving.

I get the car going and head back up the streets toward my home. A block away, I pull over.

'Friends of yours?' I say.

Esquido shakes his head. 'It's nothing. Babosos. Norteno little men.'

'How do you know they're Norteno?' I ask.

'The necklace. Fourteen. Norteno number.' Esquido looks pale. He blinks his eyes twice. I put the car back in gear but Esquido tells me to wait and make sure that we weren't followed.

'Are we in trouble?' I ask. 'Are you?'

Esquido opens his mouth and starts to respond, but then closes it and looks out at the house that we're parked in front of. Inside, past the huge picture window with its floor-length open drapes, stands a woman in a nightgown, holding a pint of ice cream and a spoon. She stands in profile, watching TV.

'Look,' says Esquido.

'I see her,' I say.

'No,' says Esquido.

And then I notice it. The polar bear. The woman stands transfixed, the spoon poised above the waxed paper pint. The corpse sinking, the bear cub. The woman sets down her items and picks up the phone. She looks out toward the street. The windowpane's backlit; I'm sure she can't see us. She is, instead, looking at herself in the glass's reflection, the phone ringing now, the taste of sugar and cream on her tongue. She will help, then go back to eating.

7

The next afternoon I head south to San José, where I am to be honored at the university there for my dedication to lessening the footprint of Man on the planet. My hybrid glides by the sewage-treatment plant, the airport, the Coliseum. To the east, on my left, are the tan and dead hills, to the right the Bay's bright and wrecked waters. A girl in her Jetta, cell phone to her ear, swings three lanes over and then back again. Her car is toy, is act, is trapeze. She is wealthy and white and the world cannot hurt her. She cuts off a cargo truck, top-heavy, bright green; the driver inside is Vietnamese, maybe forty. He lays on the horn, unblinking. A CHP cruiser, ignoring all this, blurs by with its lights on, sirens chirping. Here on the freeway we're shrunk by what we've made, reduced to platelet and neuron. We move past one another with purpose and task, through the veins of this constructed body.

I pass by San Leandro and Hayward, Union City and Fremont, zip codes that the Big Three and Big Oil built, forty minutes of blacktop towns with ad hoc culture, sprung to life with the death of the American trolley. Sandstone walls protect residents from vehicles, drivers from eyesore. Cal State University Bay South is fifteen minutes from the Downtown San José exit. The parking garage on 7th Street is enormous and dark, and a line of cars moves in an ascending square, from one floor to the next, searching for spaces. When a car pulls out, the line stops and waits. Six cars back, I watch this ballet, the reverse lights lit on the car begging departure, the car behind it giving no ground. Two days, three days, five days a week, this is what our next generation of good minds navigates, before math, before Constitutional Law, before reading Tolstoy or playing the tuba. They learn how to drive their car and then park it. At CSU-BS, there is continued commitment to practical modes of education.

I park on the roof, in a faculty spot, and hang my faculty pass from my rearview. A new one of these arrives in my mailbox each semester, courtesy of Dick Reed, CSU Bay South's President. Dick and I played football together at Stanislaus State, in Turlock. After he obtained his business degree, Dick took a job with the country's second-largest vending-machine company, working his way up from regional sales to Senior Vice-President before making the jump into education. Dick was and is round and big-boned and quite broad, and the skin just above his upper lip sweats profusely. He also has a penchant for underage girls, and because of this penchant and poor tact and bad luck, Dick Reed was caught, back in 2002, soliciting a fourteen-year-old prostitute in a part of Oakland that he had no business being in. While he sat in the seat of his dark gray Mercedes, he called me on his cell phone, seeking salvation. I, in turn, called my friend Frank Gaines, He of Much Sway at the Federal Bureau of Investigation. And because of these calls that could not be traced, and because of a complex system of want and need, of supply and demand, of greed corrected through greed, Dick Reed was never officially booked, nor fingerprinted. Instead, and by the back door, Dick was released in the middle of the night into my friend Frank Gaines's custody. In a lockbox at my house, and wrinkled from age, the handwriting faded but legible, sits the ticket that Officer Gabriel Garcia gave Dick Reed for soliciting a minor. This ticket remains there for decades to come in exchange for a voice in CSU-BS policy. For over six years, I, very quietly, have had more to do with Cal State Bay South than our governor.

It takes me two minutes of strolling campus grounds to find proof of my work here at Bay South. Heading across the groomed quad and in my direction is a tall Asian man in a bright red sport jacket. Patches and pins festoon his lapels. He's carrying a gym bag with the Nike symbol on it. The same symbol is emblazoned on his navy-blue tie and, while I can't see the back of his jacket, I know it's there, too. This man is one of the ten DCFs, Distinguished Corporate Faculty, here at the CSU-BS campus. Dressed like they're going to rent you a car, these scholars, all Ivy League grads, the best of the best, minds that at some point should be excised and studied, exist here at Bay South on six-figure salary, a sum underwritten by some of America's finest. Nike has this man; Google is here, as are Verizon and Chevron and Apple and, as part of CSU-BS's Freshman Experience, incoming students are required to take a class on the collective history of these corporations.

I walk at the DCF coming toward me. His rectangular name tag, a DCF mandate, reads Dr Hui Wu. Wu's in his mid-30s, a mole on his cheek, a slight bit of spike to his short and black hair.

'Hi there,' I say. 'You work for Nike.'

'I am Distinguished Corporate Faculty in the School of Engineering,' Hui Wu tells me.

'You don't work for Nike?' I ask, my voice lifting.

'Yes,' says Hui Wu, his jaw set, his eyes blinking once.

'Professor Wu, if I'm right, you're maybe from China?'

'I am,' says the professor.

'And you went to Dartmouth,' I say, touching the pin on his lapel with my finger.

'Yes,' says Hui Wu.

'Well, Professor Wu, I was wondering if you have time to tell me about the winter line of Nike shoes.'

Wu checks his watch. I check mine, too. It's eleven fifty-one. No class for nine minutes. I can almost smell the math skittering about this man's brain. Hui Wu takes a deep breath and looks past me.

'The Winter Nike Line will make the old new, with an emphasis on colors of the early 1980s. Nike is interested, this year, in urban culture's origins. Nike wants to take it back to the Bronx, when people played boomboxes and opened up fire hydrants and set cars on fire in defiance of living in squalor. Our shoe technicians want you to feel what it was like to be doing the Worm on a hot summer night in Harlem. We have a new shade of red that we call Shot By Cops. We have a new shade of yellow we call Crack Epidemic. We have color combinations so then that they're now. The past is the future this year at Nike.'

The grounds of the quad are teeming with life: along the narrow asphalt pathways that bisect the grass cross hundreds of students in sweatpants, in oversized jerseys. Here are sunglasses and cell phones and scooters and longboards and Juicy key chains and fake D&G purses. Every fourth student holds no backpack, no books. Dick Reed, in emails, terms this group Veal: cute and milk-fed and dead early.

'Professor Wu,' I say, 'I was wondering if you might also update me on the advances that Nike is making in athletic-supporter technology.'

'Are you on staff here?' Wu asks.

'Sort of,' I tell him. 'I sort of am. But that shouldn't matter, right? You represent a brand that holds interest for me, a brand whose products I may want to buy. It's my understanding that you know this brand. If you don't have time for me, that's fine, but I'll need, at the least, directions to the nearest Nike store so someone there can inform me.'

From his Nike gym bag, Wu pulls out an accordion map with directions to area Nike storefronts. Possession of these maps by my DCFs is a mandate. 'I'm sorry that I don't have time to say more,' says Hui Wu. 'I have a class to go teach.'

'Sure, I'm just about done,' I tell him. 'I was wondering, though, what you'll do when you leave here. What you'll take away from your time at Bay South.'

Wu straightens up at this talk of the future.

'Yes,' he says. 'I'm going back to China. I'll return to Dongguan at the end of the year, and never again in my life see this sad fucking campus. These students are idiots. Worse, they don't care. Many read at an eighth-grade level. Cell phones ring every five minutes in my classrooms. You see them,' Wu says, casting an arm, 'does this look more like a learning institution or some endless party? I have this semester and the next one, and I live, right now, in a studio apartment infested by roaches. It stands next to the freeway. It is the cheapest thing I could find. I hold two degrees from one of the top schools your country has to offer. And I will save all the money that this appointment affords and then go and do something really, truly good. I am going to help build a canal. Our river there is polluted. The water is sometimes on fire. Your skin burns if you touch it. Children play in this river and get very sick. I hope to go upstream from the city and dynamite and build so that we can get good water from the mountains, pure water, water like China used to have,' says Wu.

'That's really poignant,' I tell him, and Wu's disgust turns opaque.

'Your people, your country,' he says, 'call China a wasteland. This is poor thinking. Here is a wasteland. This place is wasteland. China gets up. China tries hard. China has begun unionizing. You look like a smart man, so I'm willing to bet that you also know that China owns most of this country's debt, and that this country's debt is enormous.'

'I do know that,' I say. I own stock in the companies that harbor this debt. Right now, they're my biggest gainers.

The campus bell rings. Wu is staring at me. He doesn't know it yet, but he won't be finishing out this semester.

'This has been really informative,' I say, and bid Wu farewell, and bring out my BlackBerry. Trung Tran, ringleader of the identity-theft ring I sometimes employ, is right now in Union City. Tonight he will be in San José, stealing mail from the box outside the front door of Wu's apartment.

I check my email on my hand-held, where a long string of jpegs has arrived. Yi-Yi was late but the wait was well worth it: Cuba Gooding Jr. getting tased in the face; Mark Hamill and Carrie Fisher tasing George Lucas in the stomach. That giant from *Dateline*, tasing himself. The Speaker of the House, a ball gag in her mouth, holding a bottle of absinthe. If these pictures could be blown up and put in the MoMA, it would be the most attended exhibition in all of art's history, and in possessing these photos – items that could destroy so many lives, that could really and truly alter history – I feel something past joy or possession or mirth. I feel, as I do through so much of my work, that I have purpose.

The last picture is of Yi-Yi herself, resplendent in white tennis dress, standing by the edge of a very blue pool. It's an image almost mythological in its beauty, a picture that aesthetes, eras from now, should put into textbooks and have the young study. The blonde tennis star and I have never had sex. It's not about that. It's that, for me, Yi-Yi's the perfect ad. She could stand next to the tall gates of hell and God wouldn't be able to give space away to the pious.

* * *

Most of the buildings on the campus of Bay South haven't been updated since *Magnum, PI* was still airing new episodes. An exception to this is the Stankowski Business Building: a glass-walled, six-story, shiny new thing endowed by one of Bay South's antiheroes, Lewis Stankowski. In an interview with *AVN Magazine*, the porn industry's standard, Mr Stankowski, head of Stank Films, which rakes in roughly one-fifth of smut's gross, said that his time at Bay South was integral to his choice of career. Raised by his grandmother after his parents were killed in a cave-in at a Nevada ghost town, Stankowski – bespectacled, rail-thin, an asthmatic – hoped to meet peers that would not haze and attack him upon his admittance into college. These hopes were false. His time in the dorms was filled with Roman games, Lewis duct-taped to a handcart and pushed toward another dork who'd had the same thing done to him, in a modern and depraved version of jousting. Girls fled at his approach. People shit in his bed. Someone stole his computer. What his tormentors didn't know was that Stankowski was rich, or would be in the very near future. Stankowski, through the death of his parents, stood to inherit nearly four million dollars from the owners of the silver mine tourist trap. This sum was not to be made available to Lewis until he turned twenty-one, at which time he could do what he pleased with the money. And what Lewis did do with this large sum of money, after four years of slander and shaving-cream wedgies, property theft and scatological miasma, was take a Greyhound to LA, and buy a two-bedroom condo just off Venice Beach, and recruit young and tan waifs in various states of poverty and addiction to live there for free, and prance around nude, and put toys in each other, all while on camera. TeenSexHouse.com laid the foundation for the small empire of smut that Lewis built for himself exactly as the Tech Boom exploded.

By 2002, Stank Films was founded, and Stankowski, now tan, now contact-lensed, now with twenty more pounds of muscle on him, took his private jet to San José for Bay South's Commitment to Excellence Campaign, a series of weekend fundraisers that up to this point Lewis had never attended. The principal funder for the new Business Building had been jailed on charges of corporate fraud, and no other alum had stepped forth to replace him. And with the state near to broke and education never high on lawmakers' to-do list, CSU-Bay South erected The Hall That Porn Built, Stankowski signing a twenty-million dollar check that very same weekend.

With class now in session foot traffic slows, and I call into work, the general line, and get Brogan. How are things there? OMG, things are GOOD. OMG, the ads for Evermore Towers come out tomorrow in the *Chronicle* and the *LA Times* and the *Tribune* and the *New York Times* and, like, other papers, too. OMG, I am learning how to decoupage.

OMG, I tell Brogan, and say bye, and hang up, sitting down on a bench in a sunken courtyard next to the Business Building. Just as I'm putting my BlackBerry away, the thing rings again: an 888 number. 888 numbers mean nothing good.

'Hello,' I say. 'You've reached Jim Haskin.' I pause here, to make it sound like a message, to fuck with whoever's about to fuck with me. At one of the foster homes before Mr Hand a bigger kid once stole my dinner from me. Later that night, I tied him to his bed and broke both his eye sockets with a square-head tack hammer.

The delay on the line lets me know this is someone in an office, someone with a thin headset on, their fingers crouched over some outdated keyboard like an evil magician.

'Ello?' says a female voice that sounds Southern and big. 'Ello ello?' the voice asks repeatedly.

'Yes?' I ask.

'Is this Mr Jim Haskin?'

'I already told you that it was,' I say.

'I didn't hear you, though,' says the woman.

'Do you want me to say it again?'

The woman ignores the question. She says that she's calling on behalf of my insurance provider. She says that her name is DePisces.

'Your name is what?' I say. 'Your name is DePisces?'

'That's right, Mr Haskin. I'm calling about your wife, Denise.'

'What about her?' I say. 'She can't come to the phone. She's in a coma.'

'Yes, Mr Haskin – from Supinal, I believe?'

'From Supinal, yes,' I tell her.

'Okay, Mr Haskin, I'm going to get right to the point? In case you have any questions? Your provider isn't covering your wife's treatment.'

'At all,' I say.

'That's right,' says DePisces.

'Okay,' I say, thinking of numbers on pages, thinking of phrases like THIS IS NOT A BILL, which, apparently, is bullshit. 'I'm ready for your explanation.'

'Mr Haskin,' says DePisces, and she sounds happy here, sounds as though she's really ready to let me have it, as her tone has gone lighter and ascended an octave, 'we've been researching Supinal ourselves—'

'Because the makers of Supinal keep you in business.'

'Mr Haskin, if you won't let me explain,' says DePisces.

'Okay,' I say, and think of my offshore account, think of selling the house, think of Connor's tuition and the Dow being down, my assets all trapped, ad revenue slowing.

'Mr Haskin, what this research has concluded is that your

wife's DNA harbors a genealogical susceptibility to the active ingredient in Supinal, a hereditary predisposition, Mr Haskin, and because of this—'

'You have my wife's DNA?' I ask.

'Yes, Mr Haskin, when you took her to Palo Alto Medical Hospital, you signed papers there, thereby granting a release that we have permanent access to your wife's DNA and can keep it on file, for our records.'

'On what piece of paper was said release?' I ask.

'Page 27,' DePisces tells me, 'near the bottom.'

I curb the nearly overwhelming desire to hit the first thing I can, to put the phone down and throttle the world, larynx by larynx.

'Okay,' I say, 'how much will it be, monthly?'

'Well, there's a retroactive charge.'

'Are you Satan?' I say.

'I'm not,' says DePisces. 'Since this genetic condition existed in your wife before she ever chose to take Supinal—'

'Supinal was approved by our doctor,' I say.

'And yet your wife consciously chose to take it, Mr Haskin. Therefore, your provider sees this as the choice of the patient.'

'So you're saying that every cent of my wife's condition I'll pay out of pocket.'

'I am, Mr Haskin. I am saying exactly that. Do you want to set up a payment plan now? I can do that for you, Mr Haskin. I can take care of that.'

'Give me the figure,' I say, thinking of my Vietnamese identity-theft ring, and that there can be only so many people on the face of the Earth with the first name DePisces.

'Four million three hundred and forty-five thousand twelve,' says DePisces. 'And seventeen cents.'

'Four and a half million,' I say.

'A little less,' says DePisces.

'If there's a hell,' I say.

'You'll see me there, Mr Haskin?'

'How long do I have?' I ask.

'To pay the bill or to see me in hell?' asks DePisces.

'The former,' I say.

'Well, it depends on the plan you set up.'

'To pay it in full. The four million,' I say. 'Fuck interest. I'm not paying interest.'

'Mr Haskin, we're willing to give you three months.'

'So, mid-Decemeber,' I say.

'We'll say the 23rd,' says DePisces.

'Fantastic,' I say. 'DePisces, enjoy life with your name. Enjoy the rest of your shitty existence.'

'I hate my name, Mr Haskin,' says DePisces. 'And I've had a pretty tough life. It's one of the reasons that I took this job. To get back at people with normal names and sane lives. People with names like Jim and Denise. Do you have any questions?' DePisces asks, but I don't, and hang up, thinking the whole of the world is boomeranging back at me: the housing bubble and easy credit conditions, over-leveraging and deregulation. The commodities boom. The incorrect pricing of risk. The lemming march of the shadow banking system. All of the things that made us rich, Lambs, that kept us so warm and cozy, all of these things have grown up. They own fangs. Their claws have come in. They are hungry.

The Business Building's banquet room is on the top floor. Hand-painted signs adorn the ground-level hallway that leads to the elevator. They read CONFERENCE ON SUSTAINEABILITY. I take a pen out from my eco-safe attaché and cross out the ees, because when people feel dumb they tend to buy things so as to feel better. The elevator's bell dings and I step in and step out seven seconds later. I walk over linoleum floors designed to look like they're marble. There are numbers on windows, students at desks. There are teachers that stand at the front of these rooms, their hands out in front of them, poised as if to catch something of very great weight that has turned out to be very late in arriving.

At the banquet room's entrance sits a girl at a table, columns of name tags spread out in front of her.

'Speaker or guest?' she asks through her smile.

'Both,' I say, and the girl screws up her face then relaxes it, like her brain just had a bowel movement.

'Totally,' she says. 'Totally.'

'I'm Jim Haskin,' I say.

'Right. I knew that,' she says. 'I think your ads rock.'

I consider how a polar bear dying rocks. 'Thank you,' I tell her.

The banquet hall has a dome that is also a skylight. The banquet hall's back wall is windows. Between them and me are rows of wood tables, covered in white tablecloths. Upon these are glasses and flower arrangements. The room is half-filled; a soft din coats the air. There's a low stage at the room's other end, a podium, a microphone, a bottle of water. I put on my mask; I leave myself. I depart from the true me of emotion, of opinion. I prick an unseen hole with an invisible pin and that self, that me, escapes as clear gas, imperceptibly hissing. It leaves and taking its place is Work Me, is Fake Me, is Me on the Stage and Me of Hands Shaken, Me of the Eyebrow Cocked to Show I'm Invested. The Me of Concern, of Finger to Chin. The Me of Long Title and Capital Letters. The Only Me Most People Ever Get to See. Please tell Me: who are You, how are You.

A fat man in shorts and white tennis shoes with a very red face and his polo tucked in over his enormous rippling belly approaches me, his hand out. I shake it. His hair is bright white, the shirt a loud red. Santa disguised and in hotter weather.

'Hi, Jim, I'm Don Keller, I'm the Chair of the Environmental Studies Department.' Don Keller says how honored he is and I say it back, how honored I am, the small part I play, just here to help, how remarkable, the campus. I'm glad; I'm so glad. Keller hands me a check for two thousand dollars. This sum is enough for me to buy dozens of Miley Cyrus CDs.

'It's going straight to Habitat for Humanity,' I tell him.

'That's great to hear,' says Don Keller.

After a brunch of goat cheese and cracked-pepper water crackers, fresh fruit and mimosas and salmon with capers, I am introduced by Fat Tropical Santa, and then take the stage to tell these students and professors and whomever else about the need for sustainability here, on our planet. That what we have reached is a true tipping point, that the things that have propelled us this far we must now view as limiting. It requires sea change. It requires a new type of thinking. It requires walking through life as through a minefield: with constant concern, with the mind truly worried, for only when we are truly worried can we change our ways, can we know and dwell on and then ultimately fix all our problems. We have been lucky, I say, as the sun floods in through the windows behind me, as silverware clinks, as the room's servers move in near-silence. We've afforded ourselves utter decadence. We live as China did, before its Revolution, as Russia, before its Revolution. But these Revolutions did come, and Rome was sacked, and these things, my friends, stand just past our horizon. The world is awake and the world is in pain. Each action counts and is not isolated. When a dolphin is killed off the coast of Japan, in a net made for tuna, it affects the price of heating oil in Boise. When Brazilian rainforest is chopped and then burnt, it affects the mating habits of Mongolian snow leopards. This notion might seem far-fetched, but for the planet and the other species upon it our actions are their nightly news at eleven, and we must learn new ways to not have each newscast be a study in and orgy of violence. We must learn that the less we are felt and are seen, the better; that by lightening our foot-print, we can walk farther.

I pause here for applause, as it is expected, before moving on to Feel-Good Solutions: solar panels for houses, windmills in backyards, hydrogen cars, plastic bag moratoriums. The applause comes too, at BS Eco-Day, presented by the BS Department of Environmental Studies. I look out and count the number of water bottles, many of which will spend the next thousand years in landfills. I look out at the laptops and digital cameras, the mp3 players and cell phones, at the closed sea of plastic before me. At its majesty. At the money that it translates to, at dire cost to the planet. None of these people will alter their ways; none will start showering every other day, none will donate their car and take public transportation. None will leave the heat off and just use a blanket. Because we obey. Because we had been told that things would be fine: we beat the Russians, we beat the Germans. Both threatened the freedom of our Golden Way. Both wanted state regulation. We would not have this. We knew much better. We understood the salva-tion of endless consumption. Let us sit here and applaud what we've done, before we get up and go out and destroy it.

I start in on a PowerPoint about drought, how we help it along, water parks and golf courses. The lights dim and, two minutes into my folly, the door to the banquet room opens then closes. I stop listening to what it is that I'm saying. I keep talking but put the talk on autopilot. I do this because standing now, in the back of the room, are my three closest friends on the planet. Frank Gaines wears a black suit and black tie, the starched collar of his white dress shirt unbuttoned. Henry Stine, returning from the set of *Coyotes*, is in T-shirt and jeans and pinstriped sport jacket. Ned Akeley, beside him, the three a short row, is in navy suit and black shirt and red tie. I look at them but nothing on my face changes. I look at them and think of the almond fields, the Home, Mr Hand and his sermons, the bunk beds, their tightly coiled springs, the scratch of the green donated Army blankets. There were ten bunks in total. Nineteen kids there. Mr Hand always left one bed open. I speak about drought, about what we've reached, about Los Angeles County at such a crisis point that they will now filter sewer water for their taps. Ned Akeley holds his hands up in front of his chest. All fingers are up. We meet in October, next month. I talk about long-term viability of the Hech Hechy Reservoir in Yosemite, its waters pristine, its purity in danger. Henry Stine holds up three fingers. Third week. And as I talk about mining effects on the Colorado River, Frank Gaines puts six fingers to chest. We are meeting on a weekend. We don't meet on weekends. I stumble in my speech. My three friends straighten up. I correct myself, and then keep talking about water rites, about flooding in the Delta, about the need for conservation in the San Francisco Bay. My head moves around the room; I employ gesticulation. People nod when my eyes fall on them. I talk for another five minutes and end, and when I look back to the banquet-room door my friends are gone. Our meeting is the same day as the Parents' Weekend soccer game at the school that my son attends. The lights come back on. I breathe in deeply.

The drive up to Piedmont is a slow and long dream, the fleet moving as if connected by strings, the traffic heavy. I dawdle through the radio stations. A twangy post-teen croons of love on the Plains. A black man raps about pimping his women. The song from the Hypo Beach Party comes on; like the events, it has been a huge hit, the song breaking Billboard's Top 40. I seek and seek as drivers drive by me, seeking. Here is the DJ who hates the GOP; here is the DJ who hates liberals. Here is the Vietnamese-language station, and here one in Mandarin, and here three in Spanish. Here is Christian Rock twenty-four hours a day. Please don't touch that dial. Please mosh for Jesus.

I pull into my driveway, where Esquido talks with my maid, Samampo. Samampo's Brazilian. I don't know what her name means. The difference between the portly and the stout is that the stout, I think, have purpose. Samampo has a duster tucked into her apron. Samampo is 7th Day Adventist. Samampo is the future of most of mankind: a menial job, a mind filled with God, trips to the Walmart with her half-dozen children, each of whom will give Samampo at least three grandchildren. I know how the math works. I've seen Sao Paolo, the helipads twenty stories above the leaning, aching slums. It will happen here. It *is* happening.

In the bedroom, I drape my suit jacket over my wife's legs. I look at the machine that assists with her breathing. Today, Esquido has dressed her in hot pink capris and white cap-sleeve blouse with black buttons. The pants, a size 4, look enormous on her frame. I run a finger down the length of one of her arms, the machine's lung gasping then lifting. Her sunken cheeks resemble pale, crumbling cliffs. Her fingers have shrunk; the wedding ring I bought her sits loose up near her first knuckle. I bought the brass band at a Reno pawnshop; five years later, I had a diamond the size of a flash drive fused to it. I pick up my wife's finger and look at her face, then push the ring down to the webbing.

8

Dear Dad,

Here is the church, here is the steeple, open the doors, and here's all the people. Here is gridlock on the tree-lined main drive on a Sunday, the Mercedes and U-Hauls and Land Rovers and Jeeps backed up to Purgatory Road, the name of which, Dad, I couldn't make up if I had to. Families pour out from cars, blinking in the mild wet heat of late morning. They lug boxes and rugs and old steamer trunks. They balance pairs of skis on their shoulders. Fathers shake the hands of fathers, their oxford shirts in lilac and salmon tucked into khaki Land's End shorts, their pert wives clucking in sunglasses. In the evening is the Annual Second Beach Clam Bake, seaweed and seawater in huge iron pots, the stones glowing red in dug pits near the shoreline. Headmaster Lynn makes the rounds in Birkenstocks and plaid madras bermudas. He and his wife have three golden labs and live in a house not far from my room's small window. Our school building is called Old Hall, four floors of classrooms and tables, the numbers on the door in some old and sharp font, and golden. The football coach, Mr Frank, teaches

American Civilization. Ted Dill, one of the two non-athletes on my floor, fell asleep in his class on the very first day and Mr Frank stood up and hit him on the side of the head with his textbook. Not the sort of thing, Dad, you see in public education. If students wear hats inside Old Hall, teachers have the right, in passing, to take them. It occurs to me, Dad, that I don't own a hat. Why is this?

The seniors here are called Seventh Form, the numbers in the nomenclature descending to Fourth Form for freshmen. Cameron Nash is Seventh Form. Cameron Nash rides the bench. This is because Cameron Nash is on crutches. We were out running and Nash went toward the playground for his normal smoke break and a long strip of land had been dug up, it would seem, for irrigation purposes, and Cameron Nash stepped into this ditch, badly spraining his ankle. We're 3-0, Dad, to start off the season. One ball past me in the first trio of matches, and this ball was kicked with such ambition and grace that it does not keep me up at night, thinking and thinking. There are some balls that are meant to go in, and this one, kicked by a foreign exchange student from Nigeria, was one of them, a ball that curved as it dropped, so that it looked like it would sail high and to the side of the goal and then didn't. The Nigerian and I shared a glance afterward and he offered me a small smile, and I smiled back. One can't put ego before beauty.

Sally Ashton's field-hockey squad, on the other hand, is faring quite poorly. At 0-5, morale has flatlined. They hunch off their bus, coming back from away games, their bags slung over their shoulders. Does field hockey exist in California, Dad? It's an odd sport, the sticks too short, the dribbling bad for the posture. Sally and I are in French class together. She wears tweed pencil skirts in brown, beige or grey. Her thin legs are long, her flat feet rather wide. At Tuck (the time after evening study hall, and before we are to lay down and sleep), I stand with the other soccer players and talk sports because I'm not brave enough, yet, to approach her. There is a basement in Main Hall and we all gather here, the boys and the girls, and buy snacks from a student manning the counter. There are Mars Bars and ice cream and small packs of chips, and cans of cold soda. People text friends at Exeter, at Westminster, at Andover. The basement has a foosball table, institutional furniture from the sixties or seventies. Down here as well is the St George's shop, where one buys their sweatshirts, their school mugs, their mesh shorts for running. Would you like a crest patch for the breast of one of your jackets? I imagine you might think it tacky. I imagine your plane ride back here, the small Earth, its farmland appearing between bursts of cloud, the hum of the cabin pressure, of engines. Milton, I've heard, is also undefeated, and their schedule easy until they meet us on Parents' Weekend. There is Chapel three times a week, the stained glass glowing in the low evening sun, Father Paulson in white robes and a purple sash sort of thing with gold crosses on it. We sing hymns and then kneel and then gather in lines, where we wait to drink wine and eat wafers, kneeling.

Ted Dill, the previously mentioned abused, and Hitoshi Ibu are the last two additions to the floor. This is Dill's fourth boarding school in three years: Groton then Taft then St Mark's, and now St George's. Dill doesn't drink and used to smoke pot, until he fell asleep in his Groton dorm room with a joint in his hand, burning to cinders a wicker trashcan and subsequently getting booted. His narcolepsy has followed him since; Dill can simply not stay awake, or get to classes on time, or to Chapel or dinner. Sleep is his tragedy, and a sad one to have, Dad, to be lost to perpetual dream, to seek rest so often it's damning. Please say hi to Mom, even though it's sort of pointless.

Ibu wears black suits with white shirts and black ties. Ibu is often in sunglasses. He has a tattoo of a dragon across most of his back, and the rumor is that Hiroshi is part of a sect of Shinjuku Yakuza. I'm less interested in the truth of this hearsay than I am, Dad, in understanding its origins: why it is that the 'other' must be branded, perpetually, as not only criminal but as part of some criminal organization, the evil group, the net of castigation spread as wide as can be, to include not only the person himself but those never met, never witnessed. Isn't comprehension the best means to disarm? We can pave roads with the greatest of ease but instead choose to always build mountains. It's odd. Dr Dimler has confirmed this oddity. He's almost worked up the courage to ask me about the fight: what got me so mad, what made me force the kid to eat glass. He asks me of 'battles,' of what sets me off; this is metaphor, yes, Dad, a ruse? A thing placed as bait in the middle of the room, open-ended on purpose? Regardless, I adhere to your advice of not talking about it until asked explicitly to do so.

With half of last spring's semester missed I had forgotten the rush and the push of it all, the burst and bloom of the class day, of thirty-second conversations, students rushing by in passing, of plans made and plans defaulted upon, of glances caught and books dropped and backpacks slung over shoulders. I watch the wind take the corner of a classmate's blue blazer one second before it takes the corner of my own. Every brick is old here, Dad, and still red and will be long after I've left. The lawns of the quads are perfectly edged, the hardwood floors waxed weekly, as I sit in a desk and listen to the squeak of rubber-soled LL Bean leather moccasins climbing the steps of the stairwell. We have classes on Saturday so Wednesday afternoons we can travel to matches or host schools here. There is breakfast then learning then practice then dinner, then study hall and Tuck Time and back to our rooms for lights off at eleven. Each dorm has a faculty monitor on its ground floor; ours is the JV basketball coach, Mr Shouse, one of the few black people I've seen in my months in Rhode Island. Weekends, he parks his VW Westfalia on the main quad's flat grass, sleeping with the van's camper roof open.

A long dipping hill on the west end of campus leads down to a road lined with modest one-level ranch houses. A block or so past is 1st Beach, the tourist beach, and Oceanside Diner. Through a grandfather clause, smoking inside of OD's is still permitted, and the bright orange booths that line the long wall of windows is often filled with St George's subversives: the small hipster crowd and black-clad ne'er-do-wells tapping their Camels on the lips of tiny tin ashtrays. I come here on weekends, and for comfort food: there are Sailor Hats, Dad, like Mom used to make, triangles of toast with holes in the middle, the yolk running out when I cut them. OD's opens at 5 a.m., a time that teenagers generally avoid, and I can get in and out before the brunch crowd tromps down the hill, hungover and recounting late Saturday nights had in secret – pints of vodka bought from sympathetic store clerks at one of the nearby Cumberland Farms, hours spent hunched near the beach's breaker wall, passing the bottle in darkness. Our three forwards are part of these weekend excursions, Ford, the Southerner, in possession of a Louisiana ID that claims he's of age, and is his brother's. I've been invited by these three for two weekends straight – you gotta come Haskin goddamnit you pussy. Punches in the shoulder, meant to convince. No one's punched me at all since I put Mark Norris into Intensive Care. I smile at my teammates and say thanks but no thank you.

Because I think making friends of any kind, Dad, is like digging holes, and one can't dig so deep that these holes become homes, and one's trapped by what's made, the pit growing too cozy. One must be prepared to abandon it all, at the very last second. Keepers know this. Keepers don't have friends. Even their teammates work unwittingly against them, perpetually in the way on penalties and corners, and the keeper, director, last guard at the gate, must push them into place and wave them away and get them at well past arm's distance. We stand and we wait, idle until it is time to be perfect. In the first match of the season, against Portsmouth Abbey, Coach Blitzer had pushed up our fullbacks to midfield and a forward got through our line of defense, the boy sprinting past with the ball lofted over. I stood on the toes of my cleats, waiting to rush him, and it's in moments like these, Dad, when I feel of true worth, my useless thoughts gone, the gravity of the singular task all-consuming. I could see each blade of grass as the boy, buzz-cut and broad-shouldered, trampled it, running past the chalked line of the goalie's box and then looking down and that, Dad, is when you let him have it, when you are not thing but unstoppable force, a wall made of wind, a flesh-toned black hole. The boy faked to the left but did not take the ball and I sprinted and then slid on my side, arms raised to face level, and came down on the ball and the boy's kicking foot a split second before he attempted to kick it, and you take everything, Dad, the ball, the foot, the boy, because you're the keeper, because you're allowed, by the rules of the game, to fuck up the person who comes in your box, to make that person pay for their brave stupid acts, and with the ball pressed to my jersey's stomach, and as the boy fell over the top of my body, I gave his ankle a short and sharp twist, the boy screaming in pain and cleating my back but the ball, Dad, was mine, and the ref blew his whistle.

I spend Sunday afternoons at the cliff above the beach; there is a chasm there, sharp and thin, the earth pulled apart by the water. I've wondered if, with enough speed built up, I could jump it. It's a thirty-foot drop and I'm not going to try, but the thought nonetheless does cross my mind when the waves crash below and send up the rock walls a fine salty mist that covers my skin so that when I walk home I can smell, on my body, the ocean. Last weekend our class toured Newport's famous mansions:

The Breakers and Chepstow and Kingscote and Rosecliff. In Chateau-Sur-Mer there's a deer-hunting scene painted on the stone around the fireplace; in Marble House there's a room half a soccer field in size done only in white and lavender. A silver heiress lived in one of these compounds, as did a coal magnate and a captain of steel, and a man who owned one of the first steamer lines, and a widow of timber, and a leader in canning. People who took all they could from the Earth and did this so well that these homes, today, are Federally protected – are National Landmarks of worth and importance, and inside of each are things so ornate, so modified from their base elements' aesthetic, that it's hard to imagine that they came from the Earth at all, that they were dug up and then molded and melted and changed, and all of these moldings and meltings and changes were done with such care and a grace so precise that they are unrecognizable as coming from nature. This is what we honor, Dad: the will of mankind to dig and extract, to turn sand into glass and tree into mantle. To take something dormant and make it awake, to lend to it shape and have it suit purpose.

All things I considered while up very early, jogging toward the park in which Cameron Nash used to smoke, a trowel tucked into the elastic band of my sweat shorts. I can make reservations for dinner somewhere; I imagine the nicer ones will book up rather quickly. Hi to Esquido – he made me a mix? Of all these metal bands that I haven't heard of? Death and Obsessed and Entombed and Unleashed? And Obituary? Lots of low growling and double bass drums and is it odd, Dad, that I find this type of music to be calming? That it moves so fast that I can slow down? It's nighttime now, a storm on the Atlantic, the lightning running like veins down some dark and wide leg, the wind shaking the windows in their worn wooden frames.

See you very soon.

Love,

Connor

9

We dropped out, stole a car, drove east for three days, away from the Pacific, our dorm, California. We bought wigs at a dime store. We bought beer at gas stations. We kept to state roads all the way into Utah, then doubled back, up to Reno, and married. It was April. It was springtime. The desert was freezing at night. The cacti were blooming. We slept under wool blankets in the Buick's back seat. We looked at the rings on our fingers and smiled. We divided the driving.

Gone from my mind was the flood pass, the deep cross, the weight of my pads and my helmet. Gone were professors, professing. We changed plates west of Elko and went north to Twin Falls. A week here under alias, a roadside motel, a nice bit of lawn for the walking of pets. The tile in the bathroom was mustard and brown; a Japanese print of a tsunami, near cresting, hung above the queen bed's headboard. We walked the five miles to Shoshone Falls, the water there roaring through the gullies. Flat bits of rainbow flashed in the mist. We shared a large apple, a bag of pecans. My wife's hair had lightened, from the sun. In the motel's dirt lot, between the blacktop and rooms, was a stand that sold fireworks, and that night we bought sparklers and drank beer with its owners, a Vet and his son, Kenneth and Weller. Kenneth had lost both arms during Tet:

one at the elbow, one at the shoulder. Towards midnight, he brought out a flask filled with whiskey and one hour later had Weller tape, to his stumps, bottle rockets. Kenneth spun in circles as the lit fuses hissed. Denise screamed when the rockets shot upwards.

We checked out the next day and went east to Wyoming. In the distance stood mountains, their tops cleaved to flat by eons of wind. We had on jean shorts, plaid Western shirts with mother-of-pearl buttons. My wife was as tan as I'd ever seen her. I thought of her parents, farmers from Fresno, Ukrainian extracts who knew by now that their daughter was missing. And above us the big sky, its blue like an ocean, its clouds like a great fleet of ships, vessels far from the coast and slow in their journey, cumulus frigates waiting for wind, for the slow push toward the Mississippi. Denise played with the hairs on the top of my knee.

'We could go home,' I said.

'Not yet,' she said.

'Are you worried?' I asked.

'I'm worried my parents are worried.'

We were twenty years old. We owned no cell phones. Slovenia wasn't a country. There was no euro, no PlayStation 3, no Tennessee Titans or MySpace. Honeybees buzzed in numbers unconsidered. The world was enormous, was breathtaking.

We wound south for two days, Cheyenne to Santa Fe, the desert a mask, the state roads nearly empty. Outside of Pueblo an Army convoy fifty trucks long passed us in the opposite direction. Camouflage jeeps held young men with stern faces, their teeth set against their vehicles' bouncing over the poorly tarred roads. In the middle of nowhere, and for no reason at all – there was no perpendicular road, no possibility of cross-traffic

– a stoplight divided the convoy in half, as my wife and I waited in the dust-covered Buick, five feet away from a flatbed semi carrying a missile perhaps ten feet in length. A duo of soldiers, one black and one white, sat with their legs over the side of the truck, staring at us, rifles on shoulders. Our time alone had starved us for talk; I waved and then rolled down the window.

'Where's that thing going?' I asked the helmeted men, who looked younger than us, barely eighteen. The soldiers looked at each other and then back at me.

'Montana,' the white soldier said.

'Where's it coming from?' I asked.

'Montana,' the black soldier said.

I turned to my wife, who was smiling.

'You're lost?' I asked, looking back at the truck.

'We're practicing,' the black soldier told us.

'What are you practicing for?' asked my wife, leaning out from her seat.

'The Soviets,' the white soldier told us. 'We're practicing for the end of the world.' The truck lurched and the soldiers' bodies leaned one way then the other.

'So when the world ends, you'll drive missiles on trucks through the desert?' I asked. The light went to green but I didn't drive forward.

'Something like that,' said the black soldier.

'But if the world ends,' I said, 'then who will you kill? Won't all the Soviets already be dead?'

'This thing can't get to the U.S.S.R.,' the black soldier said, patting the shaft of the missile with a hand.

'Then what good is it at all?' asked Denise.

'This one's for home games,' the white soldier said. The semi moved forward a foot and then stopped, the way that a train

hiccups down tracks. The sky was bright blue, the dry dirt a
tan red. There were low hills in the distance.

'Home games,' my wife said, and the black soldier whispered
in the other man's ear, and they both stared at us, their young
faces blank, the truck still not moving.

'You got a green light,' the black soldier said, and when we
asked more questions about just what they meant, they wouldn't
respond, and we kept on driving.

Fifty-five miles northeast of Santa Fe the Buick's temperature
pinned, the car chugging and wheezing as we limped off the
highway. The Aztec Café was just off the state road; a pump
bay with red awning shimmered in the heat, NO GAS signs
fastened to the nozzles' black hoses. Most of the diner's windows
were gone, but inside the abandoned café was near-perfect: five
low chrome stools were still bolted to the floor, in front of a
hardwood bar and soda fountain. There was a short row of
booths, their brown vinyl intact, the linoleum tables harboring
bottles of ketchup and mustard. I knocked on the door and
offered a hello, my wife laughing and climbing in through the
frame of the window. Grit swept every surface, our twin sets
of footprints bringing up dust as we peeked and then crept
around corners. In the back, past the kitchen, was a two-room
apartment, lace doilies over the arms of a mauve poly sofa. A
TV stood tabled, a mangled coat hanger jammed in as antenna.
In the bedroom, a quilt of bright blues and dark reds lay
perfectly flat on a bare queen-size mattress. Late afternoon light
fell in squares through the white cotton curtains.

'That quilt looks homemade,' I said to Denise, but she didn't
respond, and I realized my comment as a kind of concession
to the sudden and unwanted intimacy of the place; to the life
left behind, forever.

In the kitchen's slim pantry was a half-finished case of Tecate, the cans' aluminum cool but the beer itself tepid. We sat outside, on the café's single step, watching the sun sink down into the desert. The sofa had a bed that pulled out from its belly, and on thin squeaky springs we slept the thick and full sleep of the drunk, under wool blankets brought in from the Buick.

The next day I went out to look at the car. The sun was just beginning to get hot; it held low and white in the sky to the east. A milk truck passed on the state road's raised bridge, freckles of rust on its bumper. I opened the hood, and taped to the cap for the radiator was a letter, one I still have:

We saw your car and wanted to help. It was only the radiator. Pass this gift along or be doomed in your life. Greed eats whole worlds.
—Anonymous

A semi upshifted and the desert's silence settled back in, the heat taking all sound as I stood there in the shade of the pump bay's metal awning. Some tiny town stood to the south, the sun gleaming off its tin roofs, its windows. The air seemed to hold weight that it hadn't before. I breathed in and then out and turned to go inside. Denise was standing in the doorway.

'What's in your hand?' my wife asked me.

'A note,' I told her.

'We get mail out here?'

I handed my wife the small piece of paper.

'Do you want to go home now?' she asked.

'We don't have to,' I said, and both of us stood there and looked to the east, to the states and the places that we'd never seen, to the line on the horizon that meant forests and streams and farmlands and mountains and canyons.

'We could stay here,' said Denise. 'Reopen the café. Put a sign in the window that says "Under New Management."'

I looked at my wife and her smile made me smile. I walked over to the doorway, where she stood in the sun, and I hugged her. Her mouth was next to my ear.

'Do you want to go home now?' my wife said again.

'We don't have to,' I said, but ten minutes later we were driving.

We passed Reno and then Donner Lake and dropped down into Sacramento's hot valley. By the time that we got back to Fresno, it was late in the evening. A kitchen light shone in my wife's parents' house as I pulled into the driveway.

'What's going to happen now?' I asked Denise.

'What's going to happen now is that I'll go into my house and my parents will cry and then probably yell and somewhere in there, they'll notice the ring and then yell some more and then go back to crying.'

Denise gave me a smile, her lips over teeth.

'I feel like I could sleep forever,' my wife told me.

'Call me in the morning,' I said, and then my wife kissed me and got out of the car and walked up the steps of her parents' porch. Denise knocked on the door and I pulled away, taking my camera from out of its case and holding it out the car window. I turned the lens east, towards all that we'd seen and hadn't. I depressed the button and the shutter snapped down. I tossed the camera on the passenger seat and then drove back to Turlock.

And here is the picture of my wife sitting on the hood of the car, on the Salt Flats of Utah. The sky's a soft grey, the flat earth an off-white. There is a light in her eyes of true jubilation. She has her legs crossed. She's wearing black Keds. Her jean cut-offs jut up the side of her thigh. Her nose is still wide, her breasts still small. This years before any of her operations.

And here is the picture of my wife by a stream – we'd rented pans, had become, momentarily, prospectors. I can remember the shine of the tiny gold flakes. I can remember the swish of the water and sand, the pebbles pinging against the pan's tinny metal.

And here is the picture of my wife on a rock, a leg and an arm raised to the sky, an 'Oh!' on her face, a look of theatrical concern. Her brown hair has pulled itself free from its band. She is pretending that she's lost her grip. She is pretending that she is falling.

There are 48 pictures – two rolls of film – from our wedding trip east in our stolen Buick. I keep these in a lockbox in a wall safe in my home. When my wife wakes up, I will give her this box. We will sit on a sofa and go through these pictures.

OCTOBER

10

Ash Meadows National Wildlife Refuge is in South-Central Nevada, in the part of the state that comes up as grey on maps on the Internet. It's taken me six and a half hours to drive here. The ground on which I stand is owned by the Feds, as is nearly eighty-five percent of the state. Nye County is the third largest in all the U.S., and shaped like a hammer. The southern end of its handle lies just west of Clark County and the spending pit known as Las Vegas. The mob may have its slots and its whores, but its taxes in part come here, to Ash Meadows. Over 220 different types of birds have been logged at this refuge. The metal dragonfly currently yards overhead isn't among them.

The machine has a wingspan of over twelve feet. Its body is silver and scaly. It does two tight loops in the bright desert sky then drops fifty feet, stopping stock-still a yard from my face. The machine's red eyes are round pieces of glass, oversized and set near the top of its head. The machine, I think, is looking at me.

Today I've left my Prius at home, opting instead for my blood-colored Hummer. My friend Frank Gaines stands just yards away from the vehicle, in desert fatigues and a navy-blue baseball cap that says USMC in gold letters on the front of it. Henry Stine and Ned Akeley sit drinking iced tea at a card table under a camouflage canopy. Frank joined the Marines the year I went to college. Our birthdays are five months apart from each other. The dragonfly reascends and makes tight crazy loops; it seems tethered, a weather balloon spun by a gale. In Frank's hands is a black metal box, its antenna extended.

'Guess how much,' Frank says.

'Ten million,' I say.

'Eighty-six,' Frank tells me. He tweaks two of the controller's dials at once and the dragonfly shoots through the blue desert heavens. In place of feet is a miniaturized version of a helicopter's landing apparatus. Its wings beat as fast as a hummingbird's. Fixed to its belly are twin rows of missiles, each sleek and black and the size of a pencil. They look like the heels on Simer's Kate Spades. It's noon and one hundred and seven degrees. The glare from the sun lends the weapon a nimbus. A series of barbs, like oversized fishing hooks, hang from the dragonfly's straight and thin tail. Sweat from my armpits has bled through my dress shirt and is now seeping into my loosely tied tie and the waist of my linen khakis.

'I'm going to get some water from the truck,' I tell Frank.

'Pussy,' Frank calls me. My friend's visage resembles the face of a downturned, flesh-colored anvil. His chin is pronounced and very near sharp, his nose barely more than two nostrils. He has small eyes and low cheeks and a flat and big forehead. Frank, like our mutual friend Henry Stine, has in recent years gone totally bald. Ned Akeley's locks have also disappeared. I am the only one left who can manage a hairdo.

The loose sand crunches under the soles of my shoes. The Amargosa Desert looks otherworldly. Mountains striped brown and red stand in the distance. Tan crooked reeds grow from shallow silver pools comprising this area's hot springs. The water here is twenty times saltier than any ocean. This bit of country is known as the Nevada Proving Ground. In 1951, very near where I'm standing, Marines crouched in trenches while weapons-grade plutonium was airdropped by a Boeing B-50 Superfortress, around the same time that *I Love Lucy* debuted, the first mall in the world opened in Framingham, Mass., and direct-dial coast-to-coast telephone service reached all the way from New York to California.

Inside the truck is a dark green plastic canteen. The water is tepid; I drink it in chugs. The heat comes in waves and feels charged, and could be. Taped to the visor is my late birthday gift to Frank: a picture of news anchor Chris Matthews on a white leather couch, being tasered unconscious by the writer Tom Clancy. The shot captures Matthews mid-stun, his arms pinned at his sides by the voltage. Behind the couch stand Sean 'Puffy' Combs and Ed Schaffer, United States Department of Agriculture Secretary. Both men hold wads of money in one hand and gold-rimmed brandy snifters in the other.

My friend Frank Gaines is a big Clancy fan. It isn't so much the author's plots that Frank likes, but rather what we believe is the man's truly thrilling life story. Clancy was one of six of near-feral children found dead in the woods in remote western Maryland. A group of Army wives, all of whom had lost their husbands to World War II, made a pact to abandon their children and start over. This quintet of women, Hagerstown residents, fed young Thomas Leo and the five others sleeping pills, and then drove them out to the forest. Clancy, at nine, was the oldest of this lot, and did what he could to function as parent – the widows, it seemed, believed in sporting chance, and left each boy with a backpack, sleeping bag, jackknife and mittens. Rocky Gap State Park, just east of Cumberland, is 3,400 acres in area. For two years the boys lived here, wandering, surviving on squirrel meat and berries from bushes. Three of the boys did not last a year, succumbing to exposure with the onset of winter. A fourth was eaten by wolves the summer thereafter. Thomas kept track of all this in his journal, a spiral-bound notebook that his mom had tucked into his backpack, along with four ballpoint pens. This journal is kept today in a secret underground room of the Library of Congress. Each corpse, Clancy writes, was cooked on a spit and consumed by the remaining survivors. Thomas and his final companion, Wayne Bell, lived on in the park for another three years, shunning all brushes with human society. In 1951, the same year the bombs fell in the desert, Wayne Bell and Clancy died in a cave-in. WPA workers found the journal and bones later that decade.

Another way of saying this is that there is no Tom Clancy. Instead, and with the masses' wealth of tax dollars, an actor was hired as stand-in, a thespian who was classically trained and paid very well to pretend that he wrote and writes novels he didn't and doesn't. This is the man one will see at book signings and hear talking on conservative radio programs. The actual writers of these nationalist brochures are members of the ATF, CIA and FBI. A rotating panel of State Appeals Court judges reviews manuscripts each year, in June. My friend Frank Gaines has submitted his novel, *Terror Out West*, seven times. In 2005 it was a Finalist.

Beneath the canopy, Henry Stine's pale, egg-shaped head bounces out nods while Ned Akeley gesticulates, speaking. A gas-powered Weber stands in one corner of the canopy's shade. The dragonfly is whizzing and whizzing.

'I brought steaks,' Frank says.

'Okay,' I tell him.

'Did your kid win his game?'

'I don't know,' I say. 'It happened today. He's going to call me.'

'What's it like?' Frank asks.

'Having a kid?' I say.

'Sure,' says Franks. I am the only one of we four with a wife, or with children.

I shrug. 'Nearly over,' I say. 'He's sixteen years old.' Mr Hand was strongly against the taking on of a family. He told us in sermons, the televisions muted, that family had failed us, and to put back shards of a mirror cracked long ago would not help to create a clear image of self. Frank, Henry and Ned all took this to heart. My faith, it seems, is the shakiest.

'So when he's eighteen, you're cutting him off,' Frank says. The lines on his forehead remind me of dunes on a beach, and I imagine my son on the shore of the Atlantic, his shoes off, his pant legs cuffed, the tide pushing in and over his ankles, erasing his footprints.

'Well, not cut him off, Frank, but he'll be an adult. Mr Hand didn't cut us off at eighteen. We just moved elsewhere.'

'When I was eighteen, do you know where I was, Jim?'

I tell Frank he was in the Marines.

'Yes, but do you know what I was doing? I was in Irkutsk, in the fucking dead of winter. There in Irkutsk there were, supposedly, missile bases. And I lived in an ice house carved out from the ground in the middle of nowhere, and watched this Soviet army base to see if missiles were coming in or out.'

'Were they?' I ask.

'They were not,' Frank tells me. I wait for more information, but Frank is silent, still holding the dragonfly's controller.

'What's the point of that story?' I ask.

Frank shrugs. 'Kids that young need something to do, is all that I'm saying, Jim.'

'Connor's going to apply to college, though, Frank.'

'College, though, Jim, is a way of not doing something.'

'Henry and Ned both went to college. I went to college,' I say.

'But you dropped out,' Frank tells me.

In the sun, the air feels like it does in a sauna. Henry stands up behind us and takes off a shoe and bangs it on the top of the card table.

'We eat right now or I'll skin you,' he yells. Ned lights a cigarette.

Frank turns his head partially but keeps his eye on the machine. 'Keep watching,' he yells back to our surrogate brother. 'My point is, Jim, is that the singular task, and completing it well, outweighs all that. Do you think that your kid benefits from taking an Indian Philosophy class in the middle of Vermont? I doubt it. But learning to kill a bear with a blowgun when it's 20 below . . .'

'Is not a skill that my son will ever, ever need,' I tell Frank.

'Can you be sure of that?' Frank asks.

'Yes, I can,' I say, and with my hand in the pocket of my dress pants cross two of my fingers.

'I applaud your confidence,' Frank says to me, and stalls the dragonfly out in the air. The machine's wings beat fast enough that I'm sure they'll turn red, and then Frank tweaks the dials and the dragonfly's tail extends, the machine speeding forward without slowing down and slicing the tops off a trio of cacti. Frank lands the metal insect on top of his truck and five minutes later I and my three closest friends in the world are seated around the foldout card table, listening to the sizzle and pop of kabobs and fillets, the meat that Ned brought salted and cooking.

When I was fourteen, my parents died in the front seat of a car. I was in this car's back seat. I lived with my mom's mom for nearly four months but she died in her sleep; I found her body. And with no one else left, I became a ward of the state, and after forays at four different group homes where, terrified, I fought everyone I could, most often beating the other kids senseless and bloody, I was placed at Mr Hand's Home for Well-Behaved Boys, a last bastion of hope for the underage doomed, a place that was at once work camp and classroom, almond farm and Protestant academic institution.

We picked, clipped or planted from five until ten and then went to school until dusk fell upon us, at which point we ate dinner and the lights in the orchard went on, and we worked again until midnight or so, and then went to bed, and repeated this day over and over again for as long as we remained at the home. For me, this was just under four years. For my friends, my three closest friends in the world, the stay was much longer, as all three of these friends, Frank Gaines and Henry Stine and Ned Akeley, were orphaned at birth, and knew no other place than the Home for Well-Behaved Boys, growing up in the nursery before moving to the dorm, where we four became fingers to Mr Hand's thumb, single digits that together could lift and could grasp, with the help of our surrogate father's opposable ideologies, tenets taught to us each Sunday at dawn, in the clapboard chapel on the property's back lot, where Mr Hand, in black suit and starched collared shirt, preached from a podium carved out of oak and stained burgundy.

Leonard A. Hand was born in 1905, and was directly descended from *Mayflower* stock and, when this relative died the second winter onshore, a couple took the relative's offspring as theirs, and struck south and then west, where they wound up in what would become eventually the state of Mississippi. Three years of drought were followed by flood, and the boy was adopted again by sharecroppers, after the people who brought him to Mississippi drowned. And while the means changed from generation to generation, from one Hand to the next, each limb of Mr Hand's family tree was wiped out, eventually, by natural disaster. Great-grandfather Hand left Mississippi for Texas, where he had one boy and was killed by a tornado while running sheep over grassland. This boy, in turn, and forty years later, was killed in a rockslide that also killed his wife but not their only child, Mr Hand's father, who kept heading west, past Utah then Nevada, and arrived in San Francisco in 1888, eighteen years prior to the earthquake that would kill him and his wife but not their only child, Leonard, who spent a portion of his sixth month on this Earth in a partially collapsed building, the crib he was in breaking the fall of the rafters, so volunteer firefighters found the baby while collecting corpses to be burned, and held the baby up and passed the baby along to their firefighting brethren, and journalists took pictures and there is, in libraries, on microfiche, a crude black-and-white of Mr Hand held aloft, smoke from the fires the earthquake had caused drifting behind him, in the air of the very young century.

Mr Hand was raised by the church and grew up a thief, and by the mid-1920s was aiding rum runners sneaking booze up the coast, and raiding Teamsters' headquarters as far south as Salinas. On Sundays he prayed, prayed fully and strongly, believed in God and all God could do because Mr Hand saw God as the one force in the world that could combat Nature, and saw himself too as a member of God's army on Earth, and as a member of this army could trim Nature back by degrees, and at least partially subvert the forces that had killed off every generation of his family.

And when Mr Hand had made enough as a thief, and after (and always) returning a portion of these sums to the church that had raised him, Mr Hand washed his remaining riches clean through investment in oil, as no resource on Earth, in

Mr Hand's eyes, could typify quite as well the manipulation of Nature for societal gain, and Mr Hand became rich, and invested in guns and invested in steel, and with World War Two diversified his portfolio, investing in Kaiser and Boeing and Ford, companies that through might and through metal would drive the economy for nearly a decade and remain doing well thereafter, at which point Mr Hand, now in his fifties, opened the Home that I'd come to know every corner of, a place of hard work and the finest of teachers, instructors paid princely sums to teach the forgotten to be great and take what they could by all means necessary, and thank God for this taking each night, and wake joyful, and pious, for it's through this taking, said Mr Hand, that people find God in America.

Frank tells me to check on the meat and I get up from my seat and walk over and lift a kabob, and say two more minutes. Ned Akeley, our patriarch since Mr Hand's death, waves me over.

'Let Frank take care of that,' Ned says, as I sit down and my three friends all stare at me.

'How are you doing these days, Jim?' Ned asks.

I tell Ned that I'm doing just fine, and look around the table. Frank and Henry look back at me, unblinking.

Ned Akeley crosses one leg over the other. At Mr Hand's Home, two younger boys were paired up with two older ones who had already left and made their way in the world. In this manner, Ned Akeley and Henry Stine were mentors to Frank and myself, just as they'd also had mentors. Most guidance came in the form of hard cash; that is, the capital for my ad firm came from these men. And while I've paid this sum off, I remain indebted.

'Are you sure that you're doing fine?' Ned asks me.

'Yeah, Jim, are you sure?' Henry echoes. 'We know that you

have a lot on your plate. That your son's away. That Denise is, well, vegetative.'

'The Beach Party pulled in better numbers than expected,' I say. 'Evermore Towers will sell. Is there something I'm missing here?' I ask my friends. A lump has birthed itself in my throat.

Ned Akeley wears a black three-piece suit with soft grey pinstripes. He hasn't sweated a drop since we've been here. In the suit's pocket is a white cotton square with the monogram LAH, Mr Hand's initials.

'Well, I suppose that, in some ways, the examples you bring up yourself, Jim, they're what concern us. The Beach Party doesn't happen without Henry's help. Evermore is my own creation. Frank has given you your own nurse. And we wonder, Jim,' Ned says, 'what is it for us that you're doing?'

I stand my ground. I look straight at Ned. 'I'm selling the public on your ideas,' I say. 'I am your mouthpiece. I am your conduit.'

'Yeah, Jim,' Henry says. 'But anybody could be our *conduit*.'

Frank grunts and gets up and walks over to the grill. He rips open the plastic on a package of Styrofoam plates and pokes at the meat with the tines of a barbecue fork.

'What Henry wants to say, Jim,' Ned Akeley tells me, 'is we're ready for something original. People aren't buying, Jim. eBay is down. Intel is down.'

'Exxon's not down,' I say.

'Nor will it ever be,' Ned tells me. 'But we're in a slump, Jim, and you and I know it. And this slump is ours and China's and Japan's. This slump is going to just about kill Detroit. This slump is, for the collective consciousness of this country, very near to proof that God is dead. How's your portfolio doing, Jim? Which way are your numbers trending?'

'They're down a bit,' I say back, failing to add that reading the

Journal now is something akin to being weaponless on Hadrian's Wall and watching the Picts, swords in their hands, set up their ladders. Of my thirty-five million well over half is wrapped up in markets, in funds, in portfolios. It's untouchable. Add to this AmWe's continued bloodletting and the financial sieve that is my wife's coma, and in three months or so, in my fiscal chess game, I've gone from queen to at best knight or bishop – a piece of importance but with limited range, and dictated angle.

'They're down just a bit? Just a bit?' Henry says. 'Did you invest in the end of the world?'

'We all sort of did,' I answer.

'Look, Jim,' Ned says. 'We're stuck. We don't know what to do. We need something big and we need it to be from you, Jim. It's your turn to step up. You got married. You had a kid. None of us did, and you benefited from it.'

'This is an order or a threat?' I ask Ned. Frank walks over and drops a huge plate of steak on the table in front of me. Red juice pools around the big hunk of flesh, the desert winds bringing the hot smell to my nose, and for a moment I feel as though I'll be sick. I look up at Frank.

'What?' he says. 'You don't like steak anymore?'

'I'm dehydrated,' I say.

'You're dehydrated,' says Frank. 'You're dehydrated. You know, I was in the Congo, once? We were setting up a new government there? And I got airdropped outside of Ouesso and lost my canteen coming in and spent two days without any drinking water at all? And drank my piss?'

'Stop it,' Ned says. 'Jim wasn't in the Marines. I wasn't in the Marines. Henry is not a Marine.'

'NBC has a show coming up, though,' Henry says. '*Semper Pie*. Four of your brethren open a bakery.'

'That's bullshit,' Frank says.

'Call your people. It's real,' says Henry.

A hawk sounds from somewhere above the canopy. I look hard at Ned. He's retained a boyishness to his face, despite his hair being gone, his forehead adding wrinkles. His brown eyes still look kind, look patient. Ned looks back at me and for a moment I'm small, fourteen, newly arrived to Mr Hand's Home, angry and ready to fight for reasons I don't fully know but believe in completely.

'Jim, we can't do what we once did,' Ned tells me. 'This game's changed since Mr Hand died and, while he knew lots of people, he didn't know Wall Street, and Wall Street's all that matters. It's twenty-five people at six different firms running the country. We got left on the edge, Jim. Subprime hurt bad.'

'Tell him about Greece,' Henry says. 'Tell him about Ireland and Portugal.'

'What about them?' I say.

'Don't worry about them,' Ned says. 'Worry about us. Worry about America.'

'What do you want me to do?' I ask, and remember Ned walking up to me, for the first time, in the orchards, Mr Hand trailing behind him, and the smile he gives me now is the same one he gave then: a soft and meek thing that didn't show teeth, a smile of grace, of admittance to the fact that I had been damaged and that he understood because he'd been damaged, too.

'But that's it,' Ned says, and his soft grin stops. 'I can't. I can't tell you what I want you to do, Jim. But I need you to do it.'

11

Dear Dad,

What you missed: a 2-1 win, paradise lost and regained against Milton. The sidelines near full. The proud parents cheering. A goal against me in the seventeenth minute, the game turned to scrum after a third corner kick, the first two, well hit, pushed over the crossbar by myself, your son, and both times me screaming at the ref, who kept missing the fact that I was being wedged in by a pair of Milton forwards. But the ref wasn't listening and the third time the ball was sent through I elbowed one of the forwards in the jaw, and he went down hard as the ball hit the grass and then it was just a frenzy of feet, and someone, perhaps one of my own team members, pushed the ball past me and into the net, and the small army of SG parents went quiet. Disorganization, Dad, is a keeper's worst nightmare. And there were more attempts, too, shots blocked by myself, including a leaping, diving, fretful thing, the shot from the top of the box curving away from my body, and were it not for my three fingers on the ball, fingers that because of the force of the kick were, upon making contact, jammed back into the base of my hand, we would have been down 2-0. But I pushed the ball past as the top of my head smashed into the thick iron sidebar of the goal, the parents who did come mewing in unison, the way that crowds will when the pleasure of spectacle is interrupted, so rudely, by human condition.

We scored just before half and went tied to the sidelines. Where were you today, Dad? I called home three times. I called your cell twice and, both times, straight to voicemail.

Milton had eight corner kicks in the second half: push and set up and repeat for success. The Brazilian taking the corners had the first name José, but it was pronounced more like Zha-u-zay. There was a ball off the crossbar sent back into play. There was a ball that went wide of my goal by inches. And the sweat through my socks that soaked into my cleats. And the grass stains on my knees and my shoulders. And my fingers clenching and popping and clenching again, as the action crossed midline and crept toward me.

We won in the last ten minutes of the game: I got a ball to my chest and skied a long kick up the right side of the field, where Luke Maynard, Hartford insurance-magnate offspring, crossed the ball the width of the grass, over Nacho's head and to Hartford cohort Brit Timms, who raced down the grass and brought the ball in on his own. Timms got past two defenders as though he were oiled and toed a shot low, a ball that the keeper sent back into play off his shin guard, and Brad Hauth got his second goal of the day, and the parents who were in attendance went crazy. Have you ever seen a 45-year-old stockbroker's wife lose her shit, Dad? And throw to the ground her silk Hermes scarf and then stomp on it? I had not, until Brad scored that goal. It was a sight well worth seeing.

What you missed: Sally Ashton's field-hockey squad actually winning their match against Governor Dummer, a fact so astounding to even the victors themselves that after the final whistle was blown, the win provoked in the players an odd delayed response – they walked off the field very calmly and then, one by one, and as though stricken by plague, collapsed to the grass and raised their hands upward, and some wept and some laughed and then all got up and found on the sidelines their parents, save Sally Ashton, whose parents, like you, were nowhere to be found, and sat instead on a bench and ate the flesh out of a quarter of an orange.

How is it I know this? Because today, after all matches at SG were over and my peers had retired to their parents' hotel suites in town, to be given gifts and get taken to dinner, I wandered the unusually empty campus grounds, the light thin, the bursts of wind cold, and after traipsing over the burgundy carpet of Main Hall and the groaning wood floors of our cafeteria, I reached the long asphalt corridor that leads to the infirmary and my own room in Bismarck. The windows on the south side of this short asphalt hall look out to the JV and Middler soccer fields, and walking there was none other than Sally.

Her plain blonde hair fell over the collar of her black velvet coat and she had on heels, black three-inch heels,

Dad, the bottom hem of the coat just above the heels' straps, and was making poor progress over the grass of the field, and then I was sprinting back into my dorm and dashing down two flights of stairs to a side door, and jogging out of said door and in the direction of Sally, whose skin is so pale it cannot, it would seem, even retain a sunburn. I was ten yards away when Sally, who was sitting on the low stone wall that leads to the road to the beach, became aware of my presence, and I held my hand up and Sally waved back as my heart lurched to sick and my head went light and then heavy.

Sally Ashton has green eyes with flecks of red in them. Sally Ashton has a voice I deem almost absent, a meek, fettered thing that seems tape-delayed, Sally's long skinny lips opening a second or more before any words come out past them. She barely shows teeth when she smiles, Dad, but smile she did when I reached her spot on the wall and barraged her with questions: How are you doing? Did your team win? Where are your parents? What are you doing? A volley of queries, Dad, with no breath between them, and Sally asked which of those do you want answered first, but she smiled and I smiled back as time came to a stop in the late-afternoon light of autumnal New England.

We walked to the shore as the sky rolled to bruised, Sally leaving her heels by the Del's Frozen Lemonade stand, which was closed for the season. We talked about French class, the good Mr Prescott, his short beatnik beard and tiny round eyeglasses. We spoke of Ted Dill, perpetual sleeper, and did Sally see him pass out in

Chapel and had Sally seen, last week in the cafeteria, Ted's eyes slip to shut during dinner, the weight of his spoon suddenly too much, as he pulled down his soup bowl onto his lap and woke himself up with a crotch full of broth.

And Sally said, the sick are amusing to you?

And I said yes, since I'm sort of sick, too, I'm not scared of illness the way the well are.

And then Sally said, so what's wrong with you?

And so, Dad, I told her.

I told her about you, your ad firm, about Mom and her coma. I told her about beating the shit out of Mark Norris, Class Clown, he of the racist comedy routine and founding member of the Piedmont Young Republicans: how he pushed my head into lockers and told me daily, Fuck You, and how I ignored his abuse until the day he talked about Mom's feeding tube, and that if that thing could go all the way down her throat, he was pretty sure that something else could fit down there, too: how I tackled him head-first to the ground outside of the cafeteria, the back of his skull splitting open as I pounded his eyes and broke both his cheekbones, and grabbed a glass bottle of Snapple someone had left on a step and smashed the bottle to shards and shoved them in his mouth and beat him unconscious, at which point I stopped and found more errant shards and picked up these shards and calmly put them in my pocket, not unlike how Sally and I, earlier this night, would stop and bend down and collect small rocks from the shoreline.

So you were kicked out, Sally asked me.

I was, I said. But no jail time. I just sat at home for the rest of the semester. Purgatory, not Hell. It could have been worse.

No, Sally said, her chin pulling in and her eyes going down. No, Purgatory is way worse than Hell. Hell is definite.

But in Purgatory, I said, you just wander around, or something.

Yeah, Sally said, but that's what I mean. One wanders and wanders and then waits and waits, and then after some very long amount of time, one ascends. Or descends? Can you go to Hell after Purgatory?

I'm not sure, I told her. The wait isn't worth it to you? I asked.

No, Sally said. To me, it isn't. The one thing that's different about Earth and after is that no matter where it is that one goes, they don't have to spend another second just waiting.

And I said, but we're not waiting right now.

And Sally said, sure, we're waiting to know if we like one

another, and if we do, then we'll wait until we first kiss, and then wait again to put hands on each other, and wait even more until we first fuck while we wait to fall in love then break up.

But if you know how it's all going to end, I said.

What's the fun in it? Sally told me, and said nothing else and we walked in silence, eastward, the reeds on the dunes falling away as the sand dropped under the ocean. Out on the water, some large ship sat, its lights blinking. Sally's coat was exactly the color of night; it made her pale face and blonde hair appear floating.

What do you think's on that boat? Sally asked.

I don't know, I said. Medical supplies. One thousand tricycles.

Or fur coats, Sally said, smuggled from Russia.

Millions of marbles, I said.

Hundreds of parrots, said Sally.

And then, Dad, and I am not kidding you here, the barge's horn blew, out there on the water. I looked to the sea and then back at Sally, whose eyes had grown big and whose mouth was now smiling widely, and, somewhere during our first long kiss, the horn blew again, the waves lapping and lapping.

See? Sally said. Now we have to wait for something else, and got up from the beach and brushed the sand off her coat and then we were walking back toward the school, the lights from my dorm bright dots in the distance.

Sally's dorm, Strauss, is on the west end of campus, about as far away from my own as is geographically possible. We walked up from the beach, crossed the narrow, quiet road, climbed the low stone wall and walked over the fields, which hold a slight curve to them. We passed to the south of Bismarck itself, both of us looking in each lighted window, where dressers stood stacked with strewn ties and textbooks and uncapped sticks of deodorant. Hitoshi Ibu, parentless too, sat shirtless on his bed, lifting dumbbells.

We walked past the hedges next to the cafeteria's stained glass, then past the tall narrow windows of Main Hall. Between Strauss and Main Hall sits Dragon Quad, its trimmed square of grass divided by diagonal walkways. At the center, where all of these paths converge, is a large stone circle, the head of the quad's mythological namesake etched into a low stone riser. From above, these paths look like a gray and crudely drawn sun, its beams shining out in all directions.

We stopped at the bright red front door of Strauss and Sally turned to face me. I didn't want things to end. So where were your parents? I asked. You never told me.

At the Morgellon's Research Foundation. It's up by Albany.

They're scientists, I said.

No, my dad's a banker. My mom doesn't do much. We go out to eat. She takes me boutiquing. Sally smiled at me, waiting for the question.

Okay, I said, so what's the Morgellon's Research Foundation? I said.

It's where they do research on Morgellon's Disease, Sally told me. I have it.

I'm sorry, I said.

You might be, Sally said. I've only had three fiber appearances since I've been here, and no rash. My folks think the sun. But summer is over and I hate the sun. And I really, really hate field hockey. I think I might quit. I want autumn to get here so I can shop. There's this community-service thing, downtown? You go feed the elderly. It's a block and a half from Banana Republic.

You're going to help people so you can shop? I asked.

Shopping is helping people, Sally said back.

She did a full curtsy, irony-rich, and then said goodnight, the bright red door slapping shut behind her. I stood on the dorm's roofless brick porch and watched as the light went on in her room, the blinds closed, the lines of cream-colored plastic distorting Sally's shadow as she sat down at her desk and remained there in profile. I stood there and watched her a full minute more before I grew aware of how odd I might look and then turned around and went back to Bismarck.

What you missed, Dad, was sort of a lot, and I wish that you'd been here but suppose if you were, none of what happened with Sally would have transpired. It's late at night now, the dorm under half-full, all on my hall signing out for the weekend. A new northern squall pushes and pulls, snaking down the width of my window, shifting the frame back and forth in the sill. Three more weeks and we set the clocks back.

Please say hi, etc.

Love,

Connor

P.S. – where were you? Where are you?

12

I drive out of Ash Meadows, away from my friends, past cacti and sagebrush and curled sleeping sidewinders. The long string of road is frosted with sand, the grit audible under my Hum-Vee's tall tires. When I was young there was talk of the sun burning out, of perpetual blackness, perpetual winter. This talk coincided with the '83 slump, the Dow Jones going, suddenly, completely, to sleep – one must stock up, one must get ready. One must buy heating pads and cans of starched food; one must buy parkas and Vitamin D and kerosene lanterns.

The first time I remember getting mad at my son, he and I were on a beach in Santa Cruz with Denise. Connor was ten, and didn't want to put on any sunscreen. It was deep summer, a week or two before Connor started sixth grade and his first year of junior high school. He'd heard somewhere – perhaps from a friend, perhaps from the radio or television – that a study on sunscreen had found it produced bone-marrow cancer in lab rats.

Denise and I had been in Piedmont for over five years. My wife took our son to tennis lessons, to math tutors. She picked up the groceries and she did the dishes. I worked long hours, sometimes for weeks straight, while I did all I could to become the trendsetter for selling the Green Revolution. In short, we became what Piedmont was: a 50s holdover, a *Leave It To Beaver* community subsisting – and subsisting well – as the 20th century drew closed its curtains. And as the Tech Bubble stunned the country with wealth, and our bank accounts filled up with money, Denise began to see ruby bangles and diamond earrings as inadequate ways of confirming our wealth to ourselves and our neighbors. So the surgeries began: a new chest, rhinoplasty, and eyebrow transplants; collagen for her lips and butt augmentation. For three years of our son's life, some part of my wife's body was bandaged, and I realized that Connor thought his mom always sick, and this scared him.

On the sand that day, the waves lapping in, I tried to convince Connor that the lotion was safe, that the things that he'd heard were wrong, that how he'd get hurt was by the sun in the sky, and not the lotion that had been made in a lab, perhaps not far from where the test rats were dying.

Connor furrowed his brow, his eyes narrowing.

'But the Egyptians didn't have suntan lotion,' he'd said. 'And the Assyrians and Romans didn't have it, either.' My son's school had done a report on ancient cultures the previous year, and Connor was still obsessed with it.

'No,' I said, 'they didn't. But they knew it was important to stay out of the sun. They knew that Nature could hurt them.'

Denise sat in silence in her plastic beach chair.

'Look at mom,' I said. 'Mom's really tan and she's fine. That's because Mom uses suntan lotion.' Denise moved her feet around in the hot sand. A surfer walked by us and stared at my wife's chest. Denise smiled and touched at a strap on her bikini.

'But Mom goes to a store to get her tan,' Connor said. 'Being outside is different.'

'Connor, if you don't put this on, you're going to burn. You're going to turn very bright red and be in horrible pain, and your skin will peel off and you'll look like a monster.'

'Jesus, Jim,' said Denise, from behind her sunglasses.

'But it's the sun,' Connor said. 'How can it be bad?'

'Put it on,' I'd told him, and when Connor said no, I held him down on his brightly striped towel, put my knee in his back like I was a cop and my son was a criminal, and while Connor cried and begged me to stop, I slathered suntan lotion onto his skin, my son claiming I was trying to kill him.

State 95 takes me north past Death Valley, the mountains to the west between a milk-chocolate brown and a soft shade of pink. Over this range lies Furnace Creek Golf Course, an 18-hole par 70. Septuagenarians in plaid khaki slacks can work on their short game in 100-degree heat, the water for sprinklers pumped in through pipes affixed to the banks of the Colorado River.

At Tonopah I turn west onto State Highway 6 and link up with State 120, winding my way through Yosemite Park, wherein resides a motley collection of perverts and meth-heads and Hell's Angels and felons, their tales of kidnapping and drug peddling and abuse making national news every couple of years, while attendance numbers drop and the sides of cliffs are graffitied. I drive past Livermore Labs, University of California's nuclear research facility, then over the Altamont Pass, where sheep low and bend their heads, grazing. I want to go home, to check in with Esquido, to look at my wife as she lies peaceful, breathing. Instead, I drive by Oakland's rotting ports and am on the Bay Bridge in another three minutes. Just weeks ago these lanes were full; now, in the face of enormous recession, I could weave back and forth with no fear of collision. The City's downtown is equally still; the Financial District's skyscrapers block out the sun, the streets here almost like tunnels. I park underground and pocket my ticket, my Hummer taking up two parking spots, the security man in his sad and bright booth paid off with a fifty.

American Weather is devoid of life, its striped walls done

up in streamers. Friday was Brogan's 23rd birthday; we had a vegan cake party, the layers of fake devil's food gluten-free, the ice cream Tofutti. The frosting was soy-based and contained no added dyes. It tasted like shit. Everyone was happy.

Back in the Red Room, I brainstorm and spreadsheet. I make 3-D graphs, lifestyle and climate and product end-use overlapping. I apply cluster analysis to primetime TV. I consider Ponzi schemes, YouTube campaigns, some new Facebook game that promotes while it brings in money. I look out my window at the long span of bridge. I pick up my binoculars, spinning their scope. There are clouds in the sky, but the wind will not push. The Bay is a flat and impenetrable gray. I put down my binoculars and think again of my friends, staring at me from their seats in the desert.

The sun's nearly down when a key hits the lock to AmWe's front door. I stand up from my chair and take from a desk drawer a taser, a souvenir sent to me by Yi-Yi, from her VIP Party. I pad silently down the short hall that separates the Red Room from the rest of AmWe's interior. A two-sided mirror allows me to see out without being seen. There is the sound of papier mâché being ripped and I peek out a bit more to see the back of Simerpreet Sweeney's head, the long swish of her ponytail.

My Senior VP has on walnut knee-high leather boots, her dark denim jeans tucked into the calves of her footwear. The pants look tight enough to have bonded to her skin. Her cap-sleeve blouse is sheer and in patterns of white and orange damask. Simer repairs all the streamers to the trash. I stand stick-still, watching. She passes by Brogan's desk, then Michiko's, then DeKwan's, disappearing into her office. Simer leaves her door open and, as I turn to retreat to the Red Room, I kick the small bit of teak paneling that separates my mirror from the hallway's soft carpet. Simer hears it. She appears in the doorway, her head cocked, her ponytail swaying. My right knee, torn during my football days, seizes up and I grimace in silence, my feet starting to sweat. Simer stares hard at the glass panel that hides me. She comes back into AmWe's main office space and stops in front of DeKwan's eco-desk, constructed from cinder blocks and discarded sheet metal. DeKwan is our Earthquake Safety Guide, meaning that he keeps in the drawers of his desk a surplus of supplies that would be of use in the instance of natural or man-made disaster. On a bimonthly basis it's DeKwan's job to make sure that we have PowerBars and dried fruit, thermal blankets and batteries that still hold their juice. These batteries are for the dozen small Maglites that DeKwan keeps inventory of. The Maglites work well. Their bulbs are quite bright. Simer bends down and pulls one of them out and then turns back to the glass, to face me. While all at AmWe know about the one-way glass, not everyone knows that a bright light held up to its reflective side reveals whoever's behind it. Apparently, though, Simer knows this, and now takes five steps toward the mirror.

There's time for me to get back to my office and sit, to attribute the noise to some unknown source and put on my Work Face and claim overtime, innocence. But I don't do it. Simer's big eyes are deep brown, her face narrow, skin perfect. Each of the Maglites has a rope at one end; Simer uses this to twirl the device on her finger. She smiles, then sets the light down on the floor. I could go, I think. But I don't do it. Simer takes the boot off and pitches the length of leather to the side, her eyes locked on me. She does the same thing with the second boot, then stands up straight and pulls her blouse up over her head. Her bra is Cavalli, half leopard print, half Asian motif, the straps in bright red, the breasts underneath small, round and golden. She slides down her jeans, her boyshorts the same print as her bra. I watch through the glass, the air ducts softly humming. Simer takes her jeans all the way off, then reaches into one of their pockets, pulling out a long silver tube of lipstick. She unscrews the top and walks to the glass and writes, in reverse and backwards, EVERMORE, so the word appears left to right on my side of the mirror. Then Simer dresses and walks out of the office.

I wait ten minutes more, sweat drying on skin. I open the door and peek out my head. I walk out of AmWe's office and look down to the trio of elevator doors. The numbers above each read 1. Simer is gone. My heart slows its thumping. Any hope of solution to my friends' demands has vanished along with my Senior Vice-President. I log out and shut down and pack up and switch off, the sun now a red bulb under the fabric of the tranquil Pacific.

The fifty I've given over to the cashier has worked; my Hummer owns no ticket. I climb into the cab and turn over the ignition. My windows are tinted to very near black. I rise up and out of the garage's small mouth and turn right and head down the hill, toward Market Street and the entrance to the bridge, the power lines for the electric buses a loose black canopy over the asphalt. In St Mary's Square two middle-aged men do tai chi under a church's rose window. A trio of homeless in army fatigues sits on a bench, watching. The dinner and club crowds now fill the streets, their smiles sewn with love or merlot or cocaine, their union-made canvas Chuck Taylor knockoffs a lawsuit soon pending. At the corner of 2nd, near Montgomery BART, a large group of people, all dressed in green, wait at the corner for the street light to change. Two of them have walkie-talkies. Bracelets of hemp sit on some wrists; tattoos creep up toward some shoulders. One of the Green People points past my car and as my light changes and I drive toward the on-ramp

150

and home, I look to my right and see a second group dressed the same as the first. There are no banners, no bullhorns or signs. They don't know how to protest, whatever it is they're protesting. Amongst the crowd of fifty or so, there is a thin twenty-something and for a moment she looks so much like my wife: the wide, flattened nose, the same cocoa hair, the same narrow body. I keep staring as I guide my car down the street, looking back just in time to avoid slamming into the bumper of a mid-model Honda Accord that has slammed on its brakes in front of me, a BIODIESEL sticker stuck to its window. My blood-colored Hummer is almost as wide as the street; from tire to curb, it's maybe two inches. There's no way to pass the Japanese sedan. I honk once, long and loud, then give two quick beeps. The Honda's brake lights extinguish. The street light goes yellow and then to red and as I put on my brake, the pair of pedestrian hordes rushes toward me.

The 2008 Hummer H3 has a gross weight of roughly 6,000 pounds. The two crowds, now one, eat up the view out of my vehicle's windows. They are locusts on wheat, Georgia kudzu, crazed gaming fans on the floor of Best Buy the dawn after Thanksgiving. People are screaming. People climb on the hood. People are trying to put dents in the metal. A chant rises up as palms slam on the glass. My hands grip the wheel, my knuckles whitening. The seat rises then falls then the Hummer starts rocking. I look up and see soles of shoes coming down on my sunroof. More people climb on the Hummer's red hood, a slithering orgy of rage and organic cotton. Fifteen pairs of eyes stare through my windshield. A bearded man points at my face and then spits. The vehicle tilts and his body leans in, his nose going porcine as it hits the glass. Fists beat at my doors in crazed syncopation. The chant is Murderer, Rapist, said again and again, but the flash mob, it's wrong. I am neither of these.

I am a caring, sympathetic individual. I offer a system in which to fit in, and it is they who would murder and assault this system, and take away all of Your well-watered lawns, Your spray-aerosol body mist in Mango Vanilla. It isn't me, Lambs, scaling the walls. It isn't me rushing with spears at Your pens while You're sleeping.

The Hummer lurches. The shocks gasp. The chant's pitch ascends. My mouth's gone dry and the hairs on the back of my neck stand on end. I keep my hands on the wheel. I don't move. I stop looking. I try to gaze past the human blockade and what I see, when I do, when I retreat inside my mind's eye, is myself at fourteen, in the back seat of the Skylark that belonged to my parents. The car's upside down. The car's in a ditch. My dad's dead in his seat. My mom's been ejected. The world is completely, impossibly still. There's no hiss from valves. The engine's stopped running. I'm on my side with blood on my arm and pull myself up and sit cross-legged on the roof's cream upholstery, my collarbone peeking past the skin of my shoulder. I'm trying to figure out why the Skylark's back window looks different. It takes me some moments to figure out it's because the car's upside down. My dad's neck is snapped, his head sitting at a sad awkward angle. It's summer and I look at the ditch's dun grass then past it, at the post-and-wire fence. I make no sound at all. I am sure that the car will blow up if I so much as murmur. A crow lands on the fence post. I sit very still. I watch the crow preen its feathers.

A rock hits the back window on my pitching SUV and then the chanting stops and the car's shocks calm down and the crowd climbs down off my hood and flees into the nighttime, down side streets. The Honda is gone, though I haven't seen it leave. My car is in park, the engine still running. Here and there on the sidewalks, onlookers gawk, waiting to see what could possibly follow. I sit still for some seconds. I have been mobbed.

I have been mobbed and as my heart slows down, as my brain and then body understand they're not doomed, the smallest of smiles floats onto my face.

I have been mobbed. I must have purpose.

I put the Hummer in gear, proud of myself, and drive down to 1st Street and then take a right, rolling past Natoma and Howard and Folsom. I climb the curved on-ramp that leads to the bridge, its underpass lit by hobos' small fires. I keep driving east, over steel, over asphalt and water, past the toll lanes and parked CHP cruisers and into Oakland. I climb the steep grade to the top of my street, and park in my garage, getting out and running a finger over the crack in the Hummer's back window.

Inside, on the kitchen's island, is a note: Esquido is out, has gone to a movie. I look in my refrigerator but nothing makes sense. The light from inside falls on the brick floor. The Sub-Zero's handle presses into my palm, my skin still dry from the trip to the desert. I walk back to the bedroom, to go see my wife but, when I hear the swish and the pull of her breathing machine, I turn back around. Tonight, I just can't do it. I know the gaunt cheeks and curve to her chin. I know it's not going to get any better. Instead, I descend the brick steps to my house's west wing, and turn on the TV and DVD player, and watch one more time an ad that I've made and have watched at least five hundred times since my wife's coma. The screen goes to blue and then the test image, its long strips of bright colors like a painting by Klee, whom I loved as a child and whose work I had seen in museums. I stand by my brown banded-leather love seat, one finger stroking the smooth treated hide. The lights on Lake Merritt twinkle a mile past my window.

Cue black screen post-test. Cue AmWe's logo, the W stacked on top of the M, both consonants lower-case, the vowels in caps. Cue a circle, grass green, encasing the letters. Cut to close-up of a single white spot on a cherry-red background. Zoom out to see more of these spots. The background starts to move. The background and dots are a ladybug. The insect is wriggling over a leaf; it turns left and then right and then makes a full circle. I mute the ad's sound and say out loud the words: *Have you tried sleeping remedies that just haven't worked? Do you wake in the morning feeling overmedicated or drowsy?* The ladybug pushes out its small and bright wings; it flies from the leaf into a perfect blue sky, past animated lawn and animated trees. *If you're having trouble sleeping at least three nights a week, then Supinal may be right for you,* I tell no one. *A combination of long-known natural aids* (undersafe levels of kava and valerian) *and ground-breaking pharmacological research* (pure hyper-strong ketamine), *Supinal uses what's been around us all along and applies human medical research innovation.* Cut to human cartoon lying in bed, in the middle of a meadow. The human cartoon's eyes are chalk white, with wide and red lines, like cracks, around the iris. A second ladybug flies in from the right, the insects lifting and spinning in the sky. *Two-layer Supinal,* I say, *gets you to bed quickly and keeps you asleep. The first layer gets you asleep fast. The second layer keeps you asleep through the night, and leaves you feeling rested in the morning.* The ladybugs descend toward the human cartoon in small and tight spirals, like corkscrew, like helix. One insect lands on each of the cartoon's red eyes. They lift up again and the figure is asleep. Dissolve from stop-motion to live action, a Caucasian thirty-something woman in bed, smiling as she pulls the sheets up higher on her body. *Consult a physician to make sure that Supinal is right for you,* I say, to my wife, to the night, to the woman on the television. *In case studies, some users experienced side effects including dry mouth, nausea and dizziness. In limited cases,* I say, *more serious side effects have been known to occur, including coma and brain damage.* Pan to the sleeping woman's window, the trim painted white. Zoom in and block scene with window frame. Add animated ladybugs landing on the sill.

'I am a shell stuffed with money,' I say. Add Supinal logo. End commercial.

I walk to the TV and press the off button and go back up the wing's long flight of brick stairs to the kitchen. I take out a tall glass from one of the cupboards next to the sink and fill it with tap water. For the first night in so long it's something near cold, the air damp, the temperature in the high forties. I open the kitchen door to my deck and step out and stand next to one of my chaises. Fog shrouds the spires on the Golden Gate Bridge. The Bay is filled in with the same ghostly mist, a low bright gray sheet angling northeast, refusing to come ashore and into Oakland. Blood rushes through my cheeks, my body calibrating. I take a sip of my water. It tastes how trash smells. I set the glass down on the wrought-iron arm of the chaise. I walk over to the deck's wooden railing. My electrified fence guards in pure silence. Here and there, headlights on the Bay Bridge. No ships coming into Oakland's mute port. No ships departing.

At the base of the bridge, not far from the port, is a single bright and blinking rectangle. I'm too far away to make out what it says, but I know what it is: a digital billboard. It sits to one side of the bridge's toll entrance and is on all night, is on every day, always. It blinks blue to red to black back to blue, the colors changing every twenty seconds. National AdCo, a junk-mail firm based out of LA and with ties to Oakland's near-senile Mayor, erected the billboard four years ago, in the face of much protest. Since 2004 the bright box has blinked. I adore how it blinks. It is hope chest for those yet unmarried to thing. It is small and perpetual Christmas.

The fog sits like skin on the Bay's night-black water, the sign blinking in the foreground. Past it lies Alcatraz, site of much pain, place of the famous condemned, a landmark once occupied by American Indians, during that final time in this country's history when it seemed like capitalism might not win outright and completely. There have been repeated attempts at transforming the surplus federal land into a theme park, into subsidized housing, into any number of things other than what it is now. All these have failed; it remains just a prison, and a prison that people want badly to see, the misery of a few bringing joy to the many. In the summer months the wait for a tour is weeks deep. I place my palms on the railing's smooth wood. I look out, letting my sight unfurl, gazing until I start to see differently. The billboard is lined up with the island's tall skull, which peaks up and out of the fog. The sign, I realize, looks like tattoo, and when I have my next thought – *tattoos go on skin* – I know that I've just solved my problem.

I walk back inside and shut the door to the deck, the water glass falling from the chaise but not breaking. I descend to my office and spin my Rolodex, finding a name and a number that I hadn't considered for some time. I bring out my checkbook and write a check to my son, and put this check in an envelope, licking the flap shut. I affix Express Mail stamps and get in my Prius and drive through my dark silent village. Across from Piedmont's Episcopal church stand a trio of mailboxes, and I slide in the envelope and drive back to my house, my head full of plans the way Einstein's head must have been full of math, Stalin's head full of mirrors.

13

Dear Dad,

I am sitting on the bus next to Cameron Nash and telling him about the fight with Mark Norris. I tell him about jumping high on his chest, my weight enough to tip the guy over. I tell him about the dull thud Mark's skull produced when it hit the pavement. I tell him about my fists turning Mark's face to pulp, my knuckles' skin breaking, my hands going red. I tell him about feeling one of Mark's cheekbones give, the smallest of shifts, the slightest of movements. Nash's eyes are bright. He smiles out his wolf smile.

The bottle, he says. What about the bottle?

The bottle was too much, I say.

Tell me, says Nash. No, it wasn't.

So I do, Dad, tell Nash about the glass breaking to splinters, and me picking these up and holding Mark's mouth open, and stabbing his tongue with glass, and making sure some of the shards got down his throat, as far as I could get them. I tell Nash that Mark threw up on my hand, my fingers making him gag. I tell Nash that I made Mark swallow his vomit. And I tell Nash that when I was done with all this, I smashed Mark's head again, his eyes rolling up, the lids closing over, and then swept up the rest of the glass and put it in my pocket and went over to the recycling bin and took out the slivers and recycled them.

But the reason I did this was because of my mom, I say. The kid I beat up was talking shit about her.

That's crazy, says Nash. Glass down his throat.

No, I say, you're not listening. This kid had no right to say anything about my mom. My mom's in a coma.

A coma? says Nash, his smile disappearing.

Yeah, I say, she took this drug and it's like she's dead. It's like she's dead but she's breathing.

Crazy, says Nash, turning away.

It was really upsetting, I say. It still is. She won't wake up.

Yeah, says Nash, and puts in his iPod's ear buds, realizing the part of the story that he wanted to hear was over.

Thank you for the money, Dad: ten thousand dollars! The woman at the bank looked at the sum and then back at me, her small mouth pulled tight as she fed the check through its little machine. I bought new running shoes, a lacrosse stick, a hemp necklace. I bought a silver cuff-bracelet set with turquoise, red coral and obsidian. On one side of a bracelet is a big spiral shell; it's a fossil dating back millions of years, or so the woman behind the shop counter told me.

It's for someone you love, she'd said, boxing the gift.

I guess so, I'd told her, my cheeks turning pink. The woman was big, too blonde and too tall. She seemed both impossibly full and incredibly hungry.

This shell's waited whole eras for someone to love it, the woman had told me. Her sadness rose off her body like steam, but losers, Dad, lose, and I'm too busy being happy. Lodged in my skull is a flat, happy brain, flat happy eyes that no longer map the world's pain because nightly now I walk hand in hand with Sally Ashton.

At Tuck Time, while my team members scratch and guffaw in the basement of Main Hall, eating snack cakes, Sally and I stroll in our coats and our gloves through the mid-autumn evening. Do we all have a season in which we best fit? If so, Sally's is now: the brisk air brings a soft glow to her cheeks; she seems happy being wrapped, being bundled. She shows me her leggings, argyle, in red, gray and green. She shows me her leaf-shaped, etched copper earrings. She bought me a hat the day after I gave her the bracelet, a striped navy-blue beanie, every color of the rainbow represented. An embarrassingly large pom-pom sits on the hat's top but I wear it with pride, my hair growing matted as we head north across the football field, to the two outer fields used for lacrosse. Beyond them lie blue vervain and rough goldenrod and a small wood of bright yellow tulip poplars. On the other side of this wood is a clearing, then a fence, a country road with high grass in its bar ditch. We sit in the clearing and go over our days, our noses bright red and near-running.

You should come to New York, Sally told me. My mom opened a shop. My dad told her to wait until the economy got better, but she'd been planning the thing for a decade. She's going to just sell accessories, but like all accessories. Ties and bookmarks and hubcaps and pet leashes. She's going to call it Vox Populi. Sally turned strands of hair behind one of her ears, and the skin on the underside of her wrist rose above the hem of her sweater. A trio of bandages – butterflies – formed a short row. Sally saw me looking and I looked down at the grass, at the blanket.

I'm not trying to kill myself, if that's what you think.

Okay, I told her.

Bullshit, she said. Do I really seem that miserable?

I don't know. No, I told her. I just hate bandages. My mom, when I was a kid, she had all these surgeries.

She was sick, Sally said.

No. Or yes. She thought she wasn't pretty.

Is she? Sally asked.

She's my mom, I said. Why do you have on those bandages?

Formication, Sally told me.

Fornication? I said.

Do better, said Sally. The feeling of bugs in my skin, underneath it. Biting me inside out. It fucking sucks. It drives me crazy. Like imagine that you have a cast on your leg and there's an itch on your skin you can't scratch because you can't get to it. Then imagine dozens of those itches scratching you. It happened in Math class last week. I knocked all my books off my desk. People stared at me like I'm a leper.

So that's Morgellon's? I asked her.

That's part of it, she said. The other part's threads, these little red and blue things. And black ones; I had my first black one last summer. They're like ingrown hairs but really, really small. You need a magnifying glass to see them.

I looked at my watch. We have eight minutes, I told her.

Sally bent down and picked up the blanket, folding it neatly to quarters and holding it to her chest. We walked back through the poplars, my hand in hers.

Most people don't think it's real. Or that it isn't being classified right. That it's not a disease but just symptoms of another disease that's already in existence. Do you like my boots? They're new, Sally told me.

We reached the lacrosse fields, the dew on the grass wetting the hems of my jeans, the canvas of my sneakers. The two of us watched Cameron Nash and Heather Klootz walk out of the red-painted door of Old Hall, Nash tucking in his shirttails.

How'd they get in there? I asked.

They don't lock the building, Sally said.

You mean we can go in there whenever we want?

It's the world's cheapest hourly motel. You just have to deal with rug burn and accidental voyeurism.

Should I make us a reservation? I asked her.

You know, Sally said, what doesn't work well? And bodes poorly for you ever getting me into that building? Is when we're talking about a disease that governs my life, and you tell me how much time we have left to get back to our dorms and then start thinking about fucking. Besides, she said, once we have sex, we're just that much closer to the end of our story.

Okay, I said, but Sally stopped walking and grabbed my hand hard and pulled me toward her, and we

162

kissed for a long time before she let go, and we went on walking.

The Morgellon's Foundation, Sally said, my Dad and I took the fibers up there, and the doctors said they aren't made of any biological material whatsoever. They're not from some plant and they aren't from a sweater. People didn't make the fibers, but I think people did. We all sort of did. The shit in our streams. What we put in the soil to make our crops grow.

You're evolving, I said, my attempt at levity poor.

Sally frowned. I'm mutating, she told me. On bad days I scratch my skin off. My dad's doing all he can to disprove it's a disease. That's why he was up at the foundation over Parents' Weekend. To prove it's a lie. That it's all in my head, and the work that they do there is bullshit.

Why would he want to do that? I asked.

Because he's a banker, Sally said. The companies that put that shit in the world are also the companies that pay my dad's salary, and in turn pay for me to walk down the street with bags full of expensive new shoes.

Then don't shop, I said.

But I love shopping, said Sally.

We'd reached Dragon Quad and were standing on one of its paths, our peers passing by and calling out hi and making little mewing sounds because our hands were in one another's.

I'm going to quit field hockey, Sally said. I'm going to go do Community Service down at Beaumont Arms.

You're serious, I said.

I am, Sally told me. And I want you to quit soccer.

And I want world peace. And my own circus troupe.

Come on, said Sally. We'll have more time to hang out. I'll buy you a scarf. We'll go back to that store where you got me the bracelet.

And I told her, Dad, that I'd think about it.

Sally put her finger to my chest, and then her full hand. She leaned in until her lips almost touched mine before turning and going inside, looking back once as the door swung itself shut, my heart thrumming. I walked back to Bismarck with spring in my step, the thick paint of night burned blue by the lights, the wind bringing tears to my eyes, making everything fuzzy and larger than life. I fell asleep thinking of buying Sally things: tremendous sports cars and flowing silk scarves and some house on some beach with a pool right next to the ocean. Is love excess allowed, Dad? Greed, endorsed and accorded? As I lay on my side, the world grew too puny, and I bought Sally a spaceship, a cosmos faraway. We sped through the night in our new, fast machine, ignoring the fields and the hills and the trees, even as they were disappearing.

Please say hi, etc.

Love,

Connor

14

San Quentin State Prison sits one hour northwest of my small and expensive suburb, taking up 432 acres of otherwise coveted waterfront property. The prison's backside, opposite the lot I've pulled my Prius into, looks south toward Belvedere and Tiburon, two of the country's most affluent towns. Each day ferries pass within a half-mile of San Quentin's 5,000-plus inmates, the big boats carrying the Marin County rich to stockbroker jobs in the City's downtown, to AT&T Park and Giants games. From afar the long and low sandstone buildings look like they could be a manufacturing plant: some group of warehouses where workers canned food or ran lathes, or transformed materials mined from the Earth into combustible energy.

The first rain of autumn has fallen overnight and continues to fall at five-thirty in the morning. Up at three, I'd made coffee in my thin flannel robe, waking Esquido.

'You've been gone a lot lately,' I'd told my nurse-aide.

'I get my work done,' he'd said back, looking at the kitchen's big window, toward the Bay.

'It's not judgment,' I'd said. 'I'm just wondering what it is that you're up to.'

Esquido had looked down at the terra-cotta floor tiles. 'I saw someone last night, but I don't know if they saw me. I'm trying to find out the answer.'

'The Nortenos,' I'd said, 'from the school,' handing Esquido a red-and-gold mug from my alma mater, the word WARRIORS facing out toward me.

Esquido had shrugged. 'Maybe,' he said.

'This was in Piedmont?' I'd asked.

'Emeryville,' said Esquido. 'At the movie.'

'Should I call Frank?' I'd said. 'Do you want to give me a description?'

'When was the last time you checked your landline?' my nurse-aide had asked, ignoring the question. 'Your answering machine.'

I'd shrugged then, taking a sip from my cup. 'I'm not sure,' I'd told him.

'You should,' Esquido had said back, and returned to the bedroom where my wife dreamed of, I'm sure, wonderful things: opulent dreams, dreams refractory.

What had been on the landline's answering machine (a cream-colored box kept on my desk and a holdover from the pre-voicemail era) was a message from Connor's Dean of Students, Leslie Stephens. Dean Stephens is a middle-aged, jowled, pasty man who wears well-washed chinos and baggy tweed jackets. He drones. His glasses are huge and outdated. I bought this man a house just outside Portland, Maine in exchange for making sure that, no matter what, Connor gets a diploma from the school he currently attends. Hearing Dean Stephens's voice on my answering machine does not seem like a step in the desired direction.

North on I-580, past accidents moved to the side of the road, past Emeryville's bevy of corporate hotels, past Richmond's wrecked streets and Chevron's refinery, I consider the fact that my son has left sports to serve soup to the Newport elderly. And as I cross the bridge toward the prison and Marin, it occurs to me that I haven't talked to my son in a very long time, so much so that I can't recall, as I drive, when the last time was that we had a conversation, that it might be two months since we last spoke, that Connor's awkward cracked voice is not something I place as part of my recent memories. This thought sticks in my mind, a soft pain, until the bridge ends and the highway winds up and over the hill, and I can see the barbed wire rung around my salvation.

San Quentin is the oldest prison in the state. It's so big that it has its own zip code. It's also the only prison in California that has a Death Row for the tried and condemned. At San Quentin, there are over six hundred waiting to die, more than anywhere else in the Western Hemisphere. At the gate, I give over my driver's license, pulling up one arm of my shirt and suit so the booth guard can stamp the skin underneath. I hang my visitor's pass from the Prius's rearview, stepping out into the mist and predawn. The employee lot is large and half-full and near-silent. From one of the outbuildings, somewhere far off, hums a generator. A guard in a ball cap and dark armless poncho walks toward me. The guard is Hispanic and six-three and huge. Every item of clothing is CDC green, save for his shin-high and black steel-toed boots.

'Mr Haskin,' he says.

'Good morning,' I tell him. We shake hands. I can smell salt on the air. From somewhere nearby a gull calls. We cross the damp blacktop, the guard leading the way, stopping in front of a large metal door along one wall of a small and beige building. The guard presses the button on the intercom system next to the door.

'Do you live here, on the grounds?' I ask.

'I'm not going to tell you if I do or do not,' the guard answers.

A voice comes through the wall-mounted box, quick and low words that I can't make out but that seem to make sense to the guard on my end as he says 'Two,' then 'Eighty-seven.' The door buzzes, a bolt dropping or drawing back from its lock. The door opens onto a patch of poured-concrete floor. A thick chain-link fence stands just feet ahead of us. On the fence's other side is a second guard, this one white. He's tall but quite thin, his face young and pockmarked and too boyish for his profession. He looks at me once and then at his peer and punches in numbers on a second wall intercom unit. The door on the chain-link fence jumps and the guard pulls it open.

'Have a nice visit, Mr Haskin,' the first guard says to me, then walks back out into the rain, the door clicking shut and sealing behind him.

More doors and more keypads: the boy guard leads the way through a first and then second low-ceilinged, narrow corridor. The walls, floor and ceiling are the same institutional green, a color somewhere between mold and patina. China has the most prisoners of any country in the world. Second to China is the U.S. of A. Behind America is the state of California. I make a mental note to myself, as I walk, to find out what company it is that produces this paint, and buy stock in it as quickly as possible.

The guard and I turn one final corner and ahead of us stands another chain-link fence-and-door combination. The door buzzes, then jumps. We walk past it and, as we do, Warden Mandriel Lang opens the door to his office and stands in its threshold.

'Jimmy,' he says.

'Manny,' I tell him.

Mandriel looks at the guard and lets out a breath while

raising his bushy black eyebrows. The guard spins on his heel and walks past the link gate, closing it before he disappears back down the corridor.

'I'm going to have to strip-search you – they told you that, right?'

I blink my eyes once. Lang bursts out laughing.

'Joking,' he says. 'Joking. Come in,' and stands to one side and waves me into his office. I walk by him and onto thick burgundy carpet. Lang's office is small, and stuffed full of bookcases. *Reader's Digest* versions of authors' Great Books stand in neat rows on the shelves. A mahogany desk is tucked up against a window, diamonds of metal dividing the pane's glass. Nothing on the walls, save for another intercom system.

'Is there a name,' I ask Manny, 'for this color of green?'

Manny unfolds a metal chair standing behind the door I've just come through. He arranges it in front of his big wooden desk. 'Sool,' he says.

'Sool,' I repeat.

'Shit out of luck,' Lang says, before sitting down on his side of the desk to face me. Lang's mom is Filipino, his dad from a long line of Irish Catholics. Lang, like me, is fourth-generation Californian. His tan face has gained weight since I saw him last, at a meeting of litigants suing the makers of the drug Supinal. My wife won't wake up but Lang's wife died in her sleep, her heart hushed out of existence. Police stopped his dead wife's physician, Dr Albert J. Kass, who Mandriel blamed for the loss of his Abbey. These police found crack cocaine in Kass's car. I assisted with getting this drug into said car. Now Kass lives here, in San Quentin.

Lang and I, after the group meeting with attorneys, had gone out to a dinner at Sam's, in the City. The booths at Sam's have high wooden backs that reach up near the ceiling, along with thick fabric curtains that cordon off the booths' diners from sight. Politicians and actors dine here quite a bit, entering through the back door and eating in private. Lang and I, on that day, did the same, and spoke for some time about how money does not equal justice, and that Lang's wife, Abbey, had a weak heart, and that Dr Al Kass should have known better. Lang wanted a way to get Kass to San Quentin. I provided that way, and am back for my favor.

'So,' the warden says. 'Here we are. Here we meet.'

'Indeed,' I say. 'How's the good doctor?'

'The good doctor has learned that the medical facilities here at San Quentin are quite substandard.' Mandriel crosses his legs and turns in his chair. 'For instance,' Lang says, 'if one is coerced into sexual conduct by a very big man,' Lang says, raising a finger, 'and this very big man is quite well endowed, and tears certain parts of a certain person's body.'

'Okay,' I say, 'I think I get it.'

'What I was going to mention, though,' Lang says, continuing, 'is that these sorts of coercions happen all the time in a dungeon like this. Do you want the stats? The stats are one in five. If you come here you've got a twenty percent chance of leaving, shall we say, altered. And most get fixed up right here on the grounds. But Dr Al Kass, who's been coerced twice since his arrival here some six months ago, Dr Al Kass goes to a regular and civilian hospital. Why would I do this, Jim? For Dr Kass?'

Lang sits in his chair, smiling at me. His suit is polyester, a sort of brown-gray. His wingtips are off-brand and black and synthetic. Lang uncrosses his legs and leans in on his desk, elbows on its smooth, polished surface. He presses his index fingers together and puts them to his lips, hooking his thumbs under his plump and short chin. Outside, past the window, dawn has turned the sky cobalt.

'I don't know, Manny, why would you do that?' I say.

Lang puts a palm to either cheek. 'Because, Jim, it's more painful for the doctor this way. For others, the average scum, the house robber, the crackhead, a trip to the outside world is a treat. It provides maybe hope, maybe solace. It is, in some way, fulfilling. But for the doctor,' Lang says, 'for Dr Al Kass, it's a reminder of all that he's lost and will never regain, even when he leaves here just weeks from now, an early release for time served and good behavior. There will be, out there, no more waiting rooms, no more doctor's pay or kind, sickly patients. He'll be a felon, his license revoked, his years at Med School now useless. And I want to remind him of this, Jim, whenever I can. I want him to suffer in myriad ways. I want, for him, a buffet of suffering.'

Lang's tie pattern looks generated by some evil machine: red trapezoids descending diagonally across the tie's shiny black surface. Lang smiles again and I smile back. We are damaged men who want things not wanted by most but, when we get these things, nothing in us changes. Lang raises a leg of his suit's cheap pants, pulling up a black sheer sock by its double-stitched top.

'I'm glad to oblige,' I say to Lang. 'And if we could, I'd like to get down to business.'

Lang nods once and opens a drawer. Other than the gliding of runner on wood, the office is silent: no clock ticks, no wall unit hums with air pushed through vents. Lang slides four folders across the top of the desk. They are thick and dark green and meant to hang in some tall metal cabinet.

'Per your request,' Lang says. 'All North Seg. All killers, now peaceful. All condemned.'

'When can I interview?' I ask, looking through the folder on top.

'Today. Right now,' Lang says. 'They can be here in fifteen minutes.'

I nod my head and keep looking at the files. 'And you think that any of these four will agree?'

'Wouldn't you?' Lang says, and gets up from his desk, shifting his narrow black belt in its loopholes. 'I'll give you some time. A half-hour, perhaps? Do you want to just text me?'

I raise my hand – a mute yes – and Mandriel Lang leaves me alone in his office. I get out of my chair and sit down in Lang's, spreading the files out over his desk. In each are photos, arrest records, and comments on conduct while at San Quentin. Here is Bayliss Ford, age 29, convicted in 2002 of the murder and rape of Stephen Finn, age 10, and Charlie Bass, age 8. Finn and Bass were stepbrothers out playing along the west bank of Merced, California's Bear Creek, on a cold foggy day the first week after New Year's. Bayliss Ford, who had grown up outside Baton Rouge, and fled a home of abuse at age 15, happened upon the two boys, asking them if they wanted to 'see his pet wolf.' The two boys, according to Ford, both said yes, and he took them to a small and tight grove of walnut trees, shooting each once before having his way with them. Ford then proceeded to weigh each body with stones and dump the stepbrothers into the wide and full creek, the current taking them one hundred and two hundred yards downstream, respectively. He was arrested leaving a Fresno bar two weeks later.

But Ford will not do because Ford is black, and the tattoos just won't show up on his skin in the manner they must for my purposes.

And here is Jonathan Moon, a septuagenarian condemned in '75 for killing his wife's paramour, along with his wife and her brother. Betsy Moon was having an affair with Mr Gene Booth, the floor manager of the housewares section at the San

José Macy's. And while Moon didn't know this man, per se, he had met him once, when Moon's wife had dragged him to an Easter Weekend Sale that the department store had been having. On the night in question Betsy arrived home with her brother Michael in tow. Whether the brother knew the truth was unclear to Moon, and largely irrelevant. He killed his wife and brother-in-law as they slept, shooting Michael first as he snored on the sofa, before reloading and heading to the bedroom. Moon then fled the scene in his small yellow Datsun, parking in the garage adjacent to the Macy's where Gene Booth worked. He waited four hours, sure he'd be caught, loading and unloading his long hunting rifle. He didn't know how he'd lure Mr Booth back to the garage, in order to shoot him, but this point, as it turned out, was not germane, as Mr Gene Booth, in his last bout of bad luck, parked his navy-blue Nova two spots away from his ex-lover's husband. Moon stepped from his vehicle just as Booth did, shooting the manager once in the head and then setting down the rifle and walking to a pay phone outside of the Macy's, where he called the police and revealed his location.

But Moon will not do because he is old, and no one wants to watch the elderly die: they are reminded of parents, of grandparents. It is too actual. I clear my throat once and close up Moon's file and move on to the next one.

And here is Van Nguyen, middle son of a Vietnamese multi-millionaire. At age 12 he was sent to boarding school in Hong Kong, where Nguyen began collecting bugs: roaches and crickets and beetles and spiders, keeping them in a large iron coffee can and, according to Nguyen, 'opening the can at night, when alone, and pouring the insects over me, so they would crawl on my chest and my arms, and I could then know their feelings.' After college, Nguyen's father, connected out west via his selling of fiber-optic cable, was able to get his underachieving middle son an entry-level code job at Sun Microsystems. With an apartment and paycheck, Nguyen settled down, taking to buying himself exotic pets: Japanese hornets and huge Blister Beetles and Death Stalker Scorpions. After Hien Vu, a female co-worker at Sun, rejected Nguyen's repeated advances, he kidnapped her from her apartment's parking lot, keeping her locked in his own apartment's closet for over a week and bringing her out at night, her mouth taped, and letting the bugs crawl closer and closer to her. Vu was killed by one of Nguyen's scorpions 'somewhat accidentally; I had been wanting for her to know these bugs' feelings, but grew bored with this work and went to watch the *American Idol*, and fell asleep there on my couch, and when I woke up, the bugs' feelings were shown, and they had not liked her.'

But Nguyen's father is still trying to get him extradited, and Nguyen himself already has five tattoos, and none of the type that I need him to have, so I put down the file and pick up my final option, just as a call from my Chevron rep comes over the line of my cell phone. I let voicemail get it; I'm not ready to talk. The missed call is followed by a text from the same man: TELL ME YOUR BIG IDEA. I text back: STILL IN R&D BUT WON'T BE BY TOMORROW, a fact that I know to be true as I open the fourth and last folder, and stare at the picture of a man I've not met but have, because this man has white skin and light brown eyes, and thin and small lips and nondescript chocolate hair, and forgettable ears and a forgettable chin and not one tattoo or other identifying mark on his body. He is six-one and weighs 172.

In short, this man looks just like me.

'Please,' I say out loud, and as I read the report my prayer is answered. Robert G. Lott is forty years old. He's been in San Quentin two decades. He got to San Quentin for blowing up

175

a house on Lake Tahoe's South Side. In the early 1980s, new development had sprung up, Reagan's noveau riche wanting mansions right next to the water. An environmentalist group with the name of SeaGreen had boycotted the building of these lakefront estates through late spring and into summer, holding up building by laying down spikes in the road so contractors' trucks would blow out their tires, and also by stealing lumber and concrete, and handcuffing themselves to Bobcats and bulldozers. While this worked sometimes, SeaGreen ultimately failed: the mansions were built, SeaGreen's members arrested. Among the handcuffed was a young Robert Lott, eighteen years old and fresh from working on his parent's farm in South Dakota, Lott leaving home after his folks sold the land to Big Ag. Lott, with no one to bail him out, spent nearly a year in a Placer County jail, and was released on St Patrick's Day, 1982. Lott got a job bussing tables at Harrah's, working there for three months before he was fired for spilling fake blood on a woman's mink sable. Evicted in May, Lott slept on the beach, the newly built mansions a half-mile away. Lott took a job on a road crew as a flagger. With the money he saved he bought things for his 'moment of crisis': a string of small bombs that would go off in succession. In autumn, Lott's plan came to fruition. One night in October he took a dinghy out onto the lake, paddling silently over Tahoe's deep and dark water, the boat bobbing as he passed by each mansion's patio. Lott had chosen his house earlier that day, a Ravelais with blue LED lights in the walls of its sixteen-foot swimming pool. Lott leapt to the rocks and pulled the boat in, gathering his three duffel bags of explosives. He placed the bombs around the base of the house, twining a fuse that led back to his boat, and when nearly asea lit the single thick cord and threw it to shore, and began paddling.

176

Only one of the nine bombs Lott planted worked, but only one had to, a wiring fault in the building's downstairs carbonizing the home's insulation, and setting the Ravelais's basement home theater aflame in a matter of minutes. About the same time that Lott pulled his boat ashore on a nearby public beach, the teenaged son of the small mansion's owners was dying, along with three of his friends, from smoke inhalation. Coroner reports stated that the teenagers never woke up, their blood alcohol content five times the legal limit. The group of boys, seniors at Oakland's Bishop O'Dowd, had stolen up to Tahoe for Columbus Day weekend. All four were laid to rest at Mountain View Cemetery, an elegant graveyard in walking distance from my home in Piedmont. Lott was picked up that very same week, confessing to what he'd done but saying he thought that no one was home, and with good reason: the boys had parked their single car outside of the development's grounds, hopping the fence in the late-evening hours. Lott's spot of bad luck got him on Death Row.

But in my eyes, Lott can do no wrong. In my eyes, Lott is already an angel.

I text Lang that I'm ready and the warden comes in.

'The last one,' I say. 'Robert Lott.'

'Really,' says Lang. 'I would have guessed Bug Boy.'

'Robert Lott,' I say again, and Lang nods his head and depresses a button on the intercom system.

'Bring Number Four,' Lang says to someone, then looks at me. 'Do you want me in here for this?'

'I might prefer that he and I talk alone,' I tell the warden.

'Sure, Jimmy,' Lang says, and then he is gone, and two minutes later there's a knock at the door. I open it and standing inches away is the bearded, grinning face of my Prisoner. He wears an orange jumpsuit and has shackles on his arms and legs. The same boy guard that led me through the building's maze is standing beside him.

'Mr Lott,' I say.

'Scary suit man,' Lott tells me.

'I haven't been told how to proceed,' says the guard.

'Why don't you just bring him in here, and then leave,' I tell him. 'Will that work for you?'

The boy guard looks at the Prisoner and then nods once, moving the shackled Lott into the room. The three of us stand there, the Prisoner and guard both staring at me. I pick up the metal folding chair from near the desk and move it all the way back to the far end of the room, ten or so feet from the warden's chair.

'Can you sit him down there?' I ask. 'Is there a way to put the shackles through the chair, so he can't run at me?'

Lott remains mute, smiling. His beard is oblong and shaggy in parts and his brown hair is close-cropped, unevenly buzz-cut, but there's light in his eyes and this light is focused. This light is possessive of sanity.

'I can do that,' the guard says. Lott snorts. I set up the chair as far away from Lang's desk as I possibly can. The Prisoner sits down. The guard winds the shackles through the legs of the chair, metal banging and sifting over metal.

'Do you want me to secure his arms, too?' the guard asks.

'I don't know,' I say. 'Mr Lott, do we need this?'

Lott is looking at the long shelf of books. 'Dickens,' he says, 'was a slut.'

I look at the guard and tell him it's fine and he leaves, the door clicking shut behind him. My cell phone vibrates: a friend of Ned Akeley's, someone high up at The News Corporation. I turn the ringer to silent.

'How are you today, Mr Lott?' I ask.

178

'I'm waiting to die,' Lott tells me. Lott moves his feet, the metal chains shifting.

'And you're slated,' I say, 'for mid-December.'

Lott raises and lowers his eyebrows.

'Well, Mr Lott, I have a proposition for you. It's not going to keep you from being put to death. In fact, it might put the date forward by as much as a week, depending on some focus groups I'm conducting shortly in the future.'

'Speak English,' Lott tells me.

'Mr Lott,' I ask, 'do you have family you care about? A mother or father? A sibling?'

'I don't have to tell you that,' says Lott. His shoes are off-brand and Velcro with no arch. His socks are bright white with vertical ribbing.

'You're right, you don't,' I say back, smiling from behind the warden's desk. 'Let me phrase my question slightly differently. You are scum. You murdered four people. It hasn't mattered to society that this was an accident, as you're now here, in San Quentin State Prison. Your opportunities to make a difference in the world hover somewhere between slim and nonexistent. If you do have a family . . .'

'I don't,' Lott says. 'My parents are dead. No siblings.'

'Well, then how about your extended family of SeaGreen? You've been cut off from them. Your beliefs, like you, are held captive. If there were a way for you to forward their cause, would you?'

Lott straightens up slightly in the metal folding chair, then slumps down again. 'Are you a politician?' Lott asks.

'I am a representative for private industry,' I say. 'Politicians don't have this level of power.'

'I read the news,' Lott tells me.

'That may be true,' I say back, 'but you aren't answering my

179

question.' Morning has come to San Quentin's cold walls. Soft light streams in through the window. Lott moves his feet over the burgundy shag on the floor of the office.

'How is it exactly that you could help them? Or help me help them or whatever?'

'Money,' I tell him.

'Money for doing what?'

'For doing nearly nothing at all,' I say. 'For dying.'

'But there's more to it than that,' says the Prisoner.

'There is,' I say. 'You're right there. But I have a dozen inmates to interview today,' I lie, 'and if you're not interested, I won't waste your time, nor allow you to waste much more of mine.'

'How much are we talking?' Lott asks.

'As little as twenty million dollars,' I say. 'And as much as one hundred.'

'And what I have to do—'

'Is die,' I tell the Prisoner. 'It's just that you're dying on terms I create. You could think of me as your instructor on dying.'

'Speak English,' says Lott.

'I am and I'm not,' I say. 'I'm speaking American.'

An air siren sounds and I look out the window. A white-painted bus is passing in through the gates, new arrivals to a place of departure. Thick iron grates cover the bus's square windows. It passes from sight and I turn back to face the Prisoner.

'Mr Lott,' I say, 'what I propose is this: letting your execution be televised. Letting this act be seen by a community of viewers. Of watchers, Mr Lott. Of civilians, whose only crime is working hard five days a week and wanting, at night, a little entertainment. Just one single act to get us through these dark times, through this financial crisis. You have the opportunity here to unify the country, if not the world. And you don't have to do anything yourself. You get to just sit back and die, which, I should stress, is going to happen anyway. But in the meantime, you earn, Mr Lott. You make millions for doing next to nothing at all. And I promise you that checks will arrive in your name, and you can do what you want with them. For me, that doesn't matter. What matters to me are the perfect time slot and the right camera angles inside the Death Room.'

'You're rich,' Lott says.

'I am,' I tell him. 'But the money you receive isn't coming from me. It's coming from corporations. They're going to pay for their ad space, for their part in this show. Do you understand, Mr Lott?'

'Billboards or something,' Lott says to me. 'Decals on the gurney.' Lott's eyes are gleaming. The room glows with the promise of fiscal reward, that warm light that colors everything but is colorless.

'Something like decals,' I say to the Prisoner. 'But first let me ask you, Mr Lott, you aren't a hemophiliac, are you?'

Lott looks at me and then puts his head down. This continues for nearly a minute. I stare only at the brown hair on the top of his head. Lott brings his face up.

'Skin,' the Prisoner says. 'Tattoos.'

'Tattoos,' I say. 'That's right. Very good.'

'Tattoos,' Lott says. 'Scary suit man.'

'Scary suit man,' I tell him.

'How long do I have to think about this?' asks the Prisoner.

'About another two minutes,' I say.

'Fuck it,' Lott says.

'As in yes?'

'Fuck it,' Lott tells me.

I stand up. Lott tries to, too, then sits back down. I walk over to him. He looks at me. I hold out my hand. Lott shakes it.

'I'm going to be back here in two days,' I say. 'You'll be gone from the prison for most of the work. You'll be afforded a bed, a color TV, any food that you want but no liquor. Do you smoke?' I ask. Lott shakes his head. 'Two days,' I tell him, and walk to the intercom system on the wall, realizing that I have no idea how to use it. I turn back around.

'Do you have any idea how I call the guard?'

'Even the buttons need buttons,' says Lott, but offers no answer. I walk over and knock on the door. The door buzzes once and the boy guard opens it.

'Thank you,' I say. 'He can go now,' I say, and the boy guard untangles Lott from the chair and the Prisoner stands up and our eyes meet each other's.

'I think that all this is probably a joke,' says Lott.

'Two days,' I tell him.

Lott is led out and I fold up the chair and text Mandriel Lang, who comes in five minutes later.

'It went well,' Lang says. 'You have what you need.'

'I have the most important part,' I answer.

Lang nods and moves back behind his desk, looking out of the window. Five dozen inmates are being led single file by a guard holding a rifle.

'The human condition,' Lang says, but I don't know what he means.

'Get me to my car,' I answer.

Migrant Tattoo is in Oakland's Downtown. It's a small shop off the corner of Clay and 11th. Rudy Alvarez is the shop's owner. Rudy's older brother, Reuben, owns the service that cuts back the growth on my backyard's poplars, and cleans off the oak leaves from the roof of my house, and rakes from my back lawn leaves off my Japanese maples. Six months ago Reuben gave me Rudy's card. It has sat in a drawer; I have no tattoos, and hope never to get one. But what I do hope, today, is to have someone here give Robert Lott plenty of them.

The bell dings as I walk in Migrant's front door, the walls of the lobby covered with hundreds of drawings, each with a number next to it. Here are hearts, stars and carp, roses wound around swords, the word OAKLAND in a wide variety of fonts, along with 510 and BUMP CITY. Here are pit bulls and imps and the California state flag and Our Lady of Guadeloupe. The desk girl perks up as she sees me come in: I am a white man in a suit. Her arms are covered in a bright fluid mess, the poster-board samples caught in tornado. Her hair is dyed black and small metal horns poke through the skin just below each corner of her bottom lip. She has on a plain black T-shirt. Amongst the river of ink on either forearm are logos converted from popular types of candy. In the font used for Snickers is the word SUBVERSIVE. Near the woman's right wrist, in red on yellow, are the words SUGAR MOMMY. Small packages of Smarties wind up toward the girl's left bicep, each package inscribed with initials.

I smile at this woman. 'Is Reuben here?' I ask.

'Yeah, hang on,' says the girl, who gets up from her chair and walks back behind a thick checkerboard curtain. Her T-shirt has pulled itself up from her sitting, and just above the waist of her low-slung black jeans, at the base of her back, is a wheel divided into eight different slices, each piece its own bright color. Seven of the slices comprise the Cardinal Sins: Envy in green, Wrath in bright red, Pride in violet. The sins are spelled out in calligraphic script. The eighth slice reads YOUR NAME HERE in big black block letters.

Reuben Alvarez comes out through the curtain, along with the girl, who sits back down at the desk.

'Reuben,' I say.

'I know you?' says Reuben.

'You don't,' I say, 'but I know your brother.'

'I can't give you a discount for that, man,' says Reuben. 'Tough times, you know?'

'I know,' I say, and take from off my shoulder my faux-leather, eco-safe attaché, unhooking the small straps over its front. From inside the bag, I take out two stacks of back-bound one-hundred-dollar bills and set them down on the counter. The girl stares at the bills like she's just seen God.

'Reuben,' I say, 'tell me you want to be rich. Tell me you like San Francisco.'

15

Dear Dad,

The first snow and at three in the morning my alarm clock's light blinks, the orange strobe waking me as winds whip past my window. Here is the cold blue of silence, the radiator off. I sit up in my bunk and I listen, swinging my legs out from under my sheets before hopping down onto the top of my desk and tomorrow's history homework.

I dress in all black: my pea coat, a T-shirt, my darkest black jeans, the Converse knockoffs for which I've bought black laces. I unplug the clock: the first snow, the air filled, the air noisy with wind. I open my door and peek down the hallway, the EXIT sign casting a thick eerie red on the cream-colored walls, the brown industrial carpet. I step out, the snow lost to the sound of itself, the snow joyful and shouting.

I exit the door to my dorm and pad mutely down the concrete hallway that leads past the school infirmary, and I want to stop and talk to some dozing nurse, say my arms are heavy with adrenalin, say that my heart is pounding. I pass by the window where I saw Sally on Parents' Weekend. I open the door that leads to the hall that leads through the school cafeteria, over its creaking waxed floorboards. The lights are all off. Wind hits the big windows. Every person on campus eats here, in this room, but right now, tonight, it belongs only to me, as I creep by the huge portraits of the past headmasters, their black robes blending with the room's shadows, the stern faces looking down, floating in judgment. I stay as close to the wall as I possibly can, each squeak from the floor turning my stomach to knots as spit thins in my mouth, my hands shaking.

I walk down the long hall and past the locked office doors of Dean Leslie and Headmaster Lynn and He of Plaid Ties, the good Dr Dimler. The hallway is no more than ten yards. The hallway is endless. My heart feels like it's going to stop. It is snowing. All of my classmates, when out on a cruise, go the long way around, not through the school buildings. A good number of these people wind up getting caught, and with getting caught comes expulsion. I'd never heard of anyone just walking straight through, and I asked at Tuck, Dad, asked a number of seniors. No, they all said, you go up by the woods, you go north past the fields and cut back down on the west edge of campus. And I said, but you're out longer this way, and statistically there's a greater chance of getting caught, because of the variable of time, and they said, Look, listen or don't listen. It's snowing and I reach the big heavy doors that lead to Dragon Quad, my heart in my mouth, the hinges brightly whining, and step out onto the first of three granite steps and stare straight ahead at the door into Strauss and Sally Ashton's small and dark window.

The first snow, she'd said, Dad, we'll do it then, as the two of us chopped carrots in the commercial-sized kitchen of Beaumont Arms, with its row of gas stoves and long metal tables. The first storm because it will be loud, and no one will want to be out, and there will be low visibility, and I said okay, as we stirred soup in pots, the broth boiling then brought down to a simmer. And I thought about this, Dad, as we waited and waited, waited six days and then eight then eleven, as the leaves turned from golden to umber then fell, the air cold, the air wanting warmth, the air finding each crevice between scarf and neck, between coat sleeve and mitten. Waited while my room was broken into and vandalized, school patch torn off my blazer. Waited while staring at my clothes ripped to shreds, my wall mirror thrown to the floor and in pieces. Waited while picked on at Tuck by my former teammates, currently in the midst of a three-game losing streak that has sunk them from first place to fourth, the JV keeper called up after Cameron Nash reinjured his ankle. Waited through meetings with school personnel – I am guessing by now, Dad, that you got a voicemail, an email. Waited and waded through hard lonely days while my Coach said don't quit and my teammates said traitor.

But now it's snowing.

I open the red-painted front door of Strauss dormitory and step inside in silence, turning my body and keeping a hand on the door so that it won't bang, won't bother. It's snowing as I sneak up the steps, my lungs big in my chest, my feet, from adrenalin and the cold, barely working. I pause on the landing and take off my shoes and creep fast and mute toward Sally's door, tapping a fingernail on its white-painted wood as it opens inward. Sally's dorm parent, the elderly Ms Caroline Metz, Freshman Math, is a very sound sleeper. Sally's roommate, Perrin Thune, has slept elsewhere. With only the light from the window behind her, Sally is no more than shadow and warmth. I step into the room. Sally closes the door.

It's snowing, she says.

It's snowing, I tell her.

Two hours later, and without my coat, I step out into the black of predawn, the need to be unseen now gone: I can claim whimsy, can claim wonder – a Californian out walking in the first snow he's ever stepped in. And I do, Dad; I walk, walk down the Main Drive, past the bare maples, and turn left toward the beach and the ocean, passing by the route my former team still uses for running; past the long row of Tudors, their thick bushes of holly, and onward to the small and tight grove of pitch pines and the cliff's cold pink rock, where I sit and I wait for sunrise.

This weekend, Dad, is the SG Halloween Ball. Sally is going as Dissection. In biology class, we've been exscinding dead cats. Five days a week we stand at our lab stations, the cadavers in large metal pans that look like they could be used for baking. The first day, with small knives, we slit the cat's throats, then made incisions that ran the length of the animals' bellies. We've removed most organs. Not the lungs. Not the heart. Tomorrow, Sally is stealing her cat, and storing it in the snow until nighttime. She plans, she says, to wear it as one does a scarf, over the glow-in-the-dark skeleton bodysuit she ordered off eBay. I've told her ten times that it's a bad idea. But her logic, Dad, is quite hard to fault: they want us to take these things apart, right, but they only want us to see what we do in certain light, in certain settings. It's property theft, I tell my greatest love, my new favorite person. They'll suspend you. They'll get you expelled. I'm making a point, she tells me, and if the dead can't be involved in the day they're regaled, I'll suffer the irony.

She really said that, Dad: I'll suffer the irony. I may buy her a ring. The day of the snow, we both received brochures from Sarah Lawrence. It seems nice, Dad, and it should be, I guess: it's the most expensive school in the country. You don't even get grades. What's the point? Everyone there has already made straight As per paying the cost of tuition.

I write this letter to you from the back row of American Civilization, bleary-eyed from under three hours of sleep and pausing at regular intervals to make it look like I'm listening to Mr Frank, who is barking out facts about our Civil War, how Lincoln freed the slaves from kindness of heart and righteous indignity. All bullshit, but who cares. Sally's costume is skintight. She modeled it for me. I'm going as the War In Iraq: one-dollar bills stapled to thrift-store desert fatigues, the money stained oil-black with polish for shoes, blood-red with permanent marker.

Please say hi to Mom.

Love,

Connor

NOVEMBER

16

I have my son to thank for my ad firm's name. His year after Ritalin produced massive withdrawal, the fatigue and depression getting worse before they got better. Coupled with this was our move to Piedmont: a new home, a new school, new faces that Connor had to talk to and deal with. For a project in 2nd Grade Art, my son was to draw his interpretation of any holiday that he wanted. Connor chose the Fourth of July. I came home from the City very late one night, after dinner and drinks with my three closest friends (and now potential investors), and taped to the door of the fridge was my son's school project. Black stick figures lay under a fire-orange sky, lines of blood red criss-crossing through it. The people looked dead or asleep, some with their knees tucked up to their chin, all without eyes, all without faces. The scene was meant to depict a crowd watching a fireworks display. To me, it looked like the end of the world. Above the burning heavens, in the same dark ink in which the people had been drawn, were two words all in caps: AMERICAN WEATHER.

The Prisoner is brought into my Davis Street suite in civilian blue jeans and a grey hooded sweatshirt. Underneath these blue jeans, bought from The Gap, are leg shackles. Two plainclothes guards have accompanied the Prisoner up the New Century Commons' elevator.

At my home in Piedmont, for nearly four days, I've explained the Omnicast Execution Event to two dozen CEOs, my BlackBerry growing warm and then hot in my hand, my ear slicked with sweat, my mouth talking and talking. I explained the subscription fee would be one hundred bucks, flat. I explained the feed would come through on one of Omnicast's pay-per-view channels. I explained the profit-sharing: the Prisoner takes a cut, then the state, then the corporate investors. The percentages are 19, 40 and 40. I make a dollar for every one hundred made and while I tell this to the owners of GM and GE, of Costco and Lowe's and Time Warner and Safeway, I imagine the bills, the singles, piling up, dollar after dollar after dollar, filling my office then my house then my yard, millions upon millions of crisp dollar bills, their scent of fresh linen like spring's first full breath, their neat stacks pushing skyward.

The Prisoner is made to sit down on a chair; from a coat pocket one of the guards removes a second pair of leg shackles, threading them through the legs of the chair just as the boy guard had done in Warden Lang's office. It's ten in the morning, the day's sky a soft blue, the sun lightly warm through my balcony's sliding glass door.

'Why don't we turn the TV on,' I say to the Prisoner.

Two days ago, and from prepaid cell phone, I called the aide closest to California's Governor.

'The liberal outrage,' he'd said. 'Do Greens own guns?'

'They might or might not,' I'd said, 'but I bet they have cable. Let's not say a word for as long as we can.'

'This thing stays underground till you turn the light green. But you're being billed for the guards and the van, post-execution.'

'You're signed on, though,' I'd said, 'no matter what.'

'What choice do we have? The coffers are bare. We can't pay cops. We can't pay fire. Don't get mugged or hurt until next fiscal year, if you want to get better.'

'One more thing,' I'd asked.

'What's that?' said the aide.

'Will you watch?' I'd asked.

'My God,' he'd said. 'Are you kidding?'

The Prisoner stares at the screen and scratches his beard. The sound on the TV is off. A commercial for juice boxes is airing. Men dressed as fruit raid a child's party, knocking over cans of root beer, of cola. The mom winces in joy as stains bleed into the carpet. At the bottom of the screen are the words CONTAINS NO REAL JUICE. The children laugh and then drink and the fruit men pat each other on the back, then turn toward the camera, flexing their muscles.

'Sugar water and dye,' the Prisoner tells me.

'Good healthy juice,' I tell the Prisoner.

A talk show comes on. My tattooist is late. The glass doors that lead to my balcony face south, toward San José, its treasure chest of chips, of pixels. In four days of selling, I've had only one yes, but it's a big yes. It's a yes from the rat-eyed commander of a firm working in oil. From his office in Texas, this man gave me the thumbs-up, but he also wanted throwback, something retro and glorious, something that put on display 'his thing's past,' so instead of the words comprising the name of his multinational, there will be the old standard his company used before they were sued and forced to dissolve.

'Franklin D. Roosevelt sucks cock in hell,' Rat Eyes had said before hanging up, and after buying the most expensive part of the Prisoner's body.

The Prisoner sniffs at the air.

'Do you smell that?' he asks.

But I can only smell money, money and hope, the real possibility that the Omnicast Execution Event will not only be the most watched act in the history of man, but will affirm to my bank balance and sad, diseased mind that I am a person of worth and importance.

My suite phone rings once; the front desk is calling. I pick up the receiver – Reuben is here. I say, Send Him Up. I tell the Prisoner, Get Ready. My tattooist arrives with a black duffel bag. He's wearing black jeans and a black T-shirt that says in white letters MIGRANT. The jeans and the shirt are exactly the same shade of black. Dividing them is an orange faux-leather belt kept cinched with a white and square metal buckle.

'You parked down below?' I ask.

'I took BART,' Reuben says. For his work, I am paying him five hundred dollars an hour – a minuscule amount compared to the profit brought in, but to Reuben, a fortune.

The suite's phone rings again – DHL is downstairs.

'That's the autoclave,' Reuben tells me.

'What's that?' the Prisoner asks.

'Cleans everything, man,' Reuben says.

The guards stand in the kitchen, each drinking a Coke taken from my fully stocked fridge. I ask one of them to go down and get the package.

'Not in our job title, boss,' says one of the guards.

'Then you're both fired,' I say, taking my cell phone from out of my pocket. 'Do you see this?' I ask. 'It has Lang's home line in it. I'm not asking you two to do advanced science.'

The guards look at each other and shrug and then leave. In their absence, I leave a voicemail for Lang – I still want them gone from this job.

'Bring me that boy guard from the other day,' I say, 'the one who led in our prisoner.' I watch Reuben unpacking small bottles of ink, a package of gloves, disposable razors. A row of bright needles in a wide plastic sleeve. Two extension cords: one brown, one orange.

'How much will I bleed?' the Prisoner asks.

My tattooist shrugs. 'Depends on if you're a bleeder.'

A text comes in from Simer: EVERMORE PARTY THURSDAY, HILTON ACROSS FROM ST. ISIDORE? I write back okay, that I'll be in tomorrow. One of the guards returns, holding the DHL box.

'Where's the other guy?' I ask.

'Getting a smoothie,' he says.

'Hang on,' I say, and grab the guards' coats, both of which are slung over a single wood chair in the kitchen. I walk back to the door and take the box holding the autoclave, then hand over the state-issued outerwear. 'See you at four p.m. sharp,' I say. 'That's plenty of time to get a résumé together.'

The guard looks nonplussed as I shut the door in his face. I set the DHL box down on the desk, by the sliding glass door that leads to my balcony. My phone rings again. It's a number I know. I unlock the glass door and step out onto the balcony.

'What's a smoothie?' the Prisoner asks Reuben.

'Jim Haskin,' I say. The morning air's dry. Thirty stories up, I look down at a crowd of people making their way up Market Street. Amidst the crowd are two banners. One banner says CHANGE. The other says OBAMA.

'Mr Haskin, hello,' says a man in deep Southern drawl. 'Mr Haskin, my name is Mike Christmas. I got off the phone not too long ago with someone in oil. I think you know him a bit.'

'I do know him a bit,' I tell the Chairman of the Kingdom of Innovative Plastics and Science. 'He and I spoke.'

'He and I did the same thing,' Christmas tells me. 'I want you to know, too, that I'm calling on a prepaid phone.'

'The connection's incredible,' I tell him.

'It is,' Christmas says. 'I called our friend in oil on another of these, and I liked what I heard when he and I spoke. The connection on that call was near crystal-clear.'

'That's wonderful,' I tell him.

'At moments, though, the bottom dropped out of that call, and our friend in oil thought that you might be able to fill in those parts of our conversation.'

'Where are you, Mr Christmas?' I ask.

'The East Coast,' he says.

'No, I know,' I say, 'but more specifically. Are you outside or are you in your office?'

'I'm in my car in a hotel parking garage,' Christmas tells me.

'Great,' I say. 'Perfect. We can't be too careful.'

'Well, sure, Mr Haskin. Or Jim? How's that? But the thing that I don't understand about the privacy . . .'

'Is the fact that this is something that we want people to know about; that we want, Mr Christmas, people to see.'

'Yessir,' says Mike, in his Tennessee twang.

'The concept's no different than any other group that's looking for investors,' I tell him. 'I have a product and this product's not finished, and I want you in on the ground floor,' I say. 'Before the stock, as it were, goes public.'

'Appreciate that,' Christmas says. 'How much stock are you offering?'

'We're offering a variety of packages,' I tell him. 'Different levels of buy-in.'

'I think the analogy's getting a bit fuzzy for me,' says Mike Christmas. Thin blasts of car horns rise up from the street, very near to the place where I was flash-mobbed two weeks earlier. A rally cry that I can't quite make out is being said over and over. I wave at the pedestrians, then give them the finger.

'I think you're right,' I say. 'Here's what I mean. What I mean is placement. Somewhere in December's first couple of weeks, the Prisoner is going to be condemned to death. This death, as is standard in the state of California, will be by lethal injection. This event is going to be on pay-per-view TV, and carried only by Omnicast. The cost of this event will be one hundred dollars. Let's say only three million people watch. Do you have a calculator nearby?' I ask.

'I don't think I need one,' says the Chairman.

'Good,' I say. 'Neither do I. The Bay Area alone, Mr Christmas, has about five million people in it. So I'm going to argue that three million is far to the right, especially considering the markets in Asia and Europe. So let's say that we times that sum by ten.'

'Jim, I'm getting sort of aroused,' Christmas says. 'I'm feeling slightly horny.'

'What I'm offering you,' I say, ignoring the man's greed-fueled lust, 'is the same thing that I offered to our friend in oil – that you pay in whatever you want, and your return will be that amount at least ten times over. How much you pay is based on the placement of your logo on the body of my prisoner. An arm or a leg, the forehead, the stomach.'

'What body part did our friend pick?' Christmas asks.

'He picked the chest.'

'And we're stuck on lethal injection,' Mike asks me.

'What do you mean?' I say.

'I mean we can't hang the guy, Jim? You hang him and you got more advertising space. Dress him up in a thong or some such, and after he's dead you swing him around. Push him around with a stick or something, Jim. You could brand the stick. The Kingsford Body Tongs. The Red Bull Corpse Master.'

I look down at the rally. I want Obama to win; I've given

199

money to his campaign, bought a bumper sticker for my Prius with his name on it. I want him to win so the marchers below will understand that his winning is irrelevant: that it will not stop war, that it will not stop greed, that we are not governed by law but by money.

'The back's getting tattooed and I like the thong idea,' I say, 'but we're not going to hang him. We're staying with the shots.'

'Okay, sure, Jim,' Christmas tells me. 'You have some sort of sheet that says what costs what?'

'I do,' I say. 'I'll send it by fax. Do you have a home line? Something secure? Something private?'

Christmas says that he does, and we make arrangements for later that day. The marchers for Change down below are gone, having turned some unseen corner.

We say our goodbyes and I slide open the glass balcony door and re-enter my suite to the sound of shaving cream being pressed out of a pressurized can. The Prisoner is topless, his white Nike T-shirt laid over the side of the couch, over his gray Nike hoodie. Next to these items is a print-off of the Standard Oil logo: the red, white and blue oval laying on its side, the thin silver torch rising up over its middle, the single word STANDARD written in white over the oval's red middle. The Prisoner is still sitting, shackle-bound, in the chair. Reuben crouches in front of him.

'We need to shave you,' my tattooist says.

'Everywhere?' asks the Prisoner.

'Just about,' says Reuben.

On the TV, the talk show's host attempts to look pained. The camera cuts to a black woman and her three kids, a caption below the quartet reading, HOMELESS! ALMOST DIED IN HURRICANE! The woman is crying. The group sits in over-stuffed chairs. The camera cuts to a curtain to the right of the riser. This curtain drops to the floor to reveal a brand new, bright red sports car. The coupe has been waxed to the point that it shines. The homeless woman throws her hands in the air; her youngest child is sitting on her lap, and the woman, overcome, pushes her girl onto the floor and rushes over to look into the car's window. The camera follows her movement. There is a frenzy of cuts – the car, then the woman, then the car and the woman, then a miscue back to the riser, where the talk-show host can be seen pushing the children in the direction of the car. All three of the children, confused and scared, are crying.

Reuben applies his palm's mound of white shaving cream to the Prisoner's pale chest.

'I can keep the beard, right?' the Prisoner asks me.

The mother is jumping and jumping and one of her knees knocks into the chin of her oldest child, sending the pre-teen down to the floor.

'For now you can,' I tell him.

Reuben plugs in the ink gun and the machine starts to hum, and it is the hum of industry and profit, the hum of my past and my present and future, and for a moment, before the needle hits skin, I want to start humming along with the gun, the way someone hums some bar of a song that makes them quite happy.

By late afternoon, when both guards come back, the outline of the oil logo is done, the long ends of the oval reaching the Prisoner's armpits, the torch running up to his larynx. The guards tell me that it's time for the Prisoner to go and I say okay and they lead him out. I pay Reuben in cash and he leaves two minutes later.

Exhausted, succumbing, I lie down on the bed in my suite's

other room. The machine, the machine. Its soft loving thrum. The quiet ambition it lends me. In brief moments of confession, when we were young, Frank Gaines and I would talk about what life might have been like if we'd had full lives with our birth parents. Picking almonds, we'd posit and posit. But these talks, with time, would sputter to nothing, would devolve from fugues into dirges, and we would grow quiet and re-enter our minds, where dreams earned a higher rate of exchange and we could mint endless supplies of their coins and their paper.

An airplane roars by, either coming or going. I turn on my side and look out the window. A sliver of blue, very pale, the light fading, leans in through the space between the room's curtains. I say out loud, 'I am made safe by money.' I say it again and I shut my eyes and I say it over and over.

The light bends and I bring my knees to my chest, tuck my elbows down toward my stomach. My BlackBerry blinks and I open my eyes and turn the machine's face toward me. The area code reads 309 – Illinois. The Kingdom of Bulldozers is calling. I rub my eyes and swing my legs over the bed. I turn on the lamp sitting on the side table. I'm sick with fatigue, which means I'm not dead. I press accept and put my phone to my ear.

'Jim Haskin,' I say. 'Hello. How are you.'

17

Dear Dad,

A rhythm, as cold chews the trees bare, as the last rust-colored leaves balk at their folly. The sun dull, I wake slowly, mind lost to the heat from the radiator. I dress without thought, without feet, without feeling; brain dead, my toes catch on pant legs. In French class, we have moved on to the subjunctive. We express wishes contrary to matters at present. The classroom's five windows look south, at New York, at Sally. A dead cat sits even now in the snow, and I am one of two people on Earth who know its location. We read a poem in my English class: 'My mind is not right.' The poem had in it that sentence.

She scratched off the skin on her arms and legs. She scratched off the skin on a cheekbone. It was Friday and after time served at Beaumont Arms, Sally had wanted to go to the mall to look for an antique perfume atomizer, and also new boots and the brand new iPhone and a belt that Fendi had on back order. I'd told her that I'd see her at school.

It's the weekend, she'd said. Let's go have fun.

I'm tired, I'd said. The mall just sounds terrible.

So you don't want to hang out, Sally told me. She'd had on the bracelet I'd bought her, a black and white houndstooth scarf, a black pea coat with oversize buttons. Her blue eyes were watering from winds off of the bay.

It's freezing, I'd said. And I do want to hang out. I just don't want to go shopping.

Well, it's what I want to do, so you have a choice, Sally said, but when the van came to pick us both up, only I got in it. Through the window I watched Sally trudging away, toward the long row of marquees and signs that read OPEN. This was the day before Halloween, late afternoon, the sun floating low in the sky, long strips of black clouds breaking up the loud pink of pre-sunset. The mall's asphalt lot was washed in that light and as Sally passed by the rows of parked cars, one side of her scarf was taken by wind. It waved like a hand as the van traveled east, back to campus.

Perrin Thune found her bleeding in bed that same night. Sally had gone on a spree and then had an attack, the room filled with bags, filled with boxes. Tissue paper covered the worn hardwood floor, the pieces' bright corners like spring bulbs through dirt. There were new pairs of heels, a brass jewelry box. There were dozens of bras, the price tags still on them. The new iPhone sat in a box on her desk. By the door was an antique umbrella-holder. And in the middle of the room, rising out of the mess, was something so odd and so out of place that Perrin, at first, didn't know what to make of it. The moonlight stained the creature's bright teeth, its head thrown to the sky, its mouth open. Nearly as tall as the bunk bed itself, in the room's dark Perrin momentarily thought it alive, a monster returned to the world of flesh, to consume her. What the monster was, Dad, was a carousel horse, purchased by Sally at the same antique store where she'd bought the umbrella-holder. Its face was light blue, its mane a dark green. Perrin couldn't understand how it had gotten into the room but I asked later, Dad, down at the store, and they told me a driver had run it up to campus. Body frozen, mid-gallop, front hooves raised high, the horse ran nowhere in perpetual whinny. Perrin flipped on the light and saw Sally laying on top of her sheets, streaks of puke striping the side of the bed and dotting the base of a candlestick holder. A pill container, its cap off, lay next to her. Sally lifted her head and Perrin saw blood on her face.

I bought you something, Sally had told her.

Perrin took her to the infirmary. Dean Stephens was called. The next day, Sally's parents swept up in a Bentley they owned, cooed Sally into the back seat and then left forever. Medical withdrawal. She can return, if she wants, next fall semester. I will not be here if she does, Dad. 'My mind is not right,' which I said out loud and to no one Halloween night, sitting in my Iraq War costume in a corner, the cafeteria tables all shoved to the side, the PA system playing Britney, Beyoncé, Rhianna. I no longer know if my ex-team wins games. I sit in class but I no longer listen. I feel like the creature inside Sally's room. I am a horse that goes only in circles. I wear my blinders. I chew and I swallow my hay. When they whip me, I am to canter.

At Oceanside Diner, I take up a full booth, my iPod on the table next to my pack of cigarettes. I spent a full evening down on the beach, figuring out just how one smoked. It's a fun game to play, Dad, but does take some learning. The black-clad ne'er-do-wells think they have a new friend: there's a sextet of them, but I am no seventh. They dye their hair weekly; they wear combat boots. They are part of some self-imagined army. The disdain of their privilege is sickening to see, as I see myself in them. So I sit and I smoke and I listen to metal. I stare out the window while my French fries get colder. But the time signatures in the songs throw me off: they aren't 4–4. They do more than that. They are trying to inform the world that the world is complicated. They are angry that they are losing to game shows. They are angry that no one will listen. The black-clad ne'er-do-wells only listen to punk, or what they think is punk: to the image of punk that speaks to them. I give them an ear bud and they nod and say cool, but metal, Dad, is not cool, and no punk would say that. They hand back the bud and I smoke and say nothing.

Mr Richards, lacrosse coach, asshole extraordinaire, took from my head, just today, Sally's beanie. Or my beanie: the beanie that Sally gave me. Richards is six-four and muscled, a frat boy returned to a world of children that he can bully. In the stairwell outside my History class, I pushed him with both hands up against the brick wall. Give it back, I said. You're gone, he told me. He was smiling. You're gone, he'd said, you're nothing. And Dad, what a thing! To be nothing at all! I spat in his face and said I was honored. My disciplinary hearing is midweek, next week, but I already know that I'm being expelled, so it would seem my time here is thing between things. Please say hi to Mom, even though it's sort of pointless.

Afternoons, the school van drops me off outside Beaumont Arms, but I no longer have interest in serving any community. Instead, I wander down to a park looking out at the marina. The cobblestone streets are absent of tourists, the beaches and benches all empty. I sit outside in the wind until my eyes wet, the way Sally's eyes did as she scratched herself bloody. My eyes are expressing wishes contrary to the matter at present. They are in mutiny. My eyes are subjunctive. But were the clock to wind back, Dad, what would be different? I knew no favorite songs. I knew no favorite color. I knew she was sick and that I couldn't help her. I want to go home now. There's nothing to see here. Please tell me you're busy righting big wrongs, Dad.

My mind is not right.

Love,

Connor

18

The Home Depot says yes. Walt Disney says yes. Intel's on board, and JPMorgan Chase. Boeing, maligned, wants to pay on installment. Kraft and Verizon and Pfizer say yes – they all will buy skin, will buy space, will buy in. My plan has legs. My plan is moving. The TV is on in my carpeted suite. The Prisoner sits watching and drinking a smoothie. The boy guard's name is Sam Flanagan. Sam stopped at a smoothie place on the way from San Quentin, this morning. The Prisoner drinks down his drink, the straw sucking and slurping.

'Styrofoam cups,' the Prisoner tells me.

'Good, healthy smoothie,' I tell him. The needle gun is thrumming and buzzing. Traveler's Insurance wanted space on one arm: how will his wrists sit at the time of injection? We need maximum visibility. I'd told them back that if that's what they want, they should consider the forehead, the stomach. They weren't taking this bait but did double up: Reuben has finished, just below the Prisoner's elbow, a bright red umbrella. Today he'll ink in its symmetrical twin. In thick standard blue, my tattooist has outlined a trail of the Microsoft Windows logo running from wrist bone to shoulder. Underneath the Prisoner's chest, where the ribs start to divide, is the big golden M of McDonald's. The Prisoner's body reminds me of a felt Christmas-tree ring, slowly being covered with presents.

In between recasts of Obama's big speech, CNN is airing a report about holiday travel. It's November 9th. San Francisco is ninety degrees. Audrey Monroe, of Knoxville, Tennessee, has pulled her two young children from school, in order to save money on the flight to her parents' townhouse in Tampa. She tells the reporter that her boys will study on the beach. The segment is followed by an ad for an Internet travel agency.

'When you compute the amount of money those kids will lose, for missing that school,' says the Prisoner.

'Look at the gnome,' I say. 'Is he not cute? Is he not funny?'

Guard Sam Flanagan holds the remote in his hand. 'Change the channel,' the Prisoner tells him. Three seconds of NASCAR; the Prisoner stays mute. Three seconds of a report on global warming. Three seconds of reportage on America's credit debt; three seconds of Incredible Hulk gravy boats on *Home Shopping*. Three seconds of an ad for a new shaving cream. The Prisoner plays with the beard hairs on a cheek. I don't know if he knows he's doing it. The guard clicks again and here are chimps in a tree, pulling out bugs from another's fur. The Prisoner says okay and puts up a hand.

'I like watching animals play,' says the Prisoner.

'Me, too,' I tell him.

The afternoon workload is the logo for Walmart over the skin at the base of the neck, where the brain meets the body. I change out of my suit and into a tunic and sandals and shorts.

'Are you going to the beach?' Reuben asks me.

'No,' I say. 'I'm going to work.'

'Where do you work?' asks the Prisoner.

'Nearby,' I say, and hand the boy guard my taser. 'Do you know how to use this?' I ask.

'Sort of,' he tells me, his face turning red. We go through two minutes of instructions. 'No matter what,' I say, 'do not use your gun. You use your gun and you owe me more than you could ever repay me.'

I nod goodbye to my troupe and click my door shut and descend down my building's elevator. I walk out of the lobby of New Century Commons and up to my office in the lunch-hour rush, past plump corporate types and bald homeless women. The air smells like spring, like blossoms. The day we burnt down the Home for Well-Behaved Boys, it had been like this day, unseasonably warm, late in the year and in the low nineties. Ned Akeley and I were in Mr Hand's room, where our surrogate father lay wheezing and dying. Ned was opening the drawers of a cherry-stained desk. We'd spent the past hour soaking outbuildings with lye. Mr Hand stared at me, unblinking. He'd been diagnosed with emphysema six weeks before. It was his wish that the home not continue without him. It was his wish that he not die slowly.

Ned Akeley was shoving monogrammed kerchiefs into his suit coat's pockets. Mr Hand, with two fingers, called me to his bedside, pointing at the clear mask of his ventilator. I took it off. He breathed in sharp rasps. His skin looked like the chewed pale rock of a gulley. My parents had died with no wrinkles on them, and now, to see this, how time hung on the face, how it pulled at the cheeks and the skin on the throat and put welts on one's hands and pushed one's eyes back into their skull, it made me want to not die at all, when for so long, as a youth, it was all that I wanted.

Mr Hand raised up the frail trunk of his body, pulling a pillow down further behind him. Ned was bringing out papers from a drawer of a desk and putting them through a shredder. Amongst these was my case history, my first and genuine birth certificate. Mr Hand saw me looking as the shredder's gears turned.

'All of the past will be eaten by machines,' he told me. I'd nodded back. I was twenty-four years old. My newborn son lay in a crib miles away, in an apartment in Oakland, one block from Lake Merritt.

'I need you to know,' Mr Hand told me. Ned Akeley looked up from shredding his papers. He stared at me and then Mr Hand and then left the room, calling out to Frank Gaines. The teachers and maids had all been dismissed; no boys had been at the Home for a month. I stood hunched over Mr Hand's king-sized bed, motes of dust in the air like white, spinning plankton.

'I need you to know,' Mr Hand said, 'that I think you don't believe.'

'Okay,' I told him.

'No,' he said thinly. His blue eyes were bloodshot, scared-looking.

'All this is false,' Mr Hand told me.

'All this is false,' I repeated.

'No,' he said, and then one more time, turning his head, the word changing to a slow and high moan. 'No,' he said. 'You're not understanding.'

A crow called nearby. It was late afternoon, the light past the window growing softer, more orange. Mr Hand lowered his chin and raised both his eyebrows, mutely imploring. He bobbed his forehead out toward me.

'When,' Mr Hand asked, 'is God?' He smiled then, a wide jagged thing, his small teeth mainly gums, columns of a temple long ago turned to ruins. There was a bang in the kitchen – the stove being moved. Gas was filling Mr Hand's house. 'When is God?' he repeated.

'I don't know,' I said, starting to panic. 'You took care of me. Thank you,' I told him, thinking that this was what he wanted to hear, but was too proud to ask that I say it.

'There are only two things,' he said. 'Presence and absence. No God on this Earth because of the Earth.' Mr Hand set his palm over my wrist. His skin was ice-cold. 'God comes only once all seas are dry. God comes only once all of these forests are deserts. God comes when all oil has been leeched, and the coal is all gone, and the metal all smelted. We use it all up,' he said, 'or God never arrives, and this is how we love what we cannot see, and this is how God bestows His Trust upon us.'

Mr Hand took his palm from off of my wrist, turning his head and folding his arms over his stomach. He blinked his eyes once and opened them wide and then closed them. 'More,' he said, like he was saying a word he'd said so many times it was finally okay to no longer say it. And then Ned Akeley was pulling me out of the house, and we were setting the front porch on fire. Mr Hand's Home sat four miles off the public road and, with the structures ablaze and for the last time in my life, I passed by the long rows of thin almond trees, the sun's orange light flashing as we sped past the orchards.

The light strobes this way now as I walk through downtown, the sun blinking off the windows of cars, the sides of skyscrapers. I pass by Bay Alarm, a divorce lawyers' firm, a securities brokerage. The cathedral on St Mary's Square stands draped in shadow. Thin sickly trees with dead umber leaves bend toward the Square's patches of sunlight. I turn right on California, away from Grant Street and the Barbary Coast Trail, where bronze medallions stamped into the sidewalk honor the Gold Rush and Old Mint, the miracle of the stagecoach's arrival. Past Kearney, on Spring, on the alley block separating California from Sacramento, a white van is parked with its hazard lights blinking. From out of a freight door walks a twenty-something man with a long, contoured beard and hoops in his ears and tight acid-washed jeans and tight black V-neck T-shirt. The man opens up the van's two back doors and pulls out an over-sized canvas painting. I've slowed down my gait and now stop completely.

The first painting the man swings out of the van is a huge black and white portrait of Black Panthers co-founder Huey P. Newton. Newton, with Afro, is seated at a round wooden table, a bookshelf to one side, a window to the other. The painting is a digital image on canvas, covered with blotchy dark squares and Pollock paint splatters. Newton's white shirt, polyester and wide-collared, is unbuttoned to mid-chest. His hands sit folded on the table in front of him.

The artist catches me out of the corner of his eye as he steps down off of the van's back bumper. He nods his head and I wave a greeting as he disappears past the freight door's threshold, into darkness. I step off the smooth sidewalk and onto the rough-hewn granite of the alley. The artist comes out again half a minute later, looking at me and then climbing back into the van. The next painting out is of Harvey Milk, standing on a Castro District street corner. This image, like the last one, is in black and white. Milk's hair is windblown, his striped tie, by some gust, pushed over his pinstriped collared shirt and herringbone sports jacket. The AbEx markings cover his face and the back of his hands. The artist disappears again into the building. When he comes out, I approach him.

'Excuse me,' I say.

'Hey,' says the artist.

'My name is Nolan Ryan,' I say. 'I collect art.'

'Your name's really Nolan Ryan?' the artist asks.

'It is,' I say. 'My parents adored our national pastime.'

'Are you coming tonight?'

'To what?' I ask him.

'My show,' says the artist. 'I'm Garrett.'

The artist and I shake hands.

'I'm not sure if I can make it tonight,' I tell him. 'But I'd love to see the rest of the paintings.'

The artist known as Garrett looks back at the truck, then down at my tunic and my shorts and my sandals – an over-rich yuppie, not cool enough to understand, but cool enough to want to try to. I smile my wide, office smile.

'I could help you load in,' I tell him.

'You're not crazy, right?' Garrett asks.

'Of course not,' I say, my eyes shining.

'Why don't you come in after I'm all set up?' says Garrett.

'Okay,' I say, 'I have one errand to run. Will you still be here in ten minutes?'

'Sure,' Garrett tells me.

I nod my head and walk out of the alley and down half a block to Bank of the West, where I wait in line to withdraw half a million in cash, in one-hundreds. I tap my sandal on the burgundy rug as a man pleads to default on his home loan, thereby walking away from his mortgaged four-bedroom, a property about to be foreclosed on. The man is in his mid-thirties, a wedding ring on. His hair is disheveled. His sweater owns stains. Some code monkey that rode the '90s big waves, only to fall face first onto the wet sand of this century.

'It's in my right, yes?' asks the man. The whole line is looking.

'It is,' says the bank rep, 'but you must also consider your moral and ethical responsibilities.'

'The fuck?' says the man. 'What the fuck? Do you know that my water's been turned off? Do you know that my parents bring me groceries?'

'But your neighbors,' says the bank rep. 'The block on which you reside. Your default would mean bringing down the worth of those properties substantially. These are rough times, Mr Toal, but it's times like these that test the mettle of the individual, and thus society.'

'This morning I washed my face with my neighbor's garden hose,' says the man, Mr Toal. 'They watched me do it. My neighbors. They stood there looking at me, out the window. I used to buy them four-hundred-dollar bottles of wine.'

'Again, these are tough times,' says the bank rep.

The line moves forward swiftly, past the velvet poles, and after one minute more I am being helped by Bojana, a Serbian brunette, her white pinstriped blouse unbuttoned uncommonly low. Bojana touches at the strands of hair behind one of her ears.

'Hello, Mr Haskin.'

'Hi, Bojana,' I say. 'I'd like half a million, in cash, in one-hundreds.'

'Right away, Mr Haskin,' Bojana purrs. She is nineteen, a post-Kosovo arrival, and I imagine her family fleeing, in some dark cargo truck, the heavy and brutal air of the Balkans, the peaks covered in snow, the streets covered in corpses. The long trip west into Albania, then Italy, perhaps, past uniformed men in light blue UN helmets, the bribes, the swearing. Is Bojana too young to remember? Does she understand only the American way, her true past informed solely by grim stories told to her by her parents? Her accent was still thick when she began here one year ago. It's lessened since. She covers up less. She wears more makeup. Bojana, Bojana, please understand: the stuffed bear that you lost, that got left behind – it's America.

I tap my fingers on the well-waxed wooden counter, turning my head and surveying the crowd while I wait for my money.

Mr Toal has his head in his hands. The people behind me shift on their feet. Their faces are grim. Their faces are pleading. Their faces are saying to this bank and this street and this city and state and also this country, you promised me something and then took it away; I placed faith in you, my lazy belief, because you promised me lowest common denominator. You offered a way to get through, to get by, and now you expect me to roll up my sleeves, to work and want not, when you said you loved me because of my wanting.

Bojana comes back with a cream-colored bank bag. It thuds as she swings it up onto the counter.

'Do you want me to count it?' Bojana asks, smiling.

'Would you like to?' I say.

'I'd love to, Mr Haskin.' Our eyes lock and Bojana's stare goes momentarily, erotically grave – if you offered me this, what's here, in this bag, I would offer you anything.

'That's all right, Bojana,' I say. 'I'll come back if the machine counted wrong.'

'It doesn't,' says Bojana.

'I know,' I tell her.

Ten seconds later I'm out the glass doors and back up the street, where the white loading van still sits double-parked in the alley. Garrett comes out from the gallery and shuts the van's doors and turns toward me.

'They're all in,' he says. 'You want to come look?'

'Very much,' I say, swinging the bank bag at my hip. Garrett lowers his head and then gives a wave and I follow him into the building. We walk down a wide and dimly lit hall that opens up onto the gallery. Twin rows of benches, painted bright white, sit in the room's center. Garrett's paintings hang on three of the room's four walls: Newton and Milk along the north wall, next to Bruce Lee and Charles Manson. On the short wall behind me are Jim Jones and a sketch of the Zodiac Killer. The long wall to my left harbors Cesar Chavez, Jimmy Garcia and Hell's Angels member Ralph Sonny Barger. All of the canvases are uniform in size, all black and white, all covered with Garrett's additions of squares and paint splatters. To my right is a half-wall, above which is a wrought-iron grating. There is room behind the iron for people to stand.

'This was a bank?' I ask.

'No,' says Garrett, 'a union hall. Longshoremen.'

'The common worker,' I say.

'Yup,' says Garrett.

'We've left them behind,' I tell my young friend.

'I haven't,' he answers.

I sit down on one of the benches in the middle of the room and pretend to take in the paintings. I look over all the walls, also painted white. The room's scuffed wooden floors, nearly black from time and from wear, are smooth under my sandals. I hunch my chest out over my bent thighs, swinging, between my legs, the bank bag filled with money.

'Do you want to see an artist's statement?' Garrett asks me.

'You know, Garrett, I don't,' I tell him. 'What I'd like to do is buy this whole set. I'd like to do it right now. The errand that I ran before, where I went, was to the bank. I saw your reproduction of the great Huey Newton and thought, yes, this young man has it. I saw Harvey Milk – and those shapes, right? That's blood spatter? That's your artist's rendition of his unfair end? That's your recreation?'

'Not exactly,' says Garrett, but I cut him off.

'But it's close to that, yes? Something ideologically similar? Wow, Garrett, just wow. I want them. I want to buy all of them, right now. In this bag here,' I say, swinging the burlap sack up, 'in this bag is a half-million dollars. I know that you have this show tonight, and have invited your friends and maybe your family, to this defunct hall, but Garrett, I need these. I want the whole set, and worry that if I wait until tonight, until after the show, someone will buy one of your pieces, and I need all of them. I want the whole set. I just bought a mansion down in Belize, and its walls need a theme, and its walls must be smart and its walls must be gorgeous. Half a million is all that I can afford, and I hope, Garrett, that you'll find my price fair, and that you would do me the honor of letting me buy these.'

Garrett stands stunned some five feet away. He crosses his arms over the front of his chest as though he's been violated. During my speech he's looked away from me twice, and blinked more than a half-dozen times. I hold the Power Card. I hold a bank bag filled with money.

'Okay,' Garrett says, walking over to me and holding out his hand. 'You've got a deal, Nolan Ryan.'

'I'm honored,' I say, and hold out the bag in place of a handshake.

'Do you need to use my van to load these out? Or do you have a car somewhere near here?' Garrett's query has a lilt at the end of its asking, implying that these are the only two options I have.

'No,' I say, walking over to the portrait of Cesar Chavez first. 'No, Garrett, I don't have either of those,' I tell him, lifting the canvas from off its nail and raising it upward, so that the bottom of the canvas's wooden frame sits just above the nail's head. I look over at the bearded and earringed young man. He'll learn to change. He'll learn to fit in. He'll eat fast food and pay taxes and have babies. In time, he too will put on a tie and drive to an office park from his home's subdivision. He'll buy jogging pants. He'll have a house-cleaner. He'll pay in to dental; he'll pay in to vision. He will become what I need him to be. I'm just helping him to get there a little bit faster.

I hold up the painting with one of my hands and then slam the stretched canvas against the head of the nail. I drag down the portrait, the canvas splitting in half, the image of Chavez torn asunder. The painting's fabric splays like a felled, broken kite. Garrett looks like someone just ran over his puppy. He's tied the bag of money to one of the belt loops on his jeans. Garrett adjusts his stance and the bag swings toward his crotch, knocking him gently in his privates.

I throw the portrait of Chavez on the floor and yank Jerry Garcia down from the wall and put the bottom of one of my sandals through the musician's face. It takes two tries. The wooden frame splits. The Grateful Dead's singer and lead guitarist is a pile on the floor.

'You fuck,' Garrett says. 'You fucking asshole.'

But I own these, they're mine, and next to come down is badass Sonny Barger, followed by Jim Jones, the Zodiac, Manson and Milk. All ripped to shreds. All broken. All perfect. Bruce Lee comes down last, the canvas placed over the corner of one of the room's many benches, the frame snapping. I collect as many of the paintings as I can and walk out of the gallery, Garrett in tow. I walk past his van to a green waste-management Dumpster. I set down my bought art and swing open the Dumpster's heavy plastic lid, then lift the paintings into the belly of the metal container. Garrett stands just in front of the van, watching. I meet his stare as I stuff the paintings in deeper.

'This feels bad now,' I say, 'but that money, it's going to feel good. It's going, Garrett, to make you feel better.'

Storm clouds have gathered over downtown. The lightest of mist touches the skin over my cheekbones. I stuff in the paintings and slam the lid closed, the smack of plastic on metal followed by the sharp distant honk of a car.

'You know I can just make them all again, right?' says the young artist. 'That I have pictures of all these at home, and I can do over what I've already done? And that while I have no idea why you've done what you have, your actions, in the long run, are useless?'

'Art,' I say, walking toward my new friend, 'is useless. Art can inspire only more art. It spreads like disease, like virus. It repeats itself. Art is bad code and dumb math. And it is all swallowed up, eventually, by time or by money. Art dies, Garrett, or becomes an investment. It's one of the two. It dies or is killed. Your art is bad, and would die a long death. But I helped you. I killed it, before others had to stand in a room and watch it die. Galleries, this gallery, Garrett, is a hospital for dying art. No one wants to be in it. But because they love art and maybe love you, they gather to mourn, to speak in hushed tones, to come together and erect, for a short time, a vigil. But all that this group of mourners really wants, Garrett, is for the patient to die. To have someone cut the power on the breathing machine, and have this debt on society slip into the realm of the only-remembered.'

Garrett has his thumbs hooked into the loops of his jeans and, as I stride toward him, he tries to pull both out, unsure of my intentions. He gets one thumb free but the other is trapped between the denim strap and the tied-off bank bag. Garrett holds one arm between our bodies as I step in and hug him.

'Be strong,' I whisper. 'Buy everything.'

I walk out of the alley and toward my place of work, and for a moment the mass of clouds breaks and I imagine Mr Hand looking down at me, happy at what I have done, that I've taken moments out of my day to help the helpless.

At AmWe, Brogan is dancing in place. My smile's like a switch – OMG, what is it? Brogan informs me that a company down in San José has created a machine that allows one, through use of their gaming system, to power the room in which they are playing.

'It's totally still a prototype,' Brogan says. 'But they contacted us. They want us, no matter what, when it's ready, to do all of their advertising. Isn't that great?' Brogan says, then returns to pogoing. In front of the door to my office, Andrew sits at his desk. His eyes are bloodshot. He has on all black. He's knitting a shawl that reads GAY AND MARRIED. On the same night that Obama took the national vote, Prop 8, in California, had also gone through: there will be no gay marriage. Andrew's needles keep clicking as I approach him. He stares straight ahead, into middle distance. Behind, Brogan continues to dance. DeKwan gets up to join her and they do a half-tango.

'Hi, Andrew,' I say.

'Hey, Jim,' says my assistant.

'So, Prop 8,' I say.

'Yeah, Jim,' says Andrew.

'Forgive me here, Andrew? But you look unwell? And it's totally fine to BE unwell, but I don't know if you know that you look that way? And as something near leader of our village, Andrew, I feel compelled to tell you?'

Andrew keeps staring out at nothing at all. 'Go fuck yourself, Jim,' Andrew tells me.

'Excuse me, Andrew?' I say.

'I'm pretty sure you heard me,' says Andrew.

'You're hurt,' I say, because my mask is on, because I can't hit Andrew in the mouth without true repercussions. 'Your soul, it's weeping.'

'You know, Jim,' says Andrew, 'it's not. I keep waiting to cry.

But I don't feel anything at all. It's like my insides are pretty hollowed out, Jim.' Andrew blinks his eyes once and then looks up at me. 'Do you think I should be concerned about this, Jim? That I can't feel anything? Do you think it's okay to be empty?'

And I want to tell Andrew yes, this is how you get by, this is how you forget and give up and give in, that one's soul, now, is the ball from the Atari game *Pong*, and that it bounces uselessly back and forth inside of one's self until one's game is over. But my mask is on and it's a mask that covers not only my face but that leads down to my throat, to my heart, that pittering speck, that slicked, starving enclosure.

'I think it's okay to be anything that you want to be,' I tell Andrew.

'Could you tell that to California, Jim?' asks Andrew.

I pout out my lips, tilting my head. 'I wish I could,' I say. I pat Andrew's head twice and then walk to the door that leads down the short hall to the Red Room.

At my desk, the Internet up, I Google National AdCo, the company that owns and operates the electronic billboard near the Bay Bridge's entrance. I locate their number for New Accounts and then call this number and reach finally Brenda, who asks how I'm doing today. I tell her well. I tell her I'd like to buy ad space. She asks me where. I tell her at the foot of the bridge: ten-second spurts, three times a minute. I tell her my name is José Canseco.

'Okay, Mr Canseco,' says Brenda, brightening. 'Would you like to know our rates before proceeding?'

'I wouldn't,' I tell Brenda. 'I'd just like you to bill me, and take down what I want.'

'Well, this process takes a bit of time, usually,' says Brenda. 'We send you forms to get the ball rolling.'

'The ball is rolling, Brenda,' I say, 'and what I'm after is easy to make. I need a white background. I need the text in red. I want the red text to fill up the screen.'

'And what is the text going to say?' asks Brenda.

'The text should read, WATCH A MAN DIE. DECEMBER 15th. WWW.OMNICAST.COM/EXECUTION. Does such a thing seem accomplishable, Brenda?' But Brenda says nothing. Brenda is silent.

'If you need,' I say, 'I can talk to your boss.'

'Yes,' says Brenda, 'can he call you back? Can you give me ten minutes?'

I tell Brenda I can and the boss does call me back and after ten minutes more of swift back-and-forth, and a slightly increased per-second fee due to cloudy moral implications, my ad for Omnicast's Execution Event is ready to go live, and will be added to the ad cycle in 24–48 hours.

'Fax only. No snail mail,' I say, and then say goodbye and hang up. From my small office closet, I take out my tux. It's almost time to get ready to party.

19

The Evermore Towers UniTeeFest is an all-night event on the edge of the Tenderloin District, in San Francisco. Here, between California's State Supreme Court and Union Square's Neiman Marcus showroom, sits misery: shopping-cart fleets in silver and red, buoyed and dotting the narrow, filthy streets and captained by hunched, bearded men, their big cardboard signs, worn limp by age, written in thick and black Sharpie. The neighborhood's import is human unwell. The chief exports are drugs, liquor and pussy. I walk by a black woman with AIDS sores on her face. She asks me for change. I tell her, Obama. I walk by a crackhead in no shirt and torn jeans. He asks me for change. I tell him, Obama.

But shepherding all, giving to darkness light, and a voice to the mute, and eyes to those whose own eyes have filmed over to useless, is St Isidore Memorial Church, led, as it has been for decades, by Reverend Porfirio Gaines. Oprah Winfrey has given St Isidore her meaty golf clap, as have Maya Angelou and Bill Clinton. At Isidore, there's free testing for STDs, gratis health care and volunteer dentists. There are after-school programs for after-school teens, computer training and literacy classes. There is hope for the hopeless, grace for the scourge, joy for those who have been ground down so much and so far that joy does not feel human.

But tonight there is no St Isidore Church. If one were to look north, up Taylor, to Ellis, they would not see the house of worship's stone tower or rose window. They would not see the duos and trios of unwashed ne'er-do-wells, limping out of the church doors and back toward oblivion. In place of the church what one would see would be two sides of a brilliantly white, brand new apartment complex, the façade's thick vinyl walls held upright by air pumped out from generators. I've rented roof space on the Hilton just across the street, and now, at eight-thirty p.m., a quintet of spotlights spin wildly, illuminating the sky then the street and finally the fake walls of the soon-to-be-real Evermore Towers.

At four city blocks, from Ellis Street south to Turk Boulevard, and from Taylor west to Leavenworth, Evermore Towers, when finally built, will do more to displace the Loin's vice and graft than four generations of cops, social workers and mayors. No more shots fired, no more 5 a.m. fights, no men selling dope on vacant street corners. No longer an increase in heart rate as one walks from the bus stop to their two-room cage, trying to sleep through the melees and malaise, the indignant and incomprehensible yelling. There will be hundreds displaced, if not many more, but then the poor have always been portable.

Tonight, the Hilton's Grand Ballroom is also booked under my name: 30,000 square feet of blue and gold fleur-de-lis carpet. San Francisco loves an event, but unlike LA the event has to have real purpose: a charity concert to support runaway teens, an auction to raise funds for sustainment of biodiversity. NorCal needs cause, SoCal only mirrors. What I need more than anything else is for the very, very wealthy to buy space in my friends' real-estate investment, and there's no better ad than a party.

I'm standing near the oversized globe in the center of the

Hilton's lobby, watching the responsible rich pile out of hybrid limousines in eco-chic evening gowns and tuxedos. I sent Yi-Yi an invite but she's playing a tournament in Dubai. Here's Robert Redford, his magic hair, his visage still charmingly ruddy. Two states to the east, Park City is gearing up for this man's Sundance Film Festival, a cinematic extravaganza with Green overtones, counteracted only by the arrival of thousands of Hollywood types via private and gas-powered jets and SUVs, their exhaust roiling brown over Provo and Ogden and spreading all the way south to the heavens over Mt. Zion. And here is Hollywood's newest eco-gladiator. Her lipstick is cruelty-free, her shift dress organic. Her house off the East Coast is over 30,000 square feet, with an energy consumption rate over twenty times the national average. How does she get from one coast to another? By personal jet, the nonpareils' model using more fuel than the average Land Rover uses in a calendar year, more oil than it takes to make one million DVDs of Al Gore's *An Inconvenient Truth*, the star of the film currently arm in arm with afore-mentioned eco-warrior. The would-be President's chestnut eyes shine, his lips ichthyic. Made of Asian silk, his olive-green tie was stitched by a Cambodian woman earning thirty-three cents an hour. I shake hands with Alan Alda and then with Joan Baez. The chandeliers overhead look like jellyfish strung upside down, glowing to death as the party gets started.

Flitting hither and yon are my ad firm's bright bees, done up in the best eco-couture they possess, their hair coiffed, their nails and their faces painted. For them, getting to hug Marky Mark, or clink glasses with Google's overlords, or obtain, after small talk, the email address of Moby, are life items that outrank their own wedding day, their perfect childhood Christmas. Simerpreet Sweeney is here as well, in an all-black and backless low-cut Dior. Her Zanotti heels are patent black leather, four inches high with two narrow straps from her ankles to the base of her toes, where yellow jewels sparkle. I've booked her the penthouse suite right next to my own. On the reservation call, the attendant informed me that a door connecting her suite and mine could be unlocked or locked. I told the man locked, then called back ten minutes later and changed my decision.

Simer slinks toward me now, as I conclude talking up Evermore's in-house spa service to the Olsen twin not in *Coyotes*. I finish my tapas and I fold my small napkin in half.

'Your bow tie,' Simer says, putting her lips half an inch from my own, 'is crooked.' She straightens the accessory, her eyes a bright brown. My defenses are failing.

'How are we looking for a real start time?' I ask. 'I'd like to get this ball rolling.'

I smile at Simer and she smiles back, running a hand down the side of her hip. 'Whenever you'd like to,' she tells me.

We are both high from the promise of cash, from numbers jumping from checking accounts like lake trout at sunset on some bug-filled summer evening. We are sportsmen, are anglers, proud of our lures, and feel no twinge of remorse when the things that we've caught, have worked hard to catch, must be beat on the head, have their scales shaved to smooth, have their bellies cut open and their guts pulled out to make dinner.

The Hilton's main lobby of copper carpet is tri-tiered, descending as one approaches the desk. In an overstuffed chair tucked behind a tremendous curling fern sits Andrew, my currently sullen and very drunk assistant. He's wearing a strapless eggshell wedding dress, a NO ON PROP 8 sign hanging from his neck. His white heels have little pink bows on their straps. I lean in toward Simer, the end of my nose touching the skin just in front of her ear.

'Get him better or get him out,' I say. 'I'll be grateful.'

I lean away and Simer nods once and then her smile is gone, her lips pulling down, her eyebrows leveling. She is young enough that I could start over completely: a new family, new kids, a different rich suburb of some distant city. An acceptance that all good has drained from my life and the front I've put up is now who I am, the mask fusing with skin, the way back from this path dynamited with greed and with lies too long to traverse, the landscape too broken, too ugly. Simer walks over to where Andrew sits. She looks around once then hits him on the face, the blow close-fisted but glancing. Simer takes Andrew's drink and sets it sideways in the base of the fern. Andrew starts pouting. She gets him up and Simer looks toward me, then points one finger to the lobby ceiling. Upstairs, she mouths, and draws out her key card. I nod in approval. My walls are crumbling.

Fifteen minutes later, the Grand Ballroom's doors closed, I make my way up to the stage, to the microphone, to the podium. There is a version of me everywhere now, in every time zone, in Osaka, in Helsinki, and too in Belfast and Tel Aviv and Dallas and Hong Kong and Sydney. In Dusseldorf, right now, some German version of me is popping his sleeves and checking his smile, clearing his throat as the crowd starts to hush so that they may hear the words of their new eco-prophet, their channel to the heart and the soul of the globe, someone who through the supernatural or divine knows the path to the Earth's salvation, and can guide all those with the money to listen.

And I say, Hello. And I say, On behalf of the world, thank you for coming.

And then I say more, in tones spun, in tones golden. I tell the crowd of prospective Evermore residents that they have the chance to be part of a sea change, of one tremendous moment in San Francisco history, and since we are all now connected, are all now plugged in, and what happens here affects Rome, affects Norway, what Evermore offers, in essence and truth, is a chance to be a steward of the present, and thus the future.

'Many of you are already celebrities in the eyes of the masses,' I say, pointing my chin out to the crowd, my lips quivering in a manner where it looks like I am trying to hold back my tears, 'and now you have the chance to be celebrities in the eyes of the *planet*.'

Applause; a small roar ascends. I rub one eye with the back of my hand. I am pretending that I am crying. The last time that I actually cried I was fourteen years old, in a hospital lobby. The paramedic had dreadlocks. His first name was Paul. He told me that my parents were dead, a fact I already knew. Then he hugged me.

'You'll be okay,' he said.

'You're wrong,' I'd told him.

I turn my head partially away from the mic, making it look like I'm hiding my sniffling. I count off in my head – one, two, three, four – before turning back to the room and continuing.

'I'm sorry,' I say, and hope that the crowd can't see the dollar signs in my eyes. 'This just matters so much to me.'

I again talk of specs: the wood all bamboo, the insulation all recycled clothing. There will be rainwater-harvesting tanks, fog collectors on the roof of the building. There will be fruit trees in one corner of Evermore Wood, a small private park between the two towers, blocked off from the street by big granite walls made of 100% post-consumer waste, passers-by able to marvel only at the wall's sustainability, and not at the stars that walk inside its acres. A privatized grove. The red carpet of urban reclamation. The crowd makes little sounds as the list blooms to flower.

Ned Akeley, years back, during this country's tech boom, the epicenter of which was right here, in my region, became sure that the next piece of land to build up was the Tenderloin District. The first step in this process was buying all the small businesses in the area. My three closest friends in the world are now the co-owners of Golden Vegetarian Tofu and Yong Ling Ginseng and Daldas Grocery. They also own Club Vixen and Joy's Massage for Men, in addition to numerous coin-operated Laundromats and hole-in-the-wall pho eateries. And through the years they've added to their titles and deeds the district's apartment complexes, self-storages and auto bodies, promising, too, a brand new Police Department if the Tenderloin District Station can indeed be moved just one block southwest from where it is currently standing. The Mayor, at first, said no, but changed his mind after pictures of his model boy-toy found their way into his Montana ranch's mailbox, the week before he got married.

I go on with my speech: solar panels everywhere, pygmy turbines for the wind coming off of the ocean. A Michelin five-star bistro café in a wing just off of the lobby: the beef all grass-fed, the chickens all free-range, all happy. Evermore Towers, at present, is only half full; by the end of the evening, it won't be. I offer no slides. I speak from no cards. I know the dimensions, the layout, the numbers. And despite the Dow being down, the market anemic, and real estate of all sorts, even here, in the Bay, dropping in value from subprime and panic, Evermore Towers will succeed nonetheless. This is because of a single foundational truth: the celebrity rich want to remain who they are while assuaging all guilt for their way of being. From afar, they look powerful, but they're actually helpless. They are in charge but must be told what to do: a thousand Dauphins, their scepters bejeweled but so heavy.

I jump back and forth between logos and pathos, between fact and sentiment, the lights hot on my brow but not one bead of sweat forming on that patch of my skin, made smooth by a dozen types of near-toxic anti-aging creams, some of which are promoted by guests at these tables. Soon there will be champagne and handshakes, followed by a performance by the freshly reunited and original members of the band Guns 'N Roses. For the group's sinners and pervs a second banquet room has been rented, this one filled with the rich's playthings: whiskey and whores and cocaine, a craps table, Cohibas. I wrap up my speech with a quick quote from Brecht: 'Fear not death, but rather the inadequate life.' The house lights go up, and after the requisite round of applause, everybody starts talking.

Many clear out while the band begins to load in: I say goodbye to Robin Williams; I say goodbye to George Papadopoulos, Executive VP and CTO of Sun Microsystems. Each wants a spot, the higher the floor, the better. I say that I'll see what I can do: both are C-List, and at best good filler. Here is sound check, a bass drum, feedback from an amp. Axl Rose says Hello and Brogan starts screaming. Sean Penn wants to know when the back room opens up. I tell him, later. Near the door, as people begin to file out, is Michiko Hernandez, AmWe employee. From a row of brown boxes on a long foldout table she hands out shirts made by American Apparel. The T-shirts are black and silk-screened with grass-green eco-safe dye. Across the back are the twin Evermore Towers, their small wooded park. Across the shirts' fronts is the single word UNITEE.

Reverend Porfirio Gaines finds me during 'Paradise City.' His gray beard is thick, his hair nearly gone. His cashmere scarf sits draped over the broad shoulders of his black sport coat. His glasses look expensive.

'Is there a quiet place we could talk?' he asks me.

I tell him that there probably is, but that I have no interest in locating it now.

'I am here only to sell things,' I tell the Reverend.

'If you're invested in this community,' he says, 'then you should hear what all community members have to say, should you not?'

St Isidore itself will not be altered in any way; the Reverend and the church's other powers-that-be have agreed to the vinyl façade for the evening because AmWe had agreed to make, to the church, a very large charitable donation. And while, post-Evermore, St Isidore's walls will stay up, its doors always open, what the Reverend will lose, at least in part, is the flock over which he resides: his unwashed, his helpless. The Towers will make St Isidore more obsolete, and this means less exposure, less money from grants, less TV time to talk about the need to give to those who've been given nothing.

'The project's gone through,' I tell the Reverend. 'There's no changing change.'

'Correct,' the Reverend tells me. 'Talk goes so far and then watches action. I know a lot of people around here, Mr Haskin, and I know that you do, too, and I know that while you practice what you preach, you are, at heart, a businessman.'

'And you're saying you're a businessman, too,' I infer.

'I am saying I appreciate perspective,' says the Reverend. 'For instance, a few years ago, I was fortunate enough to ride in a hot-air balloon over the City. We saw many things: the trees in the park, the spires of the bridge from afar. And I saw, too, my church, from above, from a height and angle at which I had never seen it before. I enjoyed this height and perspective quite a bit, Mr Haskin. I am an old man now. I have aged. And I feel that I am in a position to afford myself another opportunity for height, for perspective. Do we understand what it is that I'm saying?'

GNR starts in on 'Live and Let Die' and the crowd's roar ascends, and I, too, start clapping. For a moment it's too loud to speak. Simer is standing in a back corner of a room, looking at me while she allows herself to be pawed by one of Adobe's very drunk co-founders.

'You've worked hard,' I say to the Reverend, after the decibels have dropped.

'I have,' the Reverend tells me.

'And you want reward,' I say.

'I want to be nearer to my flock,' says the Reverend. 'And want also to be on-hand – you might almost term it "on staff" – for this new community demographic. I want to be as near to them as I possibly can, while remaining loyal to those whom I already serve.'

'I can get you a suite. Nineteenth story,' I say.

'Top floor. Corner,' says the Reverend.

We smile at each other like we've both said something wise. The Reverend's eyes glisten.

'Everything on twenty and twenty-one has already been sold,' I say. 'There are signatures. There is paper.'

'And yet everyday miracles occur,' he tells me. He grasps the top of my arm with his hand, giving one pump and then letting go. 'I am glad, Mr Haskin, for the things that you do, for your good works on this planet.' Then he turns and heads for the Grand Ballroom's twin doors, taking a T-shirt and walking out to the lobby. A hotel social rep, waiting past earshot for my conversation with the Reverend to finish, now approaches.

'Mr Haskin,' the young male rep says, 'the second room's ready.'

I am thinking about profits lost, and also about what there

is to be gained by having the West Coast's most famous man of the cloth sipping brandy on the top floor of an eco-safe high-rise.

'Thank you,' I say. 'I'll tell those that need telling.'

Four hours later, the back room in full swing, the roulette ball pinging as the wheel makes its rounds, ice cubes in Scotch glasses popping and singing, I step out a side door that leads to an alley. I've had two gin martinis, the booze thinning my blood, the Beefeater and vermouth like a salve, like a potion. At the mouth of the alley, tucked close to one wall, is a McCain/Palin poster with feces spread on it. Palin is mustached; McCain wears a brown hat. Deep down, perhaps, we are all truly artists.

I finish my drink and throw the glass at the ground. It shatters to shards and I think of my son, his knees pinning Mark Norris's arms to cement, his fingers shoving glass down Mark's bleeding throat. I've never told Connor about my own bouts of violence, about snapping kids' bones in the bathrooms of group homes, about biting a chunk from the cheek of a boy who tried to steal my sneakers. And yet Connor has somehow learned this behavior – to fight before running and do all not just to win, but to make those who you fought remember those minutes of trenchant abuse for the rest of their lives, for forever. To hurt their body so badly that their psyche bears scars. To leave marks on the soul so that proof of the fight might be carried from this world into the next, and you'll be known when you're allowed into Hell, into Heaven.

I take out my BlackBerry and check my email: twenty-nine yeses for thirty-two vacancies. The Evermore Towers Unitee Fest has been the success I imagined. The side door I've come out opens again and Simer is backlit by the warm glow of the makeshift casino. She's holding two cigarettes between two slim fingers.

'Pall Malls,' she says. 'From Slash.'

'What's Slash?' I ask.

'No,' says Simer. 'The band. The guitarist.'

She sets her drink down on the alley's concrete and takes out a matchbook tucked in her bra. Simer lights both the Pall Malls and holds one out to me. I take it.

'How'd we do?' Simer asks.

'Only three more,' I tell her. I pull on the Pall Mall, my lungs filling with the smoke, the tissue expanding as it's blackened by tar. I breathe out and immediately inhale again. My head goes light and my arms go heavy. 'They're strong,' I say.

'You're not a smoker,' Simer answers. She's drinking Glenlivet and now drains her glass, letting the lowball's single ice cube slide past her lips, be pushed by her tongue, be released back into its double-walled receptacle. And then I do something that some part of me has apparently wanted to do for some time: I tell Simer everything. I tell her about my parents and Mr Hand's Home and my Vietnamese identity-theft ring. I tell her about Ned, about Frank, about Henry. I tell her about Esquido, his past and servitude. I tell her about the Prisoner, right now in his cell on Death Row, the ink on his skin sinking in, settling. I know this is something I should not do. I know that, through doing this, my future life is changing, and now, in the alley, the air cold from fog, I can feel my future self being reshaped as the words pour out of my mouth – one road closing down, a different route opening. Simer stands stunned, momentarily silent.

'You're lying,' she says. 'This is some sort of test. This is some sort of corporate loyalty thing.'

I shake my head. I tell Simer it isn't. 'Tomorrow I'm calling the *Chronicle*, the *Tribune* and the *Times*. This won't just make news into next year. This, Simer, will have its place in history.'

'Your parents,' Simer says. 'What happened to them?' Her work face is gone, that mask off her head. She looks terribly, erotically earnest.

'Car crash. I was in the car with them.'

'Someone hit you?'

'We went into a ditch.'

'Were they drunk? I mean, sorry, but were they?'

I tell Simer they weren't. I tell her no one was.

'Well, fuck, Jim, what happened?'

Out on O'Farrell, a cop car stops at the light. A fat woman, homeless, weaves into the bumper, falls down and gets up. She looks at the cruiser like it called her a name. The cop smiles and the woman keeps walking. I think of the Prisoner, alone in his cell. I think of my son in his room by the ocean. I think of myself, who I might have been, and who I am now, and the math of that difference.

'We just veered off,' I tell my Senior VP. 'There was road, then there wasn't.'

'I'm sorry, Jim,' Simer says and while I accept her condolences I'm not sure I'm sorry too, not positive that my first life, the one taken from me, would have been any better. But as I stand in the alley under patchy night fog, I decide that it's time for things to be different.

'Simer,' I say, crushing the Pall Mall underfoot, 'how would you like the firm?'

'What do you mean?' Simer asks me, flicking her butt at the side of a Dumpster.

'I'm retiring,' I say, unsure if I am until I actually say it. 'I'm moving on. How would you like to run American Weather?'

Simer looks at me slyly, her work face back on. Her mask narrows her eyes, lends her a wry smile.

'You're serious,' she says.

'I am,' I say. 'Sometime after New Year's. The sooner the better.'

'Don't bullshit me, Jim,' Simerpreet warns. 'Are we about to be broke? Are you faking the books?'

'The books are correct. We're in the black. We're down but I'm about to be richer than I've ever been and AmWe's going to feel that, I promise.'

'You promise,' Simer repeats, and points out a finger at me.

'I do,' I tell her.

'Come upstairs. Right now,' Simer says, and without smiling leads me back through the game room, past Axl Rose and Michiko and Brogan, past a tipsy Jim Lehrer and a wasted John Mayer and a security-restrained Whitney Houston, who keeps screaming the phrase, 'Gold, bitches' over and over. Through the lobby, behind the elevator doors, Simer keeps my hand locked in her own, as though my promise to her won't come true if she lets go of it. Inside my suite, clothing comes off until Simer says stop and slinks toward the door of the suite I'd booked for her. I tiptoe behind and we both peek in. On the still-made king bed, Andrew snores in his dress, his heels on the floor, his Prop 8 sign the thinnest of pillows. Simer slips the door shut and throws the deadbolt. She smiles at me and then heads for the bathroom, the shower. I take off my black leather Gucci slip-ons. I hear water start running. The door to my balcony is ajar, the midnight winds high, the cold air filling the room. It makes the bottoms of the white silk curtains jump the way that my heart is jumping.

Simer comes out of the bathroom in a thick ivory towel. I pull back the bed covers. I take a deep breath.

'Simer,' I say, but she cuts me off.

'Let's seal the deal,' she tells me.

I do what my Senior Vice-President asks. On the slick sateen sheet, the duvet pulled up over, Simer grabs my hand and then rolls on her side, her back turned toward me, my arm draped over her waist, my fingers touching her flat and smooth stomach, and it's this act, and not the one we'll do soon, that lingers with me after we've parted ways, after we've signed papers in my ad firm's Red Room, AmWe turned over to my Senior Vice-President. It's this act, the embrace, the draped arm meaning comfort, that assures to myself that I'm now machine, a dark metal thing full of diode and task, the acts I perform the sole love that I know, the deprogramming of love and of faith and belief just one of my programs.

20

And the Prisoner says, 'Once, when I was maybe ten, a van pulled up to my parents' farm while they were an hour north, up at Shopko. This was the summer after Reagan took office, I think. It could have been his second summer in, but he was definitely President. It was a drought year; it barely snowed, a dry spring. The van was a Chevy. Maroon. Silver side panels. Tinted windows. The windows went almost all the way down to the top of the wells, like the vans psychos drive in all of those movies.

'My mom and my dad got the land from my dad's dad, but they built the house we lived in themselves: four bedrooms, two levels. I was supposed to have a sister or brother, I think, but something happened. They couldn't. Maybe they chose not to, but I got the feeling they couldn't. Our closest neighbors were a mile away. The van had pulled up near our propane tank, sort of between the tank and one of the larger outbuildings, where we kept our old thresher.

'The guy driving the van was near forty, I'd say. He was no one I knew and not from my town and wasn't, I don't think, from South Dakota. The van had a Missouri plate on its front and a Tennessee one on its back door by the bumper. The man wore a white shirt and black overalls a size too big for him. From my bedroom upstairs, I watched him climb out of the van and look out toward the land, at the fields, at the fences. I'm thinking now that it was 1982. I'm thinking that maybe I was older than I thought I was when I started this story.'

It's a blue and a fine day, a break from the clouds, the air cold, Thanksgiving coming. Media for the Omnicast Execution Event has been live for ten days, the whole world agape and aghast and subscribing. The media outlets cannot get enough; all day there are live shots of Omnicast Headquarters, of San Quentin. Outside of both, protestors hold signs. Outside of both, protestors scream slogans. On most occasions prisoners, when put to death, wear standard prisoner clothing. My Prisoner, however, will wear only a thong. DKNY and Calvin Klein are vying to be the company supplying this thong. The bids are now war. The bids are increasing.

The Prisoner continues.

'And after looking around, the man didn't come to our front door straight off. He seemed more interested in the land than in people. From his overalls' pocket he took out a pad and a pen and started taking down notes while I watched him. He'd gone around to the back of the house. I'd had to leave my bedroom and go into the spare to see him. I was crouched on my knees, on top of the bed, and peeking through the blinds, looking down at him. He was back by the laundry line and our guinea coop. My parents always kept the blinds in that room closed. On a table next to the bed was this all-green lamp. Our neighbor, Len Dunkel, came up the road that our driveway connected out to. The man saw Len's truck and went around to the north side of our house, so Len couldn't see him as he went by, and I knew for sure then that something wasn't right, and I got off the bed to get my dad's gun, the pistol that he didn't keep in the big Bulldog safe in the basement. As I went to get up, I knocked over the lamp.

It broke on the floor, and the man stopped walking and looked up at the window.'

Simer sits in the chair at my desk, redesigning my ad firm's logo. Her gauzy black tunic drapes to mid-thigh, over a pair of bright silver leggings. The single Dow 30 firm that I'd not offered space to had been the biotech firm that had made Supinal. They're now on board, to the tune of six million – an outlandish fee for the skin space they receive, but the best act of revenge that I can come up with.

The Prisoner continues.

'Our living room took up the west side of the ground floor. It had cream-colored shag, super-thick, almost bouncy. I remember our coffee table was the wheel of a wagon, and we had this olive-green leather couch, the base of which was the tops of three wooden barrels. My mom collected dolls; they stood around the TV, sat on small benches under the heads of animals that my dad had shot. I never got to go back there, after they died, because I was locked up and they said I could go to the funeral but not to the house, not see all the things that we'd shared when we were family. To just see them in caskets, my dad, then my mom, that wasn't worth shit to me.

'And I walked downstairs and into that room and I'm standing there with that little .38, peeking out the living-room window. Len Dunkel's truck passed and the man went back over to his van, and opened the driver-side door, and halfway climbed in, his ass in the air, and then crawled back out with what looked to be blueprints or portraits. There was no way to tell because a white oilcloth was over them. Then he walked up to the door and started knocking. And it was so hot out and we didn't have central air, and the house, on the inside, was starting to warm up, there's that delay, you know, from outside to in, and the man, he's knocking and knocking, and

I'm not sure what to do, should I wait, should I call Len Dunkel. I wanted to do something, but didn't know what to do. I knew that things were about to go wrong, but I didn't know how I could stop them.'

The *Chronicle* now has a column, front page, devoted to the Event that I've helped create. My 1% fee sits in a high-yield IRA opened by the great State of California. The account's purpose, on paper, is Discretionary Funds, and I plan, in five years, to use them discretionarily. In the meantime the State and Omnicast take abuse, but it's abuse with payoff, abuse well worth taking. I haven't been home to the East Bay for ten days. I've only been here, watching the Prisoner gain ink, watching the boy guard watch Reuben working. The Prisoner's sent checks to the SPCA; the Prisoner's sent checks to California's Green Party. The Prisoner's sent checks to his old friends in SeaChange, but then, we all find ways to discard our hard-earned money, even my Prisoner, who now continues.

'And the knocking, I swear, kept getting louder and louder, three loud booms then a pause then three more of them. And just when I thought I couldn't take it anymore, silence. I heard the van door open and then close again. Our kitchen was on the house's north side and from its big window I watched the man in the black overalls walk over our property, touching at things: our propane tank, the lock on the shed that held our old thresher. We had a basketball hoop, too, between the chicken coop and the tank, and a little slab of asphalt that a friend of my dad's had poured, so that I'd have a court and the ball wouldn't just land on grass and bounce funny, and this man decided that before he'd do what it was he was there to do, he'd pick up the ball and start shooting, and did this ten, twenty, thirty times, this strange man in farm clothes that didn't fit him at all, standing on the land my family owned, playing with things he shouldn't.

'When I run over this again in my head, I try to figure out its purpose: why the man stopped and took shots when he was there, in essence, to destroy my family's farm and the farms around it. This detail, for me, is not unimportant, as it signifies one of two things, the intent of each very different from one another. The first of these is that the man was just further safeguarding. He was making as sure as he possibly could that no one was at home: no hiding dog, no lurking children, and the sound of the ball being bounced against the concrete might persuade the dog to come show itself, or might lower the defenses of the child – this man plays games, this man knows about the court, this man is not dangerous. But there's another possibility, too, and one I didn't consider much until later, after I was locked up and my days were just thinking. And this other possibility is that the man was safeguarding against himself, that he was making himself, consciously or subconsciously, do something human or common or fun, was remembering himself before he had to forget, was telling himself a new different story because the story of which he was part wasn't one that he wanted to be in.'

With media installed for the Prisoner's impending death, other firms have come forth to vie for space on the Prisoner's body: CVS Caremark and Berkshire Hathaway; Marathon Oil and Walgreen and Lockheed. The dinosaurs; the heavy-heavies. But in recent days, too, a new breed of firm: green industry. Here now, on the Prisoner's skin, amongst the logos for Big Coal and Burger King, for Motorola and Pepsi, are small bits of skin bought by turbine firms: Eagle West Wind, Shermco Industries. And appearing now, too, near the pits of the arms, on the lobe of one ear, on a knuckle, are some of the players in solar: Suntech Power Holdings and Solarworld AG, and here First Solar Inc., and here Yingli Green Energy Holding. And more things like this: hydropower firms; eco-safe e-malls, the space that they buy just a website address. The space they take up, by comparison, is tiny, and when one looks at the Prisoner quickly, at a glance, these firms' small ads are easy to miss, overwhelmed as they are by the MetLifes, the Macys. But when one looks more closely, when one lets the eye sit, when one gives the eye and by extension the mind the chance to draw it all in, these new things, these small firms, are there – are B-tier, but something near to collective.

The Prisoner continues.

'The man stopped shooting after maybe ten minutes. His last shot hit the rim, then the asphalt slab, then rolled off into the grass, and then stopped rolling. The man walked off the court and toward our biggest outbuilding, in the way back, where the grass was much higher and my dad kept a rusting '49 Ford, a thing that his dad once had, and drove until it died, and then used the parts out of. In the air there were swifts and shrikes, calling. At the outbuilding the man turned east, toward the coop, and as he did this he pulled from the front pocket of his overalls a single small package of seed and, once at the fence that separated our crop from our yard, poured the contents of this package in the ground, then bent down on his knees and loosened the soil, kneading the seeds into the earth and covering them back up, and leaving.

'I heard the van leave and, once it was out of sight, I walked around to our house's front door, against which leaned the oilcloth-wrapped paintings. Or I imagined them paintings: I don't know why. They weren't. What they were were aerial photos of our land: two of them, each as big as a canvas in a museum. I'd taken off the cloth and stood there, holding the photos in my hand, and at first I didn't realize it was my land – the perspective was one that I'd never seen, and I was trying to figure out why the man left these here, and whether or not he forgot them. I had shorts on that day, and the oilcloth was brushing up against my leg and, as I changed my stance, something brushed me that was sharper than cloth. It was a business card. It read: GOD'S EYE VIEW: AERIAL PHOTOS FOR FREE. GIVEN TO YOU BY THE CHURCH OF LATTER DAY SAINTS. Then there was a phone number one could call, to pledge donations.

'I put the card in my pocket and wrapped the photos back up, and then walked over to the spot where the man had put seeds in the ground. The topsoil was still loose, and lying on the dirt was one of the seeds which our entire fields would become, every last stalk, everything. In court, my dad – who had held out against using the ag firm's seed because he was smart, and saw where all this was going, and knew that this level of homogeneity in seed was the end of seed biodiversity, and was unsustainable – defended himself against the charges that were brought up against him. This is how the thing worked: the company got its seed on one's land, and then claimed that the farmer, in this case my dad, was using the seed illegally. The ag firm, even back then, had a few of these patents on their seed. South Dakotans were prototypes for what they're doing now, nearly everywhere. All that company had, really, to do, was get other farmers in the area to buy the seed, then they could make the case that the farmer who would not sign on was using a patented product illegally. There wasn't a need to buy off the courts: the firm brought in lawyers and scientists. This was years later. I was eighteen. The court awarded the company more than my dad could ever repay. We were already broke from the lawyers' fees ourselves. We owed more than what we made from five seasons of crops. My folks sold off the land but stayed in the house. My mom got a job teaching math in town, at the school.

They died in debt. They died in misery. And now, when you drive through my part of South Dakota, when you drive past the fields that families tended and still tend, you are seeing the product of one single corporation: wheat that won't grow without a pesticide that this ag firm makes; wheat that won't grow for more than one crop cycle, the seed needing to be bought again, the firm increasing its profit. When one drives through that land, now, what one's driving through isn't land at all. It's a company.'

It's 4 p.m.; Reuben turns off the ink gun. Sam Flanagan puts down his magazine. Omnicast, per my asking, has set up a password-encrypted web page that allows me to track subscriptions, state by state. Simer checks this page now, her finger clicking the mouse, the page scrolling.

'California is first still, but Texas is close,' she says. 'Then Florida. Then Virginia. Then Missouri.'

The Prisoner stands up, the guard checking his shackles. Aside from bits of the thigh, parts of the back, and the length of some fingers, the only space left is the Prisoner's pale face. These last few parts will be inked during the following days.

'Jesus,' he says, seeing himself in the mirror. He holds his arms up, the guard standing on the edge of the bed and sliding his bright orange prison-issue shirt down over his arms. 'What a mess.'

'Jesus,' I say, 'isn't here.'

Reuben leaves first, then the guard and the Prisoner, and Simer and I are again all alone, our clothes coming off as the door clicks itself shut, the moon already up in the late-afternoon sky, hazy and pale and indifferent.

21

Dear Dad,

Here's the real war: no Baghdad or Green Zones, no drone bombs in the Waziristan mountains; no surges of troops or opium fields, no Taliban, no NATO peacekeeping force, no tanks rolling down village streets, no exit strategy. Here is the real war: blood cancer in northeast PA, just off I-80 and upstream from Philly. In Hazleton, thirty years back, an abandoned coal mine was turned into a toxic-waste repository. Not far away is an active power plant fueled by waste coal. Not far from that is a recycling plant that through the decades has accepted perhaps one million gallons of used oil and paint sludge, pesticides and cyanide, solvents and BPAs and PCBs. And we've made these things, Dad: the coal mine and the waste, the oceans of unused paint, the fields of spent, crinkled pop bottles. And these things that we've made have made things in us: the type of blood cancer that's found here in droves, in virtually impossible numbers, has the nickname PV, short for polycythemia vera. What PV does is overproduce red blood cells in a person's body. There's a mutation in the gene called JAK2, causing bone-marrow cells to constantly produce red blood cells, even when the body signals the marrow stop. That is, Dad, it's a cancer of excess.

I know this because there was a town meeting at the Hazelton, PA Holiday Inn, the night that I happened to seek refuge there, pulling my newly bought used Prius into the hotel parking lot after sunset. I dropped my bags in my room and went downstairs to ask where there might be somewhere to eat, and before I even got to the desk saw the sign for the meeting. At a diner, much later, I had coffee and pie, neither of which I finished, then returned to my room, turning the TV on and off, and then getting up and running the water from the bathroom tap, and looking at it, Dad, and considering.

The next day, at a family-owned hardware store, I bought six feet of copper wire.

Here is the real war: Gary, Indiana's wrecked Methodist church, its stained glass all smashed, its pews torn apart and sold off for firewood. Chunks of stone from where the roof has caved in sit on the dirt floor (that wood also gone) like the petrified droppings of some giant and unseen mythological bird that inhabits the nave's sagging rafters. The stone cornices still stand, arched and intact, but there will be no further worship. The sacristy's door has been ripped from its hinges, and there in that small room a mop on the floor, and lying on top of the mop a moldering book of child's Bible verses, the spine shot, the covers fanned out and curving. It lay, Dad, like it was in the middle of being read, like someone had set it down for only a moment, and in that moment the world had ended.

And this feeling, too – that the end had arrived – as I walked across the street to the Gary Academy of Dance & Theater, its roof falling down, the paint peeling off of its walls, the base of the stairwells covered in three feet of rubble. A post office building was also condemned, as was the Jackson Five Theater, and they were places of such remarkable decay it was easier to imagine that I was gazing out at the catacombs under Rome, or Caracol, in Belize, or the Slope Houses of Turkey. Except that I wasn't, Dad. I was twenty-five miles from Chicago's downtown. I was in America's heartland.

I walked the streets for an hour and saw no passing cars and when a police cruiser pulled up at a bent-over stop sign and I walked toward the car, the cop looked at me and sped off up the street. Next to a bar with its name – The Old Shine – spray-painted on the door was a gun shop. Inside, everything was caged off: thick chain-link fence stood between the shop's elderly owner and me. Firearms coated the walls. Next to the register was an imitation grenade; attached to its pin was a yellow ceramic square, designed to look like a Post-It. In computer-inked script, the fake Post-It read: GARY BEAUTIFICATION SOCIETY. I nodded at the man and he nodded back. I asked him if he had gunpowder. He didn't ask why or if I had ID. He only asked, Black or Smokeless?

Here is the real war: the strip east of Quincy, Illinois, the endless enormous marquees, four miles of OPEN signs and drive-thru pharmacies, the gym next door to the Wendy's, the PayDay Cash Advance next to a law office specializing in personal bankruptcy. The pickups sleepwalk past the Bed Bath & Beyond, on their way back out to the country. And it was this way in Muncie and St Joseph, MO, in Dayton, Ohio and Liberty City: the Starbuck's, the Dollar Store, the Asian Buffet. The Blockbuster Video. Miles upon miles of roads tarred and paved, of card-swipe machines, of bank ATMs, of comic-book shops, of gentlemen's clubs, of tax-filing firms, of discount shoe marts, of telephone lines, of wireless connections, of passwords and keypads and silent alarms, of junk mail and mall lots and food wrappers; of franchised hotel chains, of sofa outlets, of new and used cars, of stoplights and walk signs, of thick painted lines in yellow, in white, of chirping electronic bells, of gas pumps and smoke shops and screensavers. Someone told us that this is what we want, so we drive and we drive toward the Best Buy, the Target.

And as I drive, Dad, I think of Sally on the Upper West Side, threads growing from pores while she shops online, the feeling of bugs crawling over and under and right through her veins while she goes boutiquing. We are possessed by strange diseases, and are thus strange disease. We see new symptoms each day or week, but can locate no accurate root of the problem. But the problem, Dad, is all around us, and inside. The man that I bought the car from in Newport, that faraway place, that place where decisions have been made about me in my absence, sold it to me for three grand, to get through his next two mortgage payments. His wife grew up in Woburn, Mass., the water there wrecked by toxic hydrocarbons. This man's wife, from cancer, had both breasts hacked off, their insurance paying squat, the condition pre-existing. The man's uncle, living downstream from a power plant in upstate New York, now has a half-dozen tumors in his brain. We are sprouting odd growth, Dad. There are parts of us missing.

In Cedar Rapids, Iowa, home of General Mills, the air smelled like burnt Cocoa Puffs. At a pet store there I bought a Co2 tank, the 50 lb. size, Dad, the biggest they had. The store clerk asked what type of fish I kept and I told I him I don't, that the tank was a present, and I suppose, Dad, that for news outlets it would have been, once combined with the car battery bought at a Sears in North Platte, the huge package of nails purchased in Rawlins, Wyoming.

In a Chevron outside Ogden, Utah, I stopped to fill up and to pee, the store clerk handing over the key though the door was unlocked, the restroom already occupied by an old man in blue jeans, his belt unhooked and splayed, pants down at his ankles. His red and white gingham shirt had mother-of-pearl button snaps, its side seams starting to tear and to fray. The old man was masturbating. He stopped his quick tugs when I opened the door and looked me in the eyes and smiled a big smile and then said, ya got me. On his head was a navy-blue mesh trucker's hat that read PATRIOT in gold lettering.

We are proud of our guilt, Dad. It lends us a self. We hold forth our criminal shame like a trophy. And there's no stopping this and there's no cure for this, no dam or moat, no leech or procedure. This is what it means to be American, now: our dicks in our hands, our minds lost to conjured, self-serving realms while our gas tanks fill up and the numbers turn over. We'd be arrested but we're the police; we'd be tried and sentenced, but we are the judges. It's being covered in blood not winning the war that has made us the victors.

I was going to head north to Twin Falls, Dad, to see where you and Mom honeymooned, but a blizzard was on its way in and so I drove south on I-15, and the next day I was at the Grand Canyon. I went on to Flagstaff and then east on I-40, not ready yet to return to the coast, to what I imagined my end, to the broken wrecked blue of the Pacific. I drove through Albuquerque and on to Santa Fe, where I spent the night and in the morning pulled back my small room's curtains. A sign, green and white, read LOS ALAMOS NATIONAL LAB, and offered an arrow, but when I checked out in the dawn light and went to my car, it was being broken into. I stood on the hotel's black asphalt lot, watching two kids no older than me try to wiggle a hanger down past the rubber over the window.

'Where do you need a ride to?' I asked, the would-be car robbers turning around, the wire, unwound, sticking up in the air like an antenna. Both boys wore band shirts and big baggy black pants. Metal bands, Dad: The Red Chord and Pig Destroyer. Bands I'd found myself over the previous months, bands of great speed, bands of great volume. Bands known by none at my previous school, that place I can never go back to.

'You going to call the police?' the taller boy said.

'What,' I asked, 'are you not understanding in my question?'

Amado and Marlon are Tucson runaways. Brothers, their parents were killed in Metro Manila, outside Quezon City, and the boys were brought to the States by Baptist missionaries when they were four and five, respectively, their native tongue loosed from the pans of their brains and their bodies used over and over by the minister at their foster parents' church. These criminal acts began at ten and ended last week, when Amado and Marlon told their surrogate caregivers what the church's leader had done, and Mr and Mrs Bill White had disowned them. The brothers were given five twenties each, two pairs of warm clothes, and had their Bibles taken. The boys took a bus east. They had no plan. They got off in Santa Fe to buy bags of fast food and did not make it back, the bus leaving without them.

The next day the two boys met more of their kind: lost desert youth who'd been sold off, kicked out, forgotten: fourteen-year-olds on their third year of meth; suicide attempts who had fled the white halls of psych wards. They caravanned through the flat and cold streets, panhandling, parsing the contents of Dumpsters. At per-night motels off of St Michael's Drive they slept six to a bed, one of the girls, Joy, only fifteen, giving head to men who would put the room in their names. At night, the TV low, the tin ashtray full, they spoke of parents who had slid under their sheets, orderlies who had burned them with cigarettes. When they ran out of money, then

253

ran out of drugs, the members of their small tribe turned on each other. Amado and Marlon went their own way, but not before hearing about the place that they were trying to get to when I happened upon them, the very same place that we're all at now, a place, Dad, where I'm staying.

The directions were sparse and cited no names of roads; in their stead were descriptions of wrecked barns and large trees, a weather tower and a field harboring emu. We climbed past red dirt mottled with snow, Amado guiding from shotgun, Marlon in the back seat, his head leaning out over the armrest. The road's asphalt stopped, the car spitting mud, the bomb-making equipment bouncing around in the trunk, lifting and dropping my heart, and after twenty minutes more Amado told me to stop: to our right, past a very deep bar ditch, were tracks made by truck tires. I got the Prius sideways on the wet county road. There were no other cars. The sky was flat gray, clouded over. Amado and Marlon both looked at me when I popped the trunk's hood and turned off the ignition.

'There're some things in the back that I have to take out,' I said. 'I'm riding too heavy.'

The three of us got out of the car, the two brothers helping me carry the CO_2 tank and nails and car battery down into the ditch, where they couldn't be seen from the roadside.

'What's this stuff for?' Marlon asked me, but his older brother shushed him.

I backed up the car as far as I could, setting the gear shift to neutral. I stamped down on the pedal, and ahead of us, Dad, was nothing at all: a dip in the road, a light beard of frost on the tracks that led out to the mesa. Amado had both hands on the dash; Marlon, in the back seat, was whispering prayers. I threw the gear into drive, and then we were flying.

And I would like to say, Dad, that faith afforded the leap, that the cosmos could understand its metaphorical worth, its importance – that it took a break from its black holes and dwarf stars in order to help us. It didn't. The front bumper of the Prius hit the ditch's far side, and the three of us were thrown forward then back, the car rolling a few feet then stopping. Somewhere near the engine, metal parts creaked. No air bags deployed. A hawk shrieked from the outlands.

We spent the next hour trying to move. The Prius had come to rest in a manner where its front wheels sat perched on the far side of the ditch and its back wheels on the side that we'd leapt from. We got the car on flat ground, parallel with the road, but runoff from snow made the ditch's flat impossible to climb out of. In my glove compartment, I had a bag of trail mix. We sat there as sleet fell, the engine on, the heater running. Near five p.m., the sky growing dark, we heard the churn of tires over dirt. I got out of the car just as the grille of an old-model Ford showed up at the lip of the ditch we were trapped in. The truck stopped then backed up, its driver moving to the left, spotlighting us in the soft light of dusk. Amado and Marlon stood to my side. The truck's driver was a white guy in black jeans and black boots, a wool-collared red and black checkered jacket. The guy's name is John Pace. I am sitting in his school bus right now, Dad, as I write you this letter.

Pace's truck had a winch and he pulled the Prius up and out of the ditch, the three of us scrambling after it. Level again, on the desert's cold dirt, Pace got out of his truck and looked at us, then down into the ditch, where he saw the bomb-making equipment.

'Who were you going to blow up?' he asked, knowing somehow to look straight at me as he said the question. Pace has a mustache and blue-silver eyes. The stubble that grows on his cheeks has gone gray.

'I don't know,' I told him, and it was the truth. 'I think what it was that I wanted to blow up wasn't really a thing but a bunch of ideas.'

Pace laughed at this answer then climbed in his truck and turned over the engine. Amado leaned in the Prius and pulled out the map. Both of the boys, still only in shirts, had goose bumps over the backs of their arms. Marlon was shaking. Pace leaned out the window, his cowboy hat off, the roof of the truck too low for him to wear it. The gray sky held a violet sheen. The truck's headlights shone in our faces.

'Follow me out,' he said, over the noise of the engine, and then the three of us were back in the Prius.

We passed by scrub brush, groves of small trees, low cliffs with their tops sheared to flat by eons of wind. Half an hour passed and then lights showed up on the horizon: an encampment, Dad, the husks of wrecked cars, old cargo vans raised up on cinder blocks, a big fire burning. Three dogs, all mutts, shadowed my car as Amado and Marlon pressed their hands to the windows. A quartet of RVs had been shaped to a square; there was a couple standing in its ad hoc courtyard. We passed more buses and cars as we followed Pace down the camp's makeshift road, toward a graffitied semi-truck trailer. Pace turned his truck off and signaled for me to cut my engine. I did. I was exhausted, the country a map in my head, parts of me still in Utah, in Nebraska, back east, where playoffs for soccer should by now be starting. Pace took a ring of keys from one of his jeans belt loops, then took a lock off the door of the trailer. Inside were eight mattresses, arranged in two rows, battery-powered LED lights, mismatched pieces of carpet. Old dirty area rugs, insulation, hung from the walls of the trailer. Coiled in one corner were a dozen sleeping bags. Pace walked over to these, pitching one to each of us.

'They've been sprayed for bugs,' he said. 'In the morning, you wash 'em.'

'I'm not staying in here if you're locking us in,' said Amado.

'Lots of folks say that,' Pace told him, then left, dropping the lock in the dirt at the lip of the trailer.

The three of us finished off the bag of trail mix over the course of the hour, our legs crossed on the carpeted floor, our eyes on the big glowing bonfire perhaps thirty yards away, near the quartet of trailers. At one point, I smelled beans. At one point, I heard a guitar being played. At one point, one and then two of the dogs started barking. But we were tired, Dad, as I already said, and Amado and Marlon had been tired for weeks, if not for most of their waking lives, and we fell asleep within minutes.

In the morning a woman in a mumu and military boots brought us bowls of oatmeal on a green serving tray that doubled as a board for backgammon. The woman was white, wore glasses, was huge, her silver hair nearly reaching her navel. She knocked on the trailer's tall iron door, Amado sitting up, Marlon rolling over.

'I'm Dotty,' she said, and we all said our names, and she nodded her head and then said mmm-hmm, and walked back toward the trailers. It was dawn. It was freezing, the sun out, the clouds gone. The world was quiet. We ate our oatmeal in silence and stared out at the camp, at the desert.

Amado, Marlon and I now have our own double-wide, in exchange for clearing acres of brush and helping to build a huge rainwater collector. Pace learned engineering in the first Iraq war: he's taught me how to weld, how to wire. Nights, we build bonfires. People sing songs. There's families here, a handful of children. The desert is the only world that they know and I imagine them, Dad, once they're grown up, going down off the mesa and into the city, the tang of pollution thick on their tongues, the bright lights of shops blinding their eyes, their vision. Is it a world they'll want, Dad? It's not one that I do. I pawned the Prius to buy a plane saw. I sold my iPod to buy lentils and flour.

No taxes, no Internet, no tap water, no bleach; no blowers for snow, no satin sheets; no hangers for shoes, no bright blue eyeliner; no porn magazines, no SATs; no DMV, no cubicle spaces; no plasma flat-screen color TVs, no bribing of public officials; no bank fraud, no cat litter, no Microsoft Word; no Red No. 5, no black-on-black violence; no brightly striped ties, no bras with rhinestones; no trade embargos, no closed-circuit cameras; no lab rats, no laugh tracks, no surgical lasers; no riot gear and no tear-gas grenades; no gridlock, no small talk, no Sick Building Syndrome; no Blackwater guards, no voting machines; no districts rezoned, no breast augmentation; no factory smog, no Porsche sedans; no modified food, no holidays sales; no sloth and no greed and no lust and no envy.

No thinking in lists, Dad, the whole world just data.

Just a cold and clear afternoon on this, the fourth Thursday in November. Pace shot two turkeys; tonight, there's a feast: homemade cornbread, squash with brown sugar. Below is the address for a PO Box where I can be reached. I'm sorry to send all these letters at once. Please, give mom my love, Dad. Then pull her plug. There is no solace in perpetual sleep.

Love, All My Love,

Connor

DECEMBER

DECEMBER

22

Lambs, it is Time. Get your cars home; stamp your boots free of snow. Set your purse down. Take off your necktie. Pour bags of chips into big plastic bowls. Fill glasses with ice for your beer, for your soda. Worry not about your mother's hospital bills, your children's homework. Caring and aid are not, for tonight, on your schedule. Order in food. Be sure to tip poorly. Invite over friends that you've known all your life and now don't really know, your lives disparate, drifting. Keep your laptop beside you for status updates. Make links to your blog; your input's important. Use spellcheck to counteract your mind's shortcomings. Slide closed your curtains; the TV is light. The TV, tonight, is a sun big enough for the full of the cosmos. Use your remote to type in your pass code. Put up your feet. Get comfy.

The color of the walls of San Quentin's Death Room are a jaundiced sort of green, a very light avocado. The gurney, green also, has black nylon straps. Its wheeled frame is black metal. There's room for this bed and standing space for five, including San Quentin's executioner, a man with a guard badge who wears no black mask, and carries not an axe but a needle. The room's steel door is side-hinged and hermetically seals and has the look of something one would see on a pod used for deep-sea exploration, its driver dropped down into cold silent depths, on a long and dark journey.

Esquido is gone. There was no note left, no words to indicate intent or destination. I am left to assume that his old gang has found him. I told this to Frank Gaines, currently seated to my left in San Quentin's Viewing Area, early this morning, after coming home briefly to my mailbox full, my brick steps plastered with banded newspapers. Frank has put out a soft search across twenty states.

'But in truth,' Frank had said, 'if your feeling is right, we won't find a body.'

Samampo, my São Paulo maid, has agreed for the short term to fill in, spending her nights on a cot in the room Denise sleeps in, my wife's physician on speed-dial on Samampo's cell, a nurse, for a large sum, coming by after her shift at Alta Bates to change the drip bags, the breathing tube, my wife's catheter. To Frank's right is Ned, then Henry. On the way in, through San Quentin's gates, our hired sedan was splashed with red paint by protestors. They lined the dirt shoulder from the bridge to the prison, hundreds of them, other cars speeding by, honking in solidarity. With our sedan past the gate, Henry had rolled down the window, sticking out a finger and then wiping red paint onto each cheek.

'Lord of the Flies,' he'd said, jubilated. 'Give me the conch.' He'd punched Frank in the shoulder, the two playful, grab-assing. Ned Akeley had looked at me and then smiled.

'Survival of the fittest,' he'd said.

'Survival of the fittest,' I'd told him.

This morning, after I'd checked on my wife, and opened the manila envelope containing eight letters from Connor, and sat down on the floor of my dining room and wept, wept fully and wholly, wept tears of failure because that's what I am – a fuck-up, an orphan who lost his way long ago and came to rely on a false set of standards, and who came to learn hope through the crushing of the hopes of others – after these tears, I went onto my deck, and looked down at the set of four weeping cherries, still and bare in their planters. Seated on the brick base of the oversized porcelain urn that stood in the center of the trees, the urn in which I plan to dump the ashes of my wife, was the Burgstroms' first son, Heath, highball glass in hand, grass-green wool slippers over his feet. He sat there in brown and orange plaid boxers, his navy-blue pea coat draped over his shoulders. He was looking down at his parents' Tudor's lap pool, swishing his Scotch around in his glass. I'd gone back inside and then to my wet bar, located just off of my kitchen, and found there a half-full bottle of Glenlivet, and walked down the wood stairs to my home's basement level and then out the door that led to the urn and the cherries. Heath turned his head sideways as I approached, the ground around the tree's planters covered in gravel of very deep grey, the small stones crunching under my feet. I sat down on the brick base, putting the bottle of Scotch between us.

'I'll leave,' Heath had said.

'It's fine,' I'd said back.

'Merrill dropped me,' Heath said. 'I just found out. Well, that's not true. I found out four days ago. I told my wife and she took off her ring. Then I flew to Vegas. The check Merrill gave me was low sixes, 250. I stayed at the Mirage. Do you know the Mirage?'

'I know the Mirage,' I had told him.

'I think that Vegas isn't where people go to feel good,' Heath continued. 'I think it's where people go to confirm that the world is insane, and that they're okay with it.'

There were goose bumps over the back of Heath's calves. I took the cap off the bottle and poured some in his glass, which

Heath handed to me. It was eight in the morning. There was fog off the Bay, long strings of damp gray drifting over the roof of my house, up towards the hills. I took a long sip of Scotch, its warmth coating the walls of my stomach.

'I got one of the Villas. Do you know those? They're five grand. Five thousand dollars for one night of sleep. It's what rich people make in a year in Ghana, in Haiti. I had my own butler, my own backyard. There was a putting green back there, a fountain. Waterford crystal chandeliers. A gas fireplace. I ordered an escort. Her name was Lisa. She showed up and I sent her back out to get coke. I put ten thousand dollars in her hand and said make it quick, and bring back a friend. I didn't feel anything when I said this.'

'Do your parents know you're here?' I asked.

Heath shook his head. 'I left the rest of my clothes in front of their house. I didn't want to wake them up. I'd never been up here, you know? I'd never seen what my childhood home looked like from this perspective. My parents always said don't go near the fence. Don't go near the fence: it's electric.'

'Sorry about your dog,' I said.

'About our puppy,' Heath said, nodding. 'Our puppy. It was a Burmese. Its name was Dollop, a dumb name, I know now. That dog would have gotten near 200 pounds. It was a name that didn't anticipate things. It was a name with no long-term viability.'

'How drunk are you?' I asked.

'I don't know,' said Heath. 'I remember the security line in Las Vegas. Then I was in a taxi. But the Mirage,' Heath continued, 'Lisa came back. Her friend's name was Jamie. Both of them looked like dolls. I mean, they had the features of dolls. They had these huge eyes. They were short, like barely five feet. They had these impossible measurements. We did the things you'd think we would do. The coke made them glow. They'd grown up in Texas. I stayed there three nights. At dawn, on the last day, we ordered Crab Louie.'

Heath drank down the Scotch like it was juice. He finished the glass and I poured another. He turned on the brick base of the oversized urn. His eyes were bright pink. They looked sad. They looked frightened.

'Do you think this is it?' Heath then asked me. 'I sold stocks. For six years, I sold stocks. I was trained to understand volatility. I was trained to diversify, to take calculated risks, to take people's money and make money with it. I want this to be it. If I can't have that power back, I don't want, I think, anyone to have it.'

'This isn't it,' I told him.

'I'm going to be getting a check from the state. I'm going to go through a divorce. She'll take all the money. I am going to have to move back home. I'm twenty-nine. My life is over.'

'Your life,' I told Heath, 'is just beginning.'

'I went out to EDD, near where the As play, right by the airport, the Coliseum. I did this right before I went to Vegas. Hordes of black people. I mean no offense. Truck drivers. Welders and shit. I sat at a computer made maybe during Clinton's first term. There was a job for a bank-teller spot in Sonoma. A goddamn fucking bank-teller spot. Hello, Mr Smith, may I cash your check? I went to Princeton.'

'I thought that was your brother,' I said, but Heath didn't respond to the question, instead standing up and taking off his coat and then putting his coat back on, this time with his arms through the sleeves.

'I don't get it,' Heath said. 'What's there to know? We're American, whether we like it or not, and profit is greed, and this country turns a fat fucking profit.'

'I'm going to go open the gate from inside,' I'd said. 'Stay here a minute.' I watched Heath nod his head then grab the bottle of Scotch, sliding it into his pea coat's side pocket.

Next to the door, on the basement's interior, I depressed a button that opened the iron gate between the drive and the cul-de-sac. At one time, Denise used to park her car up this drive, next to the four weeping cherries. I can remember standing out on the deck and hearing the wide iron gate groan to open, Denise's navy-blue Volvo sedan pulling up and parking on top of the gravel, my wife getting out – my wife, walking, and also blinking her eyes and moving her arms and tying her shoes and bending and lifting and laughing and saying, all things my wife did – and then the door on the passenger side opening, and here, Connor, six, eight, ten years old, in wet swimming shorts, in a Boy Scouts uniform, in white tennis shoes and carrying an oversized aluminum-framed tennis racquet. Long summer days. Days of true worth. Days of my wife, of my child, running toward me. But the trick of the past is in its contrast, every event made godsend or atrocity. I know this is not so but I need the past's lies. I grow fat on these lies. I eat them and eat them.

When I went back outside, Heath Burgstrom was next to my wife's small bed of roses, taking petals off a bulb and chewing them and then spitting them out.

'Don't do that,' I said. 'Why are you doing that?'

'There must be a way to get it all back, don't you think? Some laser ray? Something we're missing? Somewhere we can go and be like we were?'

'You should go home,' I'd told him.

Heath stood – he'd been kneeling – and nodded his head. He walked over to me and then shook my hand and then he was walking down the gravel drive, toward divorce and the dole and parents who would swing open their door and see fear in his eyes and smile a small smile, and then hug him.

Per court-ordered injunction, my friends and I have the Death Room's Viewing Area to ourselves: no press, no members of SeaChange, no former cohorts of the soon-to-be dying. No family of the victims. The family of the victims did get their subscription for free, and this gratis subscription included the VIP upgrade: a camera attached to the Prisoner's own head, so they can see, from inches away, his chest stop rising and falling.

'We should have brought snacks. Who has snacks?' Henry says, leaning forward in his seat, but Ned raises a hand and Henry goes silent. The Prisoner is to be led in at 11:17 p.m.; at present, it's ten after the hour. There is a camera mounted on top of the Death Room's round door. There is a camera mounted on one of the room's small square windows. There is a trio of cameras on tripods ringing the Death Room's green gurney. Through the buttons on one's Omnicast remote, one can choose the angle from which to watch the Prisoner die. One can choose to split one's screen in half; one can choose to split one's screen into quarters. Ned leans over Frank and touches my shoulder.

'Mr Hand,' my brother says, 'would be proud.' Ned pats my arm twice, closes his eyes out of pride and then nods his head, yes, this is it: our ship coming in despite the dark storm, our ship coming in because of it. The Omnicast Execution Event costs one hundred flat, and is being viewed, according to the last data I saw, by over one billion, roughly one sixth of the Earth's population. At twenty percent of total profit brought in, California's debt has been all but erased: the coffers for welfare and Medicaid full, no shortage of cops, no furlough days at the state universities. No IOUs penned by Mr John Chiang. No potholes the size of underwater mines on the interstates.

No NO HIKING signs posted in the parking lots of state parks. No rest areas closed, scared tourists pissing in scrub brush, in forest. The state legislation in an orgy of joy. All from the death of just one single person.

The Prisoner's given millions to the SPCA and Human Rights Watch, to Audubon and Earth Justice and Greenpeace, and also to Farm Aid and Bread for the World and the Heifer Project and Adopt A Platoon and the National 4-H Council. There have been others, too, and when the thank-you cards have come back, addressed to my suite in the City, I have given the thank-you cards to the Prisoner, who looks them over once, then throws them away in the trashcan. On the last day of inking, the Prisoner wrote Reuben a check for two million dollars. My artist-in-residence was finishing filling in a logo for Hertz on the Prisoner's long chin.

'I can't take that, bro,' Reuben had said.

'Yes, you can,' the Prisoner told him.

'No, bro, I really can't,' Reuben said. 'I take that and I stop inking.'

There's steam in the pipes of the prison's white walls. The room pings and knocks. The room has the feeling of knowing that the world outside exists and that it must not, at all costs, get in here. Earlier today, while I was checking the cameras, Mandriel Lang had stopped by, to say his hellos and see that all was in order.

'Will you be here tonight?' I'd asked the warden. Lang had shaken his head, no. I'd asked him why not.

'Because, Jimmy, if you knew you were going to Hell, would you want to see what Hell looks like first?'

I'd told Lang that I understood, though in my head I'd answered, yes, very much, to the question.

'Can you look through each lens? I'm going to lie down.'

The Warden had said sure. I'd climbed onto the gurney. The buckles and straps dug into my back; the Prisoner, however, will have no such discomfort. I stared at the light eight feet overhead. The walls made their small, tinny sounds.

'I just push the red button?' the Warden had asked.

'The red button,' I'd said. 'Make sure that that one's not blocked by my feet. Can you see my face? Can you see me breathing?' I looked back through the windows, my neck straining from its place on the bed.

'I think we're good here,' the Warden had said.

'Okay,' I'd said. 'The next one,' I'd said. 'Keep going.'

My three friends and I look through the windows from our brown folding chairs. A white iron wall runs floor to ceiling, separating the Death Room from where we sit, waiting. Aside from the walls, the prison is hushed, imbued with the silence afforded to churches, to libraries, to places of worship or learning. Past the Death Room's round door, down a long, narrow hall, a red light blinks on up near the ceiling.

'Do you see that?' Frank points.

'Holy shit, holy shit,' says Henry.

Ned crosses his legs and leans back in his chair. I hunch over my knees, elbows propped on the thighs of my pinstriped suit pants, a cufflink catching on my jacket's sleeve before fixing itself, the shirt cuff popping forward. Down the long narrow hall a square iron door opens, a guard I don't know coming out first, the camera set up outside the Death Room catching his entrance and beaming it outward, upward, into space, the image now wave, escaping the Earth's curve, its distortion, ascending past redwoods, the stretched wings of birds, past low stratus clouds cloaking the rough bulbous hump of Mt. Tamalpais, and now intake of breath by millions at once: Berliners just minutes ago off the tram, rushing past galleries closed for the evening, bottles of wine in their eco-chic bags, fingers depressing buttons of buzzers that ring in friends' lofts – I am here, I am here, I've come over; and millions of Brazilians in closed housing estates, the *condominio fechados* guarded and safe, spikes on their walls, men with machine guns checking IDs while copters sit parked on the rooftops of mansions; and hordes of tan boys on a Sydney gang beach, their summer sun just starting to set, their clocks and their watches eight hours ahead, the TV and cable box run out from a house overlooking the ocean, extension cords snaking over surfboards, past huge cans of Cooper's; and in kopi tiams in open-air malls, Singaporeans snacking on plates of bee hoon, necks craned toward the wall-mounted plasma flat-screens, the PAP paying for statewide subscription; and to the northwest, across the Bay of Bengal, past Kuala Lumpur, its thatched huts and Twin Towers, a Calcutta beggar with one arm and one leg panhandles for change outside of a pub with San Quentin's white hall on its wall-sized projector; and this image on screens in Auckland and Taipei, in press rooms in Antwerp; in Paris apartments; on laptops in bedrooms in Oslo and Madrid; in the dark biker bars of west central Texas; and too in Osaka and Rome and Lisbon; in suites in Moscow; in Georgetown row houses; in Brooklyn's brownstones and Toronto's townhomes; in Lima; in Glasgow; in London; this image – the guard, the long hall – laid down in matrix on DMD chip while air is sucked in and short prayers are spoken, pixels matching the mirrors on the small chip's square face, the projector processing digital light through reverse-fisheye and past slim color wheel, off the lens's main mirror and onto said chip all so fast that God, were He to exist, could not catch it, no churches now, Lambs, your alms are your eyes, and I'm talking in tongues that you don't understand but you do, very much, and with strong heart, believe in: here halide

272

and lightcast and SRAM and heatsink, here ANSI contrast and grayscale and halftoning, here spectra, reflectance, micro-fabrication, here integer values on non-linear scales, here gamma compression, here gamma encoding, here outlet couplers and splitters of beams, here golden ratio, here defraction grating, here TDM-PONs and FTTBs, here economies of scale, here integrated circuits – here a continuous fractal space-filling curve, its growth exponential while at the same time always bound by a square with a finite area, and this square now glowing in Prague and in Seoul, in Istanbul and Nashville and Tampico, and too in Warsaw and Montreal and Madrid, in Belgrade and Brisbane and Boston and Athens, this new sect no cult but indeed what we are, the fruit of our wars and our labs and our years, these are the veins of your Lord, now, Lambs – can you hear the tongues, can you hear the tongues, babbling?

The guard walks down the hallway and into the Room. A minute goes by and appearing in the threshold of the far door, the one that leads back to the cells of the prison, is Sam Flanagan, his blue pants too big, his guard badge pinned loosely to his shirt's chest pocket. His face carries the odd combination of boyish and grave. He steps past the threshold and stands near the wall, and here, with a guard flanking him on each side, is the Prisoner.

'Am I seeing that right?' Frank says, leaning in.

'Jim, oh my God, oh my goodness,' says Henry.

The Prisoner has no pink left to his skin. His head has been shaved. His beard is now gone. In place of the natural color of the dermis is a background of bright oily black and the logos for two hundred corporations: Hertz on his chin, McDonald's on his stomach, the Travelers umbrella on either forearm, where midshipmen sometimes get tattoos of anchors. Around each nipple is a Target bull's-eye. Walmart has bought the full of the neck, their logo inked twice, the golden letters ringing the space between the Prisoner's head and the rest of his body. The health giants McKesson and WellPoint bought in, their names stretching from the skin over the chest to where armpit meets bicep. The Windows logo dances down either arm, from shoulder to knuckle, passing tattoos for Lucent, for Yahoo, for Sony, for Sun; for United Health Group, for Verizon, for Chevy. The Prisoner, his head down, now looks up, staring for the first time into the camera. The contrast of his skin with the whites of his eyes is enormous, fantastic, my finest thing. Sam Flanagan stays where he is as the two guards leading the Prisoner move past him. Save for a black microfiber thong, the bid won by CK, the Prisoner is naked. His back, buttocks and thighs are like an overfull cart, one hallmark tattooed right next to another: Valvoline, Hostess and Code Red Mountain Dew; IBM and Pioneer and Folgers and Friskies. And more of them, too, so many more, all swimming in their big oily pool: Netflix and Remax and GMAC and PNC; Fanta and Sega and Epson and Apple and Shell and BMI and Del Monte and Rolex and Wyeth and Sygma and Stouffer's and Kellog's and Hilton and Cargill and Audi.

Ned clears his throat and recrosses his legs. I look over at him.

'It's really something, is it not?'

Ned looks slightly sick. 'It is,' says my brother.

The two guards pause at the Death Room's round door. The Prisoner, in shackles, is having trouble stepping over the raised lip of the entrance. He turns to the side, lifting one leg up and setting it down, then the other. Against the black background swim logos for Whirlpool and Anheuser-Busch, for Capital One and Bear Sterns and Allstate. My three friends and I sit, unmoving, unblinking, the glass windowpane now a screen, The Prisoner just a puddle of name, a notice of sale, a poster, a plug, a proclamation – a sheet of papyrus in ancient Cairo, a rock painting on a wall in Madhya Pradesh, the crude wall art depicting a man chased by a beast, and Lambs, this beast is me, I've been alive since 4000 BC, my fangs a decree, my claws edict, commanding that you know the world as unsafe, that the leaves and the seas and the stars and the trees are all out to get you, when really they aren't, Lambs, when really it's me, no beast at all, just a small and scared thing who must be seen as monster, who feeds off fear, who affixes like moss, who attaches like virus, but with time, and through might, and also through cunning, my tiny creature has grown, taken over its host, added both weight and scope, and now has more say than the body that feeds it, and Kroger and Starbuck's, they both know this, as do John Deere and CNH Global, and eBay and Eastman Kodak, and Kimberly-Clark and Heinz and CarMax, and Colgate-Palmolive and Lear and Aflac, and Liberty Global, and First Data Corporation, all here, etched into skin, skin that is soon lying down, skin that soon will be dying, skin that is coated with both word and image, skin stabbed repeatedly until it is changed, is darkened, is brightened, shaped like wet clay, molded to form by these tapeworms and flukes, by these fleas and these mites and mosquitoes, who on their own are removed and done in, are slapped at and killed and rubbed off of a palm with a finger, but whose numbers are huge, Lambs, whose wings buzz as horde, who arrive as stout group, as phalanx, as column, as army of plague that can eat through thick walls and fly over the widest of oceans, and find you, warm Lambs, let me keep you safe, and fret not that the antidote contains the disease, that the problem is also solution, that the serum you're given to solve all your pain contains the same venom that's put pain inside you. Ask not such questions. Rest your small minds. The choice has been made. There is no decision.

The guard asks the Prisoner what he wants to say. The Prisoner nods once and turns toward one camera, then turns away, picking another instead, the one on the window, past which I sit. For a moment I can't tell if he's looking at me or into the lens. The Prisoner bends downs and opens his mouth.

'I am you,' he says. 'We are dying.'

Cue More Guards' Arrival. Cue Five Guards In All. Cue Sam Flanagan Looking Unwell, Trying to Help while Staying Out of the Way of the Cameras. Cue Leg Shackles Off. Cue Prisoner Rolling His Feet, Stretching His Ankles. Cue My Heart Beating One-Two All Over My Chest. Cue the Prisoner Being Helped Up Onto the Gurney. Cue My Friend Frank Gaines Picking His Nose, Wiping It Onto the Pants of His Camo Fatigues. Cue a Guard Taking Off the Prisoner's Handcuffs while Another Guard Leaves the Room, For Now Disappearing. Cue the Prisoner Being Buckled In. Cue Black Nylon Straps Cinched Over His Body, Pressing Against His Stomach and Thighs and the Base of His Calves and His Shoulders. Cue Three Guards Leaving with This Act Complete. Cue the One Guard that Left Now Coming Back, Setting the Head Camera Down on the Prisoner's Inked Chest and Leaving Again and Returning with a Tray Lined With White Surgical Cloth, on Top of Which Sits a Trio of Syringes. Cue this Single Guard Setting Down the Tray Next to the Head-Mounted Camera. Cue the Prisoner Wincing from the Cold of the Metal. Cue Sam Flanagan Leaving His Post Near the Wall and Managing the Head-Mounted Camera in Place, His Face Pale as the White Iron Walls on Either Side of the Viewing Area Where My Friends and I Sit. Cue This Camera Turned On. Cue VIP Subscribers Accessing this View. Cue Subscribers Without the VIP View Now Upgrading. Cue the Guard Leaving Again and Bringing Back Two IV Bags on Tall Steel Rollers. Cue the Guard Setting Up the IV Rollers Over

Twin Xs of Red Tape that I Stuck to the Floor Earlier in the Day. Cue the Bags, Heavy with Saline, Swinging Like Udders On Cows, Milk-Filled, Nourishing. Cue the Surgical Tubing Leading From One IV Grazing the Prisoner's Left Shoulder, the Prisoner Raising His Head, Looking Up at the Bag, at the Roller. Cue the Guard Running Two Lines. Cue This Taking Time. Cue This, the First Line, Taking Ten Minutes. Cue Concern on Ned's Part – This Is Taking Too Long. Cue Me Whispering Back, But Think What Comes After. Cue My Brother Pleased After Considering This. Cue Henry Trying to Text and Getting No Reception. Cue the Guard, with Sam Flanagan's Help, Finding a Vein and Inserting the Line. Cue the Second Line Being Three Minutes, Much Quicker. Cue Rush of Saline Entering Blood. Cue the Prisoner Lifting His Head, Asking Sam Flanagan a Question that I Can't Hear, the Boy Guard Shaking His Head No, the Prisoner Nodding Back, the Whole World One Heart and One Brain, One Set of Eyes Waiting to See What Will Happen.

Cue Injection of Anesthetic: Sodium Thipoental Into Line. Cue this Drug's Trademark Name as Pentothal and Manufactured by Lake Forest, Illinois-Based Hospira, Their Vision, According to Their Website, Centering Around the Phrase 'Advancing Wellness.' Cue This Drug Dripping Down the Tube's Length, Closer and Closer to the Prisoner's Found Vein. Cue This Drug as Clear. Cue This Drug Looking No Different Than Water. Cue This Act Repeated in the Second Tube's Length. Cue Ten Seconds Passing, Then Fifteen, Then Twenty. Cue the Prisoner's Legs Stirring Briefly Beneath Their Black Straps. Cue the Prisoner Closing His Eyes and Opening Them, His Body Trying to Curl Onto Its Side, to Go Fetal, to Return Again to the Womb, that Position of Warmth, of Consummate Safety. Cue the Prisoner as Unable to Complete This Act. Cue the Prisoner's Flat Lips

Turning Slightly to Frown. Cue the Prisoner Going to Sleep. Cue Science, Arriving.

Cue Saline Flush. Cue the World, Watching.

Cue Injection of Paralyzing Agent: Pancuronium Bromide Into Line. Cue this Drug's Trademark Name as Pavulon and Manufactured by Kenilworth, New Jersey-Based Schering-Plough, a Firm that Believes, According to Their Website, in 'Preserving and Improving Human Life.' Cue 100 Micrograms of Pavulon Entering the Prisoner's Bloodstream. Cue the Lungs Paralyzed. Cue This Act of Paralysis Taking One, Two, Three Minutes. Cue My Eyes Watching the Prisoner's Breaths Shrink, His Body Aglow with Bright and Inked Signage. Cue My Mind Calculating How Many Clients Will Want Money Back Due to the Black Nylon Straps Blocking or Partially Blocking their Logo. Cue Sam Flanagan's Face, Green as the Gurney. Cue the Other Guard Waiting, His Eyes Set, Unblinking. Cue the Prisoner's Last Chugs as the Lungs Grow to Still. Cue No More Breath, the Diaphragm Frozen.

Cue Saline Flush. Cue the World, Watching.

Cue Injection of Final Agent: Potassium Chloride Into Line. Cue this Drug as Generic, No Patent Required. Cue Interruption of the Brain's Electrical Signaling. Cue the Prisoner's Heart Knowing Not What to Do. Cue the Prisoner's Heart, Stopping. Cue This Man, His Skin Ad, Being Watched in a Room. Cue Stillness. Cue Silence, No Sounds in the Walls, No Air and No Water. Cue Arrival of Prison Medical Staff, a Woman in Lab Coat and Nurse Scrubs and Stethoscope. Cue This Woman Nodding to Both of the Guards. Cue Stethoscope Used. Cue Death Pronouncement. Cue Time: 11:35. Cue Sam Flanagan Leaving the Room, the Other Guard Trailing Him Out. Cue the Prisoner, Now Corpse, Lying Dead on the Gurney. Cue this as Non-Standard Procedure, the Body Normally Taken when the

Guards Leave. Cue the Body as Left Behind for Effect. Cue the Body Abandoned as My Idea, Thereby Maximizing My Client's Product Visibility. Cue My Ad Campaign as Doing Its Job. Cue Success. Cue Fulfillment. Cue Me Finding My Way to the Top through Mountainous Maze, through Perilous Labyrinth, Past Subprime and Default and Job Loss and Dow Dip, Past Overhaul Plans and Unsecured Debt as the Nikkei Descends and Fear Freezes Europe, Cue Me, My Plan and My Way, My Lantern Bright, My Staff Anointed, My Robes Warm Enough for this Storm and this Winter. Cue Anyone Else as Doing the Same. Cue Fortune's Call. Cue My Howl. Cue My Answer. Cue Sam Flanagan Entering the Death Room's Viewing Area. Cue My Friends and I Turning Our Heads at Once. Cue the Boy Guard Drawing the Window's Curtain Closed. Cue Nothing to See. Cue Cameras Turned Off. Cue Point of Completion.

'What did he ask you?' I say, as Sam turns to leave.

'The Prisoner?' he asks.

'The Prisoner, of course,' I tell him.

'He wanted to know the temperature,' he says. Sam still looks unwell. He'll sleep poorly tonight. He'll have dreams of dark things that mean him great harm.

'In the room?' I ask. 'There, inside?'

'No, no,' Sam says, understanding. 'No, he wanted to know if I could find out how cold it was, back in South Dakota. I told him I couldn't. That there was no way.'

'He wanted to know about the weather?' Frank asks, and the boy guard says yes, and then stands there waiting, seeing if we have more to say, and, when we don't, Sam Flanagan exits.

Outside, there's a slight breeze, warm, from the south. It's an El Niño year, the reservoirs near full, the lows unseasonably high. My three friends and I get in our hired sedan and when we cross the bridge, back on the east side of the Bay, I tell the driver to exit, then drop me.

'We're going to Sam's,' Ned Akeley says. 'Tilapia. Don't do it.'

But I do anyway, saying bye to my friends and walking along an access road next to 580. The Bay smells of swamp, of thick putrid algae. I'm alone with large thoughts I don't seem to be thinking. I take out my BlackBerry and turn it to ON and have 41 new text messages. I imagine these handshakes and back slaps and stern words from an array of heads of corporations. I imagine at least one must be from Simer, sitting right now in her Nob Hill loft, drinking merlot, legs crossed, looking perfect. I turn the phone off and put it back in my pocket.

It takes an hour to get to the Ashby exit, the narrow sidewalk crossing under the overpass then ascending, spitting me out onto the dark quiet streets of West Berkeley. I keep walking uphill, past a lumber supply, past a small corner shop where a man, in the daytime and with a chainsaw, makes wooden sculptures of grizzlies. My son did a report on this man when still living in Piedmont, prior to his attempt at violent expression. The man's name was Alan. He grew up in Maine. I don't know why my brain lets me recall this.

I head east past San Pablo, then Shattuck, then Telegraph – some cars passing by, some people pushing carts. I want something, but I don't know what it is. I walk past College Avenue, the cars now brand new, the houses much nicer. A few porch lights are on and lamps burn in some windows, and I wonder if someone inside is waiting up, feeling forlorn or angry or forgotten. All of these people buy things I help sell, but I know only their items and none of these people.

Past Claremont Avenue, Ashby turns into Tunnel Road and heads up toward the Hills, their pines and eucalyptus. I pause at the road's crest and look out at the Bay and the City's many lights, at the glow of their yellow, their orange. A ramp descends to Highway 13 and for nearly two miles I'm walking right next to cars that slow down upon sight of me before speeding up and hurtling into the distance. I exit at Broadway Terrace, four hours in, my legs near exhausted, my stomach cramping. Redwoods lean in over the ramp, the air damp but the sky clear, the wash of stars thick. Here, in these hours, the world still owns itself, the pox and the canker less raised on its skin, the rash muted, and briefly I know it, the world, as I once did, when I was small and belief stood in me and most hours of most days slid by with soft grace, unpolluted. I've been here before, with my parents: we took an exit near here when going to a restaurant on Piedmont Avenue that we visited, as a family, perhaps once a month. The trip home was long and when I was young we'd play a game we'd made up called Little Boy Lost. I'd hide on the floor by the Skylark's back seat and my parents would posit about where I might be, and I think of them now, thinking of me – Hello, Stranger. Howdy. What happened to you? You were gone for so long. We were sad. We were worried. We hoped that you might find your way home. And we hoped that you might return as the person who left here. But you didn't. You disappeared. And we thought you were gone forever.

But you must understand we did not disappear, we were right here, the whole time, just waiting. And there was much to be done during even our grief, and we had to keep doing, and were faced, over time, with a very hard choice: let go of this weight or lose all grip and purchase. And we chose the latter and while here now you stand, you can't come in, and you better get going.

It takes one hour more to reach my Piedmont home, winding through my town's clean and wide streets, past mansions and hedgerows and Mercedes. I reach the top of my road, where my road stops. Wind shifts my backyard's trio of poplars. I put my key in the lock and open the door and look at the ascending flight of brick steps. The house smells like food. A light's on in the kitchen. Beside me is Connor's old bedroom, then the door to my office. The brick steps are thirty-seven feet long, their surface made glossy with sealant. A half-wall topped with shutters and a small garden room separates these stairs from my deck and my kitchen. A faucet is running. My maid Samampo speaks in hushed tones. From the Bose speakers mounted high on the kitchen's white walls comes a Portuguese radio station. In between words I don't know at all, again and again is the single word Deus. The man speaks with conviction, with knowledge and fear. I walk through the garden room at the top of the stairs and push open the kitchen's white swinging door. My wife sits in a chair ten feet in front of me. A juice box, its straw in, leans on her lap. She's wearing a white cotton bathrobe. For the first time in twelve months her eyes meet mine, and I want to run toward her and crush her with hugs, to say her name until my tongue stops working. Samampo is breathless. I stare at Denise. The dead, it seems, can rise. The dead have risen.

JUNE

23

My name is Jim Haskin, except that it's not. I had a different name, once, and while this name was never surrendered by me, I did let it be taken. The difference is at once subtle and huge. The difference, at this point, is worthless. On a Sunday in June, when I was fourteen, my parents and I were returning from a stay at a cabin on Fallen Leaf Lake, in the Sierra Nevada. We were near home. It was past three. The sun was high and the air dry and hot and there were thin washes of cloud across the sky, streaks I could see through. We were east of Modesto, on North Empire Road. In my Walkman's tape player was a movie soundtrack, something that like me I once used to love and now can't recall more than a single song of, a single chorus.

The dun grass sat cut on the low bluffs near the road; it was fire season, and the State had come through and trimmed everything back. We crossed a short bridge and drove past Turlock Lake, a single tree shading a small patch of grass, a picnic table. Summer was like this: the gray of the road and the blue of the sky and nearly all else some gradation of tan: endless parched grass, the beard of the valley. At County Road J we cut south toward Merced along Cox Ferry Road, a ten-mile stretch that linked up with Highway 59, which my family and I lived just off of. This road, once a shortcut, was now scenic byway; a new road had been built that was faster. But Cox Ferry was what my mom and dad knew, so we took it.

Two miles ahead, on the narrow road's asphalt, was a pickup with a flatbed trailer hitched to it. The trailer was carrying something metallic and tall; the sun's light washed the object in brightness. I stuck my head between the Skylark's front seats. My dad sped up. My mom had been sleeping.

'What do you think it is?' I asked.

'I bet we can find out,' my dad told me. For the last time in my life, my mom smiled at me, and it wasn't a smile that I got to see; I was looking at her eyes look at me in the car's rearview mirror. I saw them get thinner, and widen. Our car closed the distance between us and the truck, the flatbed's ball hitch locked in, the trailer, on the road, slightly swinging. As we drew closer, the object lost its glare. It was perhaps fifteen feet tall, and bedded down to the flatbed with lengths of black nylon rope, not dissimilar to those used to tie down the Prisoner. My family and I looked on in awe. What the object was was the Statue of Liberty.

In shape the replica seemed exact: there was the stola, the sandals and crown, the torch raised in the right hand, the broken chain trampled. There was the tabula ansata, the Independence date etched. There was the pedestal in the shape of an eleven-point star, points that my mom had me count after telling my dad to slow down, to get some space between us. My dad said okay but the gap didn't grow and my mom said no more as the three of us – father, mother and son – stared at the statue, its face, its patina.

We were behind the truck for nearly ten minutes. My parents had met in an Art History class at Stanislaus State and for this maintained an interest in painting, in sculpture. They did nothing special: my dad fixed cars, my mom taught third grade at the elementary school that I went to. But what they did for jobs was not who they were. The world, I think, is not like this now. The world now, I think, is different.

And as my parents told me about terms, dates and names, about AbEx and chiaroscuro, about Michelangelo's notion that the sculpture is already inside the stone, a white plastic shop bag floated down from somewhere on high, flying in front of the truck's windshield. The trailer's brake lights came on, the statue leaned forward then back, my mom said my dad's name – Bill – said it once, and then we were off the side of the road, my mom's body hurtling through glass, my dad's neck breaking on impact, the rest of my life spelled out in terms I did not yet understand but that I knew as a contract, rewritten.

I consider this now from my seat on a wrought-iron chair at an outdoor café in the heart of the Ivory Coast's capital. The air in Abidjan is like a damp cloth, paper-thin and made of white cotton. My linen shirt is wet in the pits, and my seersucker pants feel as coarse and as thick as those suits crafted from animal hair and worn by the Calvinist faithful.

On a side road around the corner from where I sit is an all-white school bus, its engine in idle. Mr Emmanuel Kanga captains this bus. Mr Emmanuel Kanga works in cocoa.

The café that I'm at, Café Bijoux, has excellent coffee. It's brought in from countries nearby: from Ghana, from Burkina Faso, from Mali. My hotel room, a suite, has a mahogany ceiling fan, a mosquito net around its king four-poster bed. I've been here four months. I have no intention of leaving. Feet away from my seat, where the narrow sidewalk ends, diesel sedans weave past foot traffic. There are open-air stalls where men sell mobile phones. There are multiple kiosks of sneaker vendors, the shoes hung by their laces from the frames of umbrellas.

The air here is so wet that blue skies are rare. The country is in the midst of its rainy season.

Yet no rain today as I sit with my cup and my *Wall Street Journal*, one leg crossed over the other. Past dusk, fruit bats take to the skies in numbers reserved, Stateside, for flocks of starlings, of sparrows. The lagoons around which Abidjan has been built harbor green mango trees and during the day the bats sleep in their canopy, and at night take to the sky in the hundreds of thousands. They leave for the suburbs, in search of food, raising and circling in the last of the light. Some of the bats have the wingspan of eagles.

I fold my paper in half and now set it down and look out at the street, where the man managing the cell-phone kiosk has waved a street orphan over to him. The man reaches down under the cell-phone display and brings out a slingshot, which he gives to the boy, along with a one-franc coin. The man points to the trees behind him, on the lip of the lagoon. The boy nods once and scans the dirt street for rocks. He walks like a hen, bent over and leading with his head. He selects a rock, discards it, keeps looking. Past the mango trees, the lagoon's water is blue, with patches of vibrant green marsh grass growing from it. I text Mr Emmanuel Kanga on my phone. My text says: *One More in Ten Minutes.*

My ad firm, the thing that I made, the thing that I built, the thing to which I brought pride and innovation, has been turned over to Simerpreet Sweeney, my Senior Vice-President. She has taken over, as well, my place as the fourth in my small group of three friends, the five of us – myself and Simer and Frank, Ned and Henry – all meeting in the backroom of Sam's, which has the best tilapia of any restaurant in the City. Ned hemmed and hawed but in the end could do nothing – Simer was already in on the game, and leaving her out translated to her explaining its rules to the public. I gave her a cut of the profits from the Omnicast Execution Event, enough to do all that she would need with the Bleach Boys, or the next problem like them. She's even considering buying my house in Piedmont, currently on the market.

The child finds a rock and loads the borrowed slingshot. He walks over to the edge of the lagoon and stands beneath a small grove of mangoes. He looks up and sights and pulls back the shot's band. The rock flies and a bat falls stunned to the ground. The boy crushes its head with his foot's bare heel, picking the corpse up and taking it over to the mobile-phone vendor. The man wraps the bat in beige burlap cloth and takes back the slingshot, nodding at the boy, who stands there with palms cupped, hoping for another franc coin, which the seller then gives him. The wind off the lagoon is the same temperature as the air. The wind here, in Africa, does nothing.

To the west, the Atlantic is bringing in clouds, huge thunderheads, black-gray and roiling. In forty-five minutes, maybe less, the streets will be drenched, the shallow gutters filling. The storm will pass through and the streets will then dry and no one will know that the storm was ever here. No one will remember. The Ivory Coast has had six civil wars in five years. The Ivory Coast is a place of forgetting.

I finish my coffee and set the cup down and walk across the street, to where the orphan, who is perhaps ten, perhaps twelve, is buying a kabob from a vendor whose stall is a propane stove on wheels. The child eats the food delicately.

'Salut, salut,' I say, 'ou sont vos parents?'

The child shakes his head, looking up at me past the hunks of meat, the iron stick on which they've been skewered.

'Vous êtes seul, ici?' I ask. *You are alone, here?*

The boy nods his head. The vendor won't look at me, at what's playing out. The vendor has made his money.

'Votre maison?' I ask. 'Ou est-ce-que vous habitez?'

The boy's eyes are big and they blink at me once and he then looks around as he finishes chewing. He sweeps his hand out toward the lagoon.

'Ici,' he tells me.

'Là-bas?' I ask. 'Dans l'eau? In the water?' I smile a big smile so the child knows that I'm joking. He smiles, too. He'll soon work in cocoa.

'But don't you want a home?' I ask, in French. 'Don't you want a job and friends who work, too? And someone who can cook meals for you? And a bed of your own? That you can dream in?'

The boy blinks again and then turns his head, considering. It may be that my French and his understanding thereof are forcing him to pause to compute all the questions. Or it may be that by ten or twelve years of age, he's been tricked and lied to so many times that he's about to stab me with the skewer or run as fast as he can, his heart rate picking up, his hypothalamus thrumming. Or it may be that, at some level, the boy comprehends and believes in the idea of predestination, and that all of his days and his dreams and his meals have happened in order to lead him only here, to this street and this moment – that the boy understands sovereign grace, and that the divine intervention of God changes unwilling hearts from defiant and fractious to governable. This tenet was central to Mr Hand's creed, and I've come to see my true role on this Earth as that of a missionary.

'Peut-être,' the boy says. Maybe.

'Peut-être!' I exclaim, like a clown, like a whore. 'Mais "peut-être" n'est pas un réponse! Si vous voulez tous des choses, je peux les donner à vous! But,' I say, 'I need you to say yes. I need you to say it's okay, and that you want them!'

The street vendor rolls his stove stall away, looking at me once from over his shoulder. The first few drops of rain are starting to fall, the white light of the sky turning gray, turning darker.

'D'accord,' says the boy.

'D'accord?' I say.

'Oui,' the boy says. 'Okay.'

I nod once and smile and put my hand on his head, rubbing his hair as I once tousled Connor's. The boy and I traverse the street's slow, busy traffic, and then we are around the corner from the Café Bijoux, and in sight of Mr Emmanuel Kanga's white bus, black smoke leaking from its long exhaust pipes. Emmanuel Kanga is large and quite dark and the whites of his eyes are perpetually bloodshot. He sees me coming and opens the vehicle doors, their hydraulics swishing. I move my hand from atop the boy's head to the scruff of his neck just as the boy stops walking. He looks at the bus and then up at me. Ninety percent of the world's cocoa production happens here, in the Ivory Coast, and it's not adults that produce it.

'Quoi?' I ask. 'This is the bus that takes you to your house. This is the bus that will make you happy.'

The boy, as most are, is skeptical. Amongst the black leather seats, row after row, are twin pairs of eyes, twin bodies of orphans. They look down at us through the bus's side windows, the panes of glass filthy and streaked by the smudged prints of dozens of children.

'Bonjour!' says Emmanuel Kanga.

And then the boy and I have a moment where nothing is said, where we speak with our eyes, where we say things with our eyes that we can't say to each other in French or in English or any language on Earth, and what the boy says is, I'm alone and I'm scared, and as a person, on Earth, I am meant to be with other people. But the people I've met have done awful things to those whom I loved and I know that you have done awful things, too, and that you are evil.

And what I say back, with my eyes and my mind and small stupid heart filled with all the wrong things is, that's fine and you're right, I am evil.

I break stare first and look up at the orphans and then grab the boy's narrow neck a bit harder, guiding him up the grooved rubber steps. Mr Emmanuel Kanga nods once and then the bus doors shut and the gears crank in the belly of the vehicle. Mr Emmanuel Kanga gives the bus gas and gets to the intersection of the street, making a right and disappearing, just as the boy takes a seat near the bus's back window. In an hour, a day, the boy will be at work in the cocoa plantations, picking beans that, once ground and processed and shipped, will become part of candy bars and cookies and muffins, delectable treats we unwrap and consume, the chocolate so perfect, so creamy and sweet, so divine, so dreamy, so delightful.

I walk back to my hotel as rain dampens the streets. At Café Bijoux, a waiter in dress shirt and tie carries my table inside, putting my copy of the *Journal* in the pocket of his apron. I walk four blocks, past noise and exhaust, past painted wood signs in French, in Dioula, in English. The Hotel Now is owned by Chinese investors. The building is nouveau and chic and neon-lit, twenty-seven stories. Ungambe Basson is one of the men who works the front desk. I ask him if the flight in from Charles de Gaulle is on time. He says that it is. I give him fifty dollars.

The drive from Cocody down to the true coast takes about forty-five minutes. I go over a bridge and pass by more lagoons on the Express de Bassam and then I am passing through the airport's road entrance, under the twin white elephants standing on their back feet, their trunks intertwined and forming an archway, the word BIENVENUE etched in the center of its stone. It's pouring rain now, the car ahead just rough metal shape and the red glow of its brake lights. It seems hard to believe that a plane could land in this storm. It seems hard to believe that my son could be one of its passengers.

Denise read Connor's letters and moved down to Santa Fe: there were months of intense physical therapy, to recoup from muscles so atrophied, from eyes that for so long had stopped working. I stayed in the States for two of these months, and what we discovered, once Denise was something near well, was that we thought that we had something we didn't at all, that our love was erroneous. It's a story most Americans already know. It's a story that needs no explaining. When I told her about Simer, she said that she wasn't surprised: not by who the person was, but that such an act had transpired.

Our divorce is now pending, but will involve no flight home – all will be done through email, through lawyers, through faxes. My ex-wife will take much of what I've earned through my work, or at least what's findable. I've nonetheless bought her a six-bedroom gem, nestled high in the hills, looking out at the Sangre de Cristos. Once, every couple of weeks, my son comes down from his trailer on the mesa, and my wife and Connor have dinner. Denise is nice enough to give me reports in the form of handwritten letters. My son, for instance, has grown a beard. My son, for instance, is reading de Tocqueville. He's on the second of the three volumes. In Denise's last letter, which arrived just this week, was a quote from the Frenchman, in my son's handwriting:

'In the United States, the majority undertakes to supply a multitude of ready-made opinions for the use of individuals, who are thus relieved from the necessity of forming opinions of their own.'

I apologize, Lambs, for my son's harsh words. He is still young. He knows not sovereign grace. But I promise: he is mutable.

I've sent plane tickets in Connor's name to my former wife's home. I've sent one every couple of weeks. So far, my son is a no-show. But I, for some reason, have a feeling about today. Perhaps it's the storm. Perhaps it's filling my quota for the cocoa firm. I park my car in a lot near the VIP Lounge and then jog inside, the rain like a wall, the thunder arriving in washes. The plane, it turns out, is already on the ground. The plane is early.

The lounge seats are low and turquoise and round-backed. They sit in threes and fours on maroon carpet, around black oval tables. A long bar is against the lounge's far wall, and I walk up to the bartender and ask for a Mamba, the national beer. The bartender says that he's out.

'What do you have?' I ask.

'Budweiser,' he says.

'Budweiser,' I tell him.

The bartender nods once and pours beer into a stein. I nod my thanks and put down my money. Save for this man, I'm the only one here. I sit down on a tall black leather stool, swiveling around so that I can face out at the lounge. Across from me, past the sea of low turquoise chairs, is a window that looks out at the terminal hall. If Connor is on the plane in from France, he'll have to walk by here. The flight from Charles de Gaulle is the only one this hour, and now, as I sip from my beer, people begin to drift by in the slow hazy way that travelers do when afforded the grace of walking again, of reaching, finally, their destination. I know nothing of them. They know nothing of me. And we have no way of changing these terms. What changes these terms is one of two things: blood, or commerce. I'm not their family and have nothing to sell, nothing that they'd choose to buy from me. I'm a rich white man in a rumpled silk suit, sitting in a lounge, drinking Budweiser. I imagine my dad, on the stool next to me. He asks what I'm doing, and I say, I'm waiting for my son. My son is coming to visit. He's flown a long way. He's done improper things. He's spoken with those who do not speak his language. He nearly got lost because I was not there. He's landed in storm. I don't want to miss him.

Behind me, the bartender turns on a fan. There are more people now, the push of the crowd, the surplus of passengers. Connor, I'm sure, was in a seat near the back. I hold the huge stein on my lap with both hands. I look out the window.

Thank You

Thank you to my family, my friends, my students, and my teachers. Thank you Harvill Secker/Vintage UK for doing this, and thanks especially to Ellie, Fiona, Frances and Stuart. Thanks to CPL for making it happen. Thanks to Brian and Emily at Joyland, who I forgot to thank the first time and who run a darn good magazine, and thanks again to the UVA, MFA, the FAWC, and the Steinbeck Center at SJSU. And you—thank *you*.